AMBER FLAME

Amber Flame: The Flame Series - Book 4

By Caris Roane

Formatting and cover by Bella Media Management.

ISBN-13: 978-1530598786

AMBER FLAME

The Flame Series - Book 4

Caris Roane

Do you enjoy free e-books? I love giving them away, especially as a benefit for my newsletter subscribers. To claim your free e-book today, subscribe to my newsletter on my home page! http://www.carisroane.com/

Hugs,
C. R.
January, 2016

Dear Reader,

Welcome to the fourth installment of the Flame Series called AMBER FLAME! If you've read DARK FLAME (Book #3), you will have met Fergus briefly, the alpha of the Gordion Pack. I've looked forward to embracing the shifters of Five Bridges for a long time and here's the first one just for you!

Against his alpha wolf principles, Eric Fergus seduces a beautiful fae woman in the dreamglide and soon discovers she's the only woman who can save his life…

Fergus has been without an alpha-mate for three years, from the time his wife was murdered. He's failed repeatedly to bond with the female wolves of the Gordion Pack. When he rescues a fae woman from a sex club, his need to bond with her goes into overdrive. But how can an alpha bond with a fae? Can his pack ever accept her as his bonded mate?

Mary has lived a solitary fae life in the Territory of Revel. As a veterinarian, she's established a thriving small animal practice. Having survived a recent abduction, she's leery of entanglements of any kind. But when Fergus contacts her through a dreamglide, asking her to save his life, she hurries to the Graveyard and rescues him from certain death. But when she discovers that for the past month he's been her lover in the dream-world, she's appalled. Mary doesn't like wolves or anything to do with Savage Territory. She wants him out of her life, but soon realizes if she doesn't serve as his bodyguard the whole territory will go to war and hundreds of innocent wolves will die. But how can she align herself with the wolves of Five Bridges?

I hope you're enjoying the Flame Series. I've had a wonderful time developing a world inspired by my love for bridges and of course, hunky warrior types of every *alter* species!

Caris Roane

PS: For the *latest releases, free e-books* and *great giveaways,* be sure to sign up for my newsletter!!! http://www.carisroane.com/

CHAPTER ONE

FERGUS SAW A GLINT of something metal slide out of his challenger's black leather wrist guard. Before he could move, the skewer pierced Fergus's gut, then punctured the base of his heart.

A searing pain drove through his abdomen.

His whole body seized.

A blow followed as Sydon, the contender in the wolf dominance battle, used his fist to knock Fergus into the sand.

Fergus landed on his side and the air fled his lungs.

He had only one chance of surviving the illegal skewer stab; he had to shift. With a thought, he transformed into his wolf shape.

Since Fergus's heart was leaking blood, he couldn't move and he couldn't defend himself.

But Sydon didn't stop. He added more blows with his fist to Fergus's head.

Fergus watched Sydon leap into the air.

Shit, this was going to hurt.

Sydon came down hard, jumping onto Fergus's ribs.

Fergus heard the bones crack. He couldn't breathe, he couldn't think. He couldn't do a damn thing.

Sydon howled his victory.

Fergus heard a shrill whistle which ended the Savage Territory dominance battle. About the same time, Fergus passed out.

When he came back to consciousness, he was still in wolf form.

Instead of the sand pit, though, he was on the bed of a truck being bounced to hell and back. His tongue lolled out of his wolf mouth.

His heart barely beat, and he couldn't breathe very well, except for small puffs of watery air.

He passed out again.

When he woke up, he'd been thrown onto a heap of broken up cement, dirt and weeds. He heard a lot of male laughter and the roar of a truck engine. A spray of gravel hit him as the vehicle wheeled out of what he recognized as the Graveyard.

So, this is where he would die.

He knew the place well. As a Savage Territory Border Patrol officer, he was familiar with the central part of Five Bridges where at least a dozen *alter* creatures were dumped every night. Most were dead. But the few that arrived still breathing, yet unable to move, would perish once dawn arrived. Long-life came with an aversion to sunlight.

Thirsty, cold and shaking, Fergus knew he didn't have long to live. He was already half separated from his corporeal being.

But he didn't want to die, and he sure as hell didn't want to leave the Gordion Pack in the hands of a fucking psychopath like Sydon. Worse, he'd felt his bond with the pack break, a sudden severing that felt as painful right now as the puncture in his heart.

Sydon.

Bile filled his mouth.

The rogue alpha would send the female wolves into the sex and drug trade along Savage Strip, he'd rape the women at will, believing it was his due, and he'd order the strongest male wolves to begin moving drugs in and out of the territory.

Sydon represented everything evil in their world.

His thoughts took a sudden hard turn.

Mary.

Oh, God, he didn't want to leave her.

For the first time in years, since his wife's murder, he had a woman in his life. Over the past month, since he'd helped rescue Mary Somers from a despicable sex club in Revel Territory, he'd been sharing her bed. Sort of.

The problem was, she didn't know about their relationship in real-time, only in what was called a fae dreamglide. When he'd fabricated his first dreamglide, something a wolf shouldn't be able to do, he'd had one purpose in mind: To bed the woman he craved. Having reached the peak of his mate-hunting cycle, he'd wanted Mary as though she was rain to his parched earth.

A woman's voice penetrated his fading mind. It wasn't Mary's, but sounded a lot like his dead wife. *Fergus, use the dreamglide. Mary can save you. Let her save you.*

Sharon?

Yes, I'm here. But don't waste time on me. Focus on Mary.

What did he have to lose?

With the last ounce of his strength, he formed a dreamglide. Once within it, yet weaker than he'd ever been before, he stood up in his human, non-wolf form, and took the helm. Focusing on Mary, he located her, then piloted the dreamglide swiftly.

He found her sitting on the floor of her family room going through photos of her life from before her *alter* transformation. She'd been in Revel Territory five years. All of her family was gone. He'd learned a lot about her over the past month.

Three of her several rescue cats lay stretched out near her, one with his paw on a photograph.

For a moment, Fergus didn't know what to do. He usually reached Mary in her dreams, but right now she was awake. Could he even make contact with her?

He had to try.

He called to her telepathically. *Mary?*

She straightened her back and grew very still, definite signs that she'd heard or felt something.

Mary, it's Fergus and I need your help. I'm dying. Hell, I may already be dead.

She rose to her feet and turned in a full circle, wild-eyed. The cats scattered, running away from her obvious distress. One of them bumped a bird cage near the window and set the inmates chattering as well.

She must have heard him. Hope sent a flame through his chest.

"Fergus? You mean the wolf from Savage?"

He was surprised, then realized they'd never even met in real-time. He might have carried her out of Roche's hellhole, but she'd been unconscious the whole time.

Yes, the wolf from Savage.

It seemed strange that she didn't know him. How many times had he had made love to her in the dreamglide? Dozens, yet the blocks she'd put in place kept her from knowing who he was.

"Where exactly are you?" She searched the room.

In the dreamglide, the one we share.

At these words, she grew very still once more. "What do you mean, the one we share?"

He'd never expected that these would be the circumstances under which Mary would come to learn what they'd been doing together. She had no idea right now how much he'd grown to care for her or how many times they'd talked and shared their thoughts with each other.

Was it possible he'd fallen in love with her?

For a moment, as he watched her, he forgot about his plight in the Graveyard or how dizzy he felt or that death was riding his heels. Instead, his wolf was all about the barefoot woman in jeans and a purple silk tank.

She had large light brown eyes and a rich scent that captivated him, layered with roses and a sharp, wood-like yarrow. His nostrils fluttered. Even in the dreamglide he could catch her scent.

Her long, blond hair hung around her shoulders and down her back. He'd loved holding her thick hair in his hands when he made love to her, especially when he took her from behind. He'd slowly wrap the length around his forearm to control her. She'd howl softly, like a wolf despite the fact that she was a fae woman from Revel Territory.

"Fergus? Answer me. Are you still there?"

Sorry. Got distracted. Can you come to my dreamglide? I need to talk to you.

"Okay, but I don't get it. How can you create a dreamglide? You're a wolf. And are you saying we've been together in the dream-world?"

Yes, that's exactly what I'm saying. But you didn't want to know what we were up to, so you set up blocks.

She put a hand to her breast. "You mean, you and I have been together?"

Yes.

"Physically? As in sex?"

Yes.

The full month that they'd been lovers, since he'd helped rescue her from Neal Roche's perverted sex club, had been the most satisfying and intense four weeks of his life. Mary had been a willing, enthusiastic participant in the dreamglide, but she'd refused to let her real-time self know that she was involved with him.

Mary didn't like wolves.

"Fergus, I'm so confused. Wait a minute, what did you mean, you're dying?"

The dizziness increased as he explained about Sydon and the dominance challenge.

Mary blew the air from her cheeks a couple of times. "And you say you're in the Graveyard?"

I am, but I'm fading.

"All right, let me think." He watched her move to the couch and stretch out. "Okay, I want you to pull me into your dreamglide, then take me where your body is."

Got it.

As Mary began dropping into a meditative state that would allow her to join him, his dizziness grew more intense. He felt the dreamglide falter. Summoning his strength once more, he pulled the remnants of his consciousness together and kept his dreamglide intact. But he could tell he was slipping away.

~ ~ ~

Mary lay on the couch and breathed deeply. She didn't understand what was happening at all. Fergus was here, in a dreamglide, one that he said he'd built, which was impossible. Fergus was a wolf from savage Territory. Wolves didn't have the power to even enter a dreamglide by themselves, never mind build one.

Worse still, how could she have been with him in his dreamglide for the past month and not have had an inkling in real-time? Talk about denial.

But if what he said was true, and he was near-death, she'd worry about their sexual relationship later.

As she fell deeper into her meditation, she focused on Fergus. Though he'd saved her life over a month ago, she'd never really met him. She'd been unconscious when he'd carried her out of a prison-like cell where Neal Roche had held her captive. Later, she'd done a search on the web, so she knew what he looked like. He was a handsome man, with long, thick, black hair that had an intricate braid on the right side.

She held that image now in her mind.

As she began to sense the presence of Fergus's dreamglide, her blocks started to dissipate.

A new image arrived, something from the past, of being with Fergus, one arm slung around his neck, her fingers tracing the flow of the three separate braids into one larger one and the thin amber leather cord that held it in place. His wife, Sharon, had created the design.

He'd loved his wife, who had served as his alpha-mate until she'd been murdered three years ago. Her neck had been bitten almost in half by an unknown wolf, her spine shattered. Mary had learned about the brutal attack from accounts on the web as well.

The deeper she dropped, the more the memories began to return. She could see him more and more clearly as well.

The next moment, she was in his dreamglide and there he was. He stood in front of her, deathly pale. But his dark eyes were lit with an amber glow, very wolf.

The air left her lungs in a one long worshiping sigh. Fergus was ungodly handsome.

Memories of her time with him rushed through her mind, of making love with him repeatedly. Chills traveled up and down her body and a sudden overwhelming desire for him raced through her blood. Without a moment's hesitation, she moved into him and slung her arms around his neck. She kissed him, nothing held back.

She was so into this wolf.

In return, he wrapped her up in a powerful embrace. He had massive corded arms and shoulders, and a beautiful wolf's body, athletically perfect, including washboard abs she'd kissed and licked dozens of times.

She and Fergus really had been lovers for the past month.

As quickly as the passion had bloomed, however, it began to dissipate. No, that wasn't right. The passion wasn't fading, it was Fergus. He was fading.

Just as he'd said, he was near-death.

She drew back. "There has to be something I can do. Fergus, tell me what to do?"

The dreamglide began to move like a swift rush of air, then stopped suddenly. Fergus glanced at the floor of the dreamglide and pointed.

She followed his line of sight. Through the dreamglide, she could see into the Graveyard. And there was Fergus, in wolf form, his black fur dusty. He lay on his side as still as death.

Glancing back at Fergus, she finally put all the pieces together. "You're almost gone."

He blinked slowly. "Get Warren. My heart was punctured. I need wolf blood."

With that, Fergus's eyes rolled back in his head and he faded to nothing. At the exact same moment that his dreamglide vanished, she was right back in her home on her couch.

She sat up. The blocks to all the former memories fell into place again, but she still retained the image from this dreamglide. The recollection would remain vivid, including the kiss she'd shared with Fergus and the tremendous wave of emotion she'd felt the moment she'd seen him.

She also knew she had only a handful of minutes left to save his life.

Her heart pounded and her hands shook.

Fortunately, her job as a veterinarian afforded her certain tools that would allow her to get him out of the Graveyard. She would need help moving him. She would need Warren and some of his men.

Her phone lay on the floor next to her photos. She grabbed it, then froze. She knew Warren was one of Savage's most powerful pack alphas, but how was she supposed to reach him? In real-time, she'd never even met Fergus and definitely not Warren.

She released a cry of frustration that sounded strangely like a yelp, more wolf than fae. She wondered at the weird reaction, but her need to reach Warren kept her focused on the task at hand.

The alpha of the Caldion pack, like Fergus, was part of the Savage Territory Border Patrol. She could start there.

She put her feet in motion as she contacted the station. She asked for Warren and was given the runaround until she said she had information on Fergus.

The woman on dispatch grew very quiet. Mary grabbed the keys for her Four-Runner off the peg near her surgery. As she headed to the garage, she focused on the dispatch operator, extending her fae senses. She could detect both grief and rage for what had happened to Fergus.

Mary spoke quietly, "Listen to me. I know where Sydon dumped Fergus's body, and I might be able to save him, but I need Warren and I need him now. Can you get word to him and can you keep this between us?"

"Yes." The word came out hushed and was spoken with the wolf gravel. "I'm in his pack and we're in trouble. We thought he was dead."

"He's not, but don't tell anyone. Fergus asked me to bring Warren over to Revel, where I live."

"You're not a wolf?"

"No. I'm fae. Please, can you connect me with Warren?"

"I'm not supposed to, but I'd do anything if it meant getting Fergus back. Give me a sec."

Mary got in the cab of her modified Four-Runner. She'd had a long bed installed as well as a sling apparatus she used for transporting big animals.

She set her phone on the dash-holder. She tapped 'speaker', hit the automatic garage door and cursed the damn thing for being so slow.

Turning the key, she revved the engine and as soon as she had clearance, she drove out, bouncing off the curved driveway and shooting down the street.

A deep wolf's voice hit the airwaves. "Warren, here. Who's this?"

"Dr. Mary Somers from Revel. I'm a friend of Fergus's and a trained veterinarian. He contacted me." She debated for a moment. She didn't want to get into the whole dreamglide situation, especially since she didn't understand why Fergus had the ability to even create one. He was a wolf, not a fae. "That is, Fergus reached me telepathically. He's in the Graveyard and he's still alive, though barely. There's a chance we can save him. But I'll need your help getting him into the sling and back to my surgery. He said he needs wolf blood."

A long, tense pause followed, then, "Where in the Graveyard?" Exactly the words she needed to hear.

"Not far from the bombing that took place about three months ago, you know, the one involving the witch, Iris."

"I know the location. I'm on my way."

The Graveyard was the roughest part of Five Bridges, full of ditches and cacti. Dozens of small makeshift bridges were the only means a four-wheel-anything could get through the no-man's land. The large central part of their province kept all five territories separated. But it was a hellish place, given to death.

She drove like a madwoman, but her powerful fae instincts told her every second counted.

When she found Fergus, she screeched to a halt and sent dust, rocks and bits of concrete into the air. She backed up close to him, ignoring the fact that she couldn't detect the rise and fall of his abdomen.

He looked dead.

She didn't care. She knew what she knew.

By the time she was using the controls to guide the sling over to Fergus, she felt a vibration in the air and knew Warren was close. "That you, Warren?" she called out. She didn't turn to look.

"Flying in behind you," he shouted. "I've brought two of my men with me."

"Thank God for that."

Warren landed and slid across some of the debris to grab for the far end of the heavy rubber sling. He moved it next to Fergus.

As soon as it was in position, she hurried to unlatch the closest side to her so that it lay flat.

The men wasted no time as they picked Fergus up and slid him onto the sling. Mary worked around them as she grabbed the latches, then locked them in place.

She stumbled heading back to the truck, picked herself up and with bleeding palms worked the machinery.

The wolves kept the sling steady. Like the garage door, the damn thing couldn't move fast enough. She let loose with a long string of beautiful words. She sensed all the wolves staring at her, but she only had eyes for the sight of Fergus's black and way-too-dry snout as the sling drew close.

"Warren, get up here on the back of the vehicle, your men with you. Take the Goddamn controls and keep Fergus steady. I'm taking off."

Warren levitated swiftly toward her. "I've got it, Mary."

She jumped over the side of the truck, landing in the gravel. She slid into the driver's seat, started the Four-Runner and put the vehicle in motion.

The large tires gave it the traction she needed through the shitty roads and wobbly bridges.

She once more drove like she'd escaped from an institution.

As she turned down her street, tires squealing, she contacted Warren telepathically. *I need one of you to give him blood right away.*

I'll do it, unless blood-type matters.

Not with wolves. She knew at least that much about the species she disliked so much.

As she pulled into the garage, she hopped out of the truck. "Warren, you and your men haul him to the surgery while I get the transfusion equipment set up. This way." She gestured with a flip of her arm in the direction of the double swinging doors.

She didn't wait for Warren to say anything. She ran up the ramp and into the surgery and propped the doors open. She raced around and gathered tubing and needles. She locked in the feet of the surgical table to make sure it didn't slide around. She could hear the men moving in her direction.

Seeing them levitate up the ramp, she called out, "In here."

They carried him straight to the surgical table. Though she'd cared for great Danes on this table, it still wasn't big enough for Fergus in his wolf form. One of the wolves held his hindquarters in both hands. She directed Warren to pull up a second smaller table and place it beneath Fergus's hind end.

Afterward, she threw a rubber tourniquet in Warren's direction. "Tie yourself up. I need a strong vein."

"You got it."

From the corner of her eye, she watched him wrap the rubber strip around his arm.

She ignored Fergus's open, glassy-eyed look. He was hanging on by a thread, but he wasn't dead yet. She quickly shaved his front right foreleg, then waved Warren in her direction.

She wasn't messing around with cleaning anything up. Time was her enemy.

She inserted a needle into Fergus's vein, though with difficulty. Not much blood was moving through his body.

Without once making eye-contact with Warren, she began the transfusing process. She complimented him on the size of his vein, drove the needle home and watched as gravity did its thing and Warren's beautiful red blood began to flow along the tubing.

As soon as it reached Fergus's vein, she felt a roll of energy move through the wolf's body and the blood began to flow.

Her eyes started to burn, and her throat felt tight.

Warren's wolf-voice sounded through the space. "This is a good sign, isn't it? I mean, that the blood is going in."

"It is. It's the best."

She took a moment to breathe and to give thanks for small miracles.

With the most critical element in place, she began a careful examination of Fergus's body. She quickly discovered the broken ribs. She couldn't imagine what had done this kind of damage.

With Fergus unconscious, she felt the individual ribs then carefully pulled each one back into place. There was no way she could perform any kind of surgery, not with how close he was to death. But she also knew that as soon as he was able, he could self-heal the bones. Her greater concern was making sure his lungs weren't torn up.

As more of Warren's blood flowed into his system, she watched Fergus take a decent breath, then another and another. Her sense of relief increased.

But she remembered what Fergus had told her about being skewered. She ordered Warren to stay put and got her ultrasound equipment.

Once again, she shaved Fergus, though this time on his chest. Using the gel, she ran her wand over the area that allowed her to see his heart.

"Why are you doing that?" Warren asked.

"Something Fergus told me about how he was injured. I understand there was a dominance battle."

"Yes. Sydon, a rogue alpha, challenged him. I was sure Fergus could take him. I wasn't there during the battle, but I was on the phone with one of his betas and got a blow-by-blow. Sydon caught Fergus below the sternum with a heavy right punch, or at least that's what we thought it was. Fergus seized while in the air, fell, then shifted, which indicated he'd been badly wounded. Sydon went in for the kill and punched at his head, then jumped on his ribs. I don't know how Fergus survived."

She kept moving the wand over his heart, and there it was—a small perforation, partially healed but leaking blood. "Well, here's the problem. He was stuck with a metal implement, like a large needle, straight into the bottom of his heart."

The atmosphere in the room changed, as surely as if electricity poured through the space. The air smelled harsh like heated metal and came from the wolves.

Warren's voice dropped an octave as he said, "Are you saying Fergus was skewered?"

"Yes, that's what he told me had happened, but he was lucky. If the puncture had been any deeper, he would have died instantly."

Mary replaced the wand and turned off the machine. "What I don't understand is how this happened. I mean, I've seen photographs of what you wolves wear during dominance fights, something like a pair of wrist guards and a leather loin cloth."

"Gladiator briefs."

"Right. I knew there was a word for it." She felt her cheeks heat slightly. Fergus would look really good in a loin cloth. Or out of one for that matter. The man she'd met in the dreamglide was built.

That she could even think of him in those terms was a good sign he was leaving the danger zone. She still didn't say anything to Warren, however, in case something else went wrong.

She cleared her throat. "With so few clothes, how could Sydon have had a skewer on him?"

Warren grunted, a rough wolf sound. "His wrist guards, if long enough, could have disguised hidden metal pieces. Jesus. Sydon must have done exactly that."

Mary didn't want to say anything, but because her sister had died as fall-out from a dominance fight, she wasn't all that surprised at the treachery of secret skewers. It seemed in keeping with her opinion of wolves generally.

She had a deep prejudice against Savage Territory. She didn't want any part of a culture so easily moved to violence. Now that she had a partial awareness of what she'd been doing with Fergus in the dreamglide, she also knew why she'd set up the memory blocks in the first place. If she'd allowed herself any real-time awareness of Fergus, she would have refused to engage in the affair.

She got out a bag of saline. Using another tube set-up, she hooked the needle beneath Fergus's fur, the same way she would a dog or a cat. Hydration would help.

She checked his vitals. His blood pressure was low and heartrate too rapid, but she sensed he'd begun the long journey back. Other than cracking open his chest and suturing the wound, she didn't have another option. She was convinced, however, that surgery would have been far worse than letting him self-heal.

"Will he live?"

She realized she'd been so intent on Fergus and consumed by her own fear for his life that she hadn't shared enough information with the men in the room. "Yes, he'll live."

"Thank God."

She finally made eye-contact with Warren, but gasped softly. She knew very little about the alpha of the Caldion Pack and hadn't known he was partially disfigured. The left side of his head was partially bald, a few inches back from the scalp line. Though the area was heavily tattooed, she could see he'd been burned, badly. His face was scarred as well, all the way to the area around his left eye, especially on and over the socket. However, he had full use of both eyes. The same side of his face also looked as though it had been burned. The rest of his head seemed normal. He had long blond hair, very thick and straight not unlike her own. His eyes were an unusual emerald green and very beautiful.

The physician in her tried to understand what had been done to him. Some of the scars looked like a wolf had bitten him. But the rest was caused by either a fire of some kind or chemicals. "Any of that causing you pain?"

He shook his head. "It happened a few years ago."

"Here, in Five Bridges?" He should have been able to self-heal.

"Yes. A dark witch's spell made it permanent. Fergus pulled me to safety, otherwise the spell would have eaten through my entire body and I would have died." His gaze drifted to the line of red connecting him to Fergus, then back to her. "I owe him my life."

She saw in his features the extremely handsome man he'd once been. Despite the disfigurement, he exuded a similar quality as Fergus, the strength and power of the alpha wolf.

His gaze narrowed and his jaw worked. When his nostrils flared and elongated slightly, she wasn't surprised that he shifted his gaze away from her. He even side-stepped to create distance, though he was careful to preserve the tubing.

Sniffing the air herself, she detected his mating musk, the same kind of scent all alphas released. She sensed that Warren needed to establish a boundary with her because of Fergus. By way of clarifying the situation for him, she drew close to Fergus and settled her hand gently on his wolf-shoulder. "I belong to Fergus right now."

She watched him release a sigh of relief. "I can smell his scent on you. He's spoken of you often, but you have to understand, until you're bonded every unmated alpha will be attracted to you."

She was surprised. "Because of your mating cycles?"

He shook his head slowly and met her gaze, the emerald of his eyes glowing slightly. "No, Mary, I'm afraid not. This is about you. You have alpha-mate capacity, a rare thing even in Savage Territory and something I would have never believed possible in a woman from Revel Territory. Yet here you are."

She noted the slightly pale appearance of the skin around his eyes. "You've given enough blood, Warren. But Fergus should have more." Wolf blood was one of the greatest healing agents in Savage Territory.

Because the hole in Fergus's heart was small, he hadn't lost a lot of blood. The surplus provided tonight was more about restoration and would go a long way to bringing Fergus back to full health within the next few hours.

A terrible chill went through her. For a brief moment, she could feel the entire landscape of Savage Territory and that the wolves would soon erupt in chaos and violence. Again.

Her gaze shot back to Fergus. She had a terrible premonition what was about to happen in his world would hinge on the decisions Fergus made over the next forty-eight hours.

Warren gestured for one of the other wolves to come forward. "Alessandro, you're up." The shorter male didn't hesitate.

Though Mary didn't understand why, she knew instinctively this wolf was a beta. He could also be an alpha-in-training, but he definitely served in a more supportive capacity within Warren's pack.

She shook off her visit with the future and carefully created a new transfusing line with Alessandro.

Mary saw that Fergus's breathing was much easier now. She used the ultrasound again and saw that the hole was completely healed. She told Warren the good news.

"Thank God."

Mary? Fergus's voice entered her mind.

She gasped, then glanced at the black wolf. But he didn't seem any more alert than before, though his eyes definitely weren't as glassy. She touched his forehead and rubbed his ears very gently. *Fergus? Are you able to communicate with me now?*

Not exactly. I'm in the dreamglide again since I'm still too weak to do this through simple telepathy.

Do you want me to come to you?

No, it's not necessary. But right now I need you to ask Warren a few things.

Sure. Give me a sec.

She kept her hand on Fergus's head but turned to Warren. "I'm able to communicate with Fergus. He's alive but still deeply unconscious."

"I don't understand. Then how are you talking to him?"

Mary drew a deep breath. "It's a fae thing. Actually, it's through the dreamglide."

Warren scowled. "That makes no sense."

At that, Mary smiled. "I know it doesn't. It's a fae thing. But humor me, Warren. Fergus has questions. Is that okay with you?"

He nodded but looked skeptical. "Of course." She sensed he didn't quite believe her.

Mary, tell Warren to take the stick out of his butt. When she hesitated, Fergus added, *Go ahead. It'll help.*

Mary knew her brows were sitting high on her forehead. "I mean no disrespect when I say this, Warren, because it comes from Fergus. But he said to tell you to take the stick out of your butt."

Warren laughed, then lifted a hand. "Okay, now I believe you."

"Is Fergus always saying things like that to you?"

"I'm a little, how shall I say this, inflexible."

Mary reverted her attention to Fergus. *So, what do you want to ask Warren?*

I need to know where my pack stands, what Sydon has done.

She relayed the information to Warren, adding, "Fergus can hear everything you say. I don't need to pass it along."

"Good to know." Warren took a step closer. "Your beta told me on the phone that as soon as you were taken away, the representative of the

Savage Pack Council pronounced Sydon the new Alpha of the Gordion Pack. You've never heard such silence before. Shortly after, however, some of the women began howling their grief.

"Sydon, by rights, had you hauled out to the Graveyard and left you there for the sun to do its work. I want you to know that your best men were in constant communication with me. I needed to know what Sydon's first decrees as alpha were and it's not good. He expects the youngest female wolves to form a harem and service his needs exclusively."

What? Fergus's distraught voice punched through Mary's mind.

She pressed her hand against his forehead to calm him. *Fergus, a little less forcefully, please, though I understand your distress.*

Warren continued. "He announced to your wolves that he has plans to make the Gordion Pack more powerful than any other in Savage. He told the older unmated females to prepare to work Savage Strip, that he would expect them to earn money for the whole pack. The male wolves have been given a choice. They can either serve as drug runners or work in a local amber flame drug factory. Everyone in the Gordion Pack will work for the good of all."

Were those his words? Fergus asked.

Mary addressed Warren. "Fergus wants to know if those were his words or yours, the last part I think, 'the good of all'."

"His words."

Fucking bastard.

Again, Mary rubbed his head. *Ease down wolf, you're too powerful for my poor brain.*

Sorry, Mary. But I need to get out of here.

When she felt the wolf move beneath her fingers, she immediately pressed a hand down on his neck. Hard. *Fergus stop this. You're not going anywhere yet. You've only just healed the damn hole in your heart.* To her words, she added the force of her fae ability and felt Fergus grow calm once more.

You're right. Again, I'm sorry. He relaxed beneath her hand.

That's better. She felt a powerful affection for him in that moment. She barely knew him in real-time, but it would seem some of her experience in the dreamglide had already started slipping through her blocks. Besides, it was clear he spent his life protecting his pack wolves and she admired him for it. He was a force for good in Savage.

She added, *I'm going to send your friends away. You won't be able to unseat Sydon until you're on your feet again and that will require an entire day of healing. Understood?*

She could feel his frustration as he battled within himself. Finally, he ground out a quiet, *Understood.*

She shifted a little to face the wolves in the surgery. "Now listen up. Fergus needs time to heal, probably the entire day before he can even shift back to his man-physique. He won't be able to do anything during these last few hours of the night except to heal himself. I'll keep him here and I'll tend to him through the day as well.

"No one knows he's in Revel and certainly not that he's alive. Except the dispatch operator at the Savage Border Patrol, so you might want to have a word with her."

Warren nodded. "I'll take care of it."

Mary continued, "Because you're from a different pack, you won't have pack-based loyalty to Sydon, so you won't be breaking any laws by keeping silent about Fergus's condition. Am I right?"

"You are," Warren responded.

"Good. I want you to head out. But Warren, I'd like you to pull some things together for Fergus since he won't have anything here to wear once he shifts back. Bring whatever you think he'll need in the way of clothes. He'll probably want shaving gear, maybe his weapons. I know that's important to all you border patrol men."

She then gestured to the southern end of the house, down a hall that backed up to the garage. "There's a side door that I'll leave open for you, but I'll expect you to return well before dawn with his stuff."

Warren inclined his head. "Yes, Ma'am."

Fergus's voice intruded once more. *Mary, tell Warren that if he wants to risk it, I've got a stash of weapons in my compound—*

Fergus, knock it off. Your only job is healing right now. And I'm not about to send Warren to your compound with a wolf like Sydon in charge. Get well, then you can go after Sydon yourself.

Right. Okay.

Enough talking. But she petted his head.

She then moved to Alessandro and unhooked the line.

"You're sure he doesn't need more?" Warren asked.

"His heart is healed, and he's on the path to recovery. But he needs to be quiet now and not stirred up about his pack. Do you understand?"

Warren nodded slowly. "I do. I'm distressing him."

"Only because he's anxious about his wolves."

"All right then. We'll head out."

Mary watched Warren heave a deep, laden sigh. She could feel the concerned weight in him, the same one Fergus carried for his pack and for Savage. If tonight's events hadn't happened, she would never have believed that wolves existed who wanted good things for their territory. She'd thought them all a bunch of wild animals. Literally.

"Come with me," she said. "I'll show you to the side door so that you can bring his things back there when you return."

She checked the garage first and was relieved to see that one of the wolves had already lowered the door. She took all three men out through the hall between the garage and her office space. She had a supply room and a small kitchenette as well as two examining rooms on this side of the house.

As she moved down the hall, time seemed to slow. She had the oddest feeling that her life was about to change in ways she would have never believed possible.

Warren's voice disrupted the sensation. "You've got a solid set-up here. I'll bet you see a lot of animals."

"I do. It was the one of the few things the *alter* serum didn't take from us as humans; we can still enjoy our pets." She waved a hand straight ahead toward the side door. "My clients and their animals come in through this entrance. I'll leave the door unlocked for you so that when you come back with Fergus's things, you can just set the satchel inside the door, lock it then leave."

Reaching the door, she pushed it wide for him.

Warren thanked her for saving Fergus. "You've done a tremendous service for Savage tonight, Mary Somers." He even smiled. "We won't forget it."

With that, Warren and his men moved onto the cement walk, then rose into the air.

She watched Warren for a long moment. Once he cleared the neighbor's trees, he headed swiftly toward the southwest, his blond hair flowing behind him like a wave. Within seconds, all three wolves had disappeared from view.

She closed the door but as promised, left it unlocked. She heard a yelp from the direction of the surgery and ran back to find Fergus's entire wolf body spasming. She again put force on his neck, using a pressure point that helped him once more to calm down.

She spoke to him telepathically. *You're okay, wolf, I'm here.*

Her words helped and his entire body relaxed.

The return to life wouldn't be simple for Fergus and given what he'd been through, Mary knew she had several rough hours ahead of her.

CHAPTER TWO

FERGUS KNEW HE was healing, but each time he rose to a minimal level of consciousness, he felt as though someone had set fire to his veins. He ached all over. His broken ribs made breathing a misery and his head felt like Sydon was still pounding on his skull.

He remained in wolf form, knowing it wouldn't be wise to change back to his human shape until he was almost fully healed. His wolf metabolism made healing a faster process.

If he'd been human, and cared for in a hospital, he would have been pumped full of drugs and kept in a coma. But as an *alter* wolf, remaining drug-free would speed up the process. And right now he had only one goal: To retake the Gordion Pack as fast as he could.

So pain it was.

He tried to control himself, but when the suffering became unbearable, he thrashed and howled out a series of moans.

Each time, Mary would reach for him and squeeze his paw or put pressure on his neck. Though she didn't have an essential healing ability as some of the witches did, her touch as well as her presence provided a kind of comfort he doubted anything else could have. Once she made contact, he would focus on her rose-yarrow scent, which triggered a pleasure response in his brain. His nerve pain would in turn settle down enough for him to fall asleep for a brief stretch.

He had a constant sense that Mary lay next to him, but he didn't really know where he was. When he'd been in the dreamglide earlier so that he could learn from Warren what had happened with Sydon, the space had been full of mist. Basically, he was still in such a deeply unconscious state that he couldn't see anything, not even in the dreamglide.

The table on which he lay was solid and cold, but felt just right for his super-heated wolf body.

As the hours wore on, he knew when the night passed and dawn came, but little else.

By the time it was midday, his healing finally began to coalesce. His heart pumped as it should and his bones had straightened and mended. His ribs had been the most problematic, but now he was breathing easily.

Toward late afternoon, he started thrashing again despite the growing wholeness of his body. This time, his distress had nothing to do with his physical state. Instead, his fears for the Gordion Pack under Sydon's rule tormented him. He felt a profound, desperate need to return to the compound and protect those he'd cared for during the five years he'd served as alpha.

As fears for his pack peaked again, the thrashing returned and he howled his agony. He didn't know how, but he sensed that some of his wolves were being hurt right now, though the sensation felt more fae than wolf.

He felt Mary's touch as she once more took his front paw in her firm grip. *You're safe, Fergus. I'm here.*

What was it about Mary that eased him so completely?

He settled down quickly and his breathing evened out. He let his fears go with a determination to return to Savage as soon as he could.

Sometime later, concern for his pack caused him to thrash all over again. Once more, he felt Mary's touch as she held his paw. "You're okay, Fergus. Sleep, now. That's it."

He calmed at once, then for the first time finally came to full consciousness. He opened his wolf-eyes and looked at her.

Her eyes remained closed as she sighed heavily and her hand slid away from his paw.

He'd worn her out.

God, she was beautiful. Her skin was like cream, her lips full and kissable, her brows arched. Her nose was straight except for a slight lovely curve near the bridge. He wanted to touch her, but he didn't want to wake her up. She needed her sleep.

She lay an arm's length away from his wolf body on a similar stainless steel table. She had a pillow under her head and was covered in a gray blanket. Maybe she was warm, but she couldn't have been comfortable.

He took a deep breath and with a thought transformed back into his human shifter shape, though he remained on his side so he could face her.

He stayed in the same position for a long time, his gaze fixed to this extraordinary fae woman who had been his lover for the past month and who had now saved his life.

When he'd seen her for the first time almost five weeks ago, she'd been unconscious since Neal Roche had shot her up with dark flame to subdue her. She'd been lying on a prison cell cot where he'd held her captive.

At the time, her flowery scent, layered with an edge of sharp yarrow, had put his feet in motion and he'd caught her up in his arms. But the moment he'd held her body against his, he'd howled long and loud. He'd sworn he'd found his mate, yet that seemed impossible. Mary was fae.

He'd never forget how overwhelmed he'd felt with his arms holding her tight, as though he'd found a treasure he'd been searching for his entire life. But in letting loose with a howl, he'd jeopardized the rescue operation. Despite his screw-up, he'd gotten her out of there anyway and had taken her to an extremely well-guarded safe house in Revel Territory.

Barely three days after he and Brannick had fought and killed Neal Roche, and long after the worst of the drugs had cleared Mary's system, Fergus had awakened with his mind full of nothing but Mary. He had a hard-on like few he'd known. He lay in bed, completely naked, shaking with need. He wanted her and needed her. He'd reached the peak of his mate-hunting cycle and every ounce of his being knew she had alpha-mate potential.

But as he'd focused on her, the strange dreamgliding phenomenon that the *alter* fae could create, had taken him over. He'd somehow accessed Mary's essential fae power and all her ability suddenly became his own. Without ever having done it before, he'd given shape to his first dreamglide, something a wolf shouldn't have been able to do. But he followed his instincts and while reclining in his Savage Territory bed, he'd closed his eyes, fallen into a deep meditation, then fabricated the fae dream-world vehicle.

Because his thoughts were all for her, the dreamglide took him directly to her bedroom. He'd found her uncovered and sprawled on her stomach. She'd been wearing only a t-shirt. He'd had a view of her ass that still undid him, smooth skin, full shape, kissable and ready for his mouth and tongue. Even now his mouth watered.

His alpha drive had taken over. He'd been all about the sex, his cock, and getting into her as deep as he could. The part of him that had strangely become fae knew he could make love to her in the dreamglide and that's exactly what he'd intended. He'd lowered the bizarre dream-world vehicle over her and made a kind of contact that allowed him to enter her dreams. Once he had, he began calling to her telepathically, then slowly seduced her.

Breaking into her dreams had been highly illegal. She could have taken him to court and had him imprisoned. Instead, she'd all but leaped into his dreamglide and the vehicle took on the exact appearance and shape of her bedroom. She was only a couple of feet away.

He'd never forget how she stood in front of him, wide-eyed, her breathing high in her chest. She blinked several times as though confused.

He remembered thinking he needed to introduce himself. "I'm Fergus. I got you out of Roche's prison cell."

She'd nodded and glanced around. "Oh, my God, you built a dreamglide."

"I did. But don't ask me how because I don't know."

She got a funny look on her face and her lips parted. Her gaze moved slowly down his chest and abdomen to finally rest on his erection. Her eyes widened. "You're a big man, aren't you?"

Her words had pleased the hell out of him. He'd slid his hand around his cock, thumbing the broad head for emphasis. "I am."

Even then, he'd sensed her openness came from being in the

dreamglide and that she wouldn't be this uninhibited in what the fae called real-time.

She'd taken off her shirt. The rest became a whirlwind of his body covering hers, his hips moving like wildfire and her moans turning into a series of wolfish howls that had him ejaculating hard.

Afterward, she'd been more subdued, even shaken. She'd told him she didn't like wolves and that this could never happen again. She'd gone around the perimeter of the dreamglide and built up what looked like a steel cage, something she called blocks. She'd explained that with the blocks in place she would have no memory of what they'd done.

She asked him politely to never visit her again in her dreams then she'd kissed him, a slow lingering kiss that told him how torn she was about what they'd just done. He could still feel her lips on his.

Of course, the next night, he'd been unable to control his need for her and despite her request, he seduced her again in her dreams. Only this time when she'd responded, they'd spent hours together. Though she'd kept the blocks in place over the next few weeks, she'd never again asked him not to come to her.

As he watched Mary now, exhausted and asleep, he wondered if it was possible she would be capable of bonding with him as his alpha-mate or was he wishing for the moon? After all, Mary was a fae woman. If the female wolves of his pack couldn't do it, how could she? And would a pack ever accept a woman from another *alter* species as his bonded mate?

He checked his internal clock. The hour was well into the late afternoon. Though he still ached and was as stiff as hell, he had to get moving. The safety of his pack called to him and Sydon needed to be sent to perdition.

He slowly slid off the surgical table. He wore his gladiator briefs, which were bloodstained. He saw a tan leather satchel by the door and recognized the emerald green logo of Warren's Caldion pack. He sensed in a manner that felt fully fae that it contained clothes for him, toiletries, and hopefully a Glock he could use until he took possession of his own.

What he'd really like, however, was a skewer and he knew exactly where he'd put it. Damn Sydon to hell.

Picking up the satchel, he moved into the family room. He saw the familiar three large bird cages near the windows, full of chattering birds. Because of the dreamglides he'd shared with Mary, he knew her home inside and out, though this was the first time he'd been here in real-time.

She made a habit of rescuing both cats and birds. No dogs, though. Just one beat-up wolf.

As he headed toward the kitchen opposite, several cats came running up to him. He was surprised given that he was a wolf. But as each meowed and rubbed around his legs, he realized he must have carried enough of Mary's scent to set them at ease.

Holding the leather bag away from the cats, he dipped down and petted a couple of them. When one of the cats raced in the direction of the kitchen, then paced in front of a row of five small ceramic purple bowls, he got the hint.

"You kids hungry?"

One of them had the intelligence to meow loudly in response.

"Okay, I get it. Mary was so busy taking care of me, she didn't feed you earlier this morning." All the cats began milling around their obvious feeding area.

He crossed the room and set his satchel near the hallway that led to the master bedroom and a second bedroom. He'd take care of the cats first and maybe look for something to eat. He was feeling famished, but almost dying would do that to a wolf.

He went into the kitchen and opened three cans of cat food. He had no idea about the portions, so he began slopping tablespoons into each bowl.

Several of the cats purred as they chowed down.

Imagine, a wolf feeding house cats.

After rinsing the tins and putting them in the recycle bin, he went to the fridge and found a half-gallon of milk. He hunted for a glass, then poured it almost to the brim. He drank it down, then another.

When he'd poured a third, he moved back to the family room area. He saw the photos still lying on the floor, of Mary with her family. For a moment, he was reminded of his own life with Sharon before coming to Five Bridges.

Sharon had been happy back then. So had he. He'd built a resort in Sedona that they'd both loved, with a spectacular view of the Mogollon Rim. They'd had money and had even planned on starting a family soon. But one night, fifteen years ago, the wolf *alter* serum had been injected into their salad dressing, an act of treachery that had put his former business partner in prison for life.

Once he and Sharon had transformed into *alter* wolves, they'd been required by law to liquidate their assets and sell off the resort. The U.S. government, by long-experience, knew it was best if *alter* beings severed business ties to the human community. Fergus understood the wisdom of it. *Alter* creatures needed to embrace their kind and their world.

He'd saved their money for the future, however, for the day he'd become alpha. From the moment he and Sharon had been assigned to the Gordion Pack, he knew eventually he'd rise to the top.

Sharon had wanted him to build them a large home right away, but all his human ambitions had transferred to his alpha drive. He'd told her they would have to wait. He had a goal and one day soon he'd be the alpha of the Gordion Pack then they'd build a beautiful house attached to a massive complex.

Becoming alpha, however, had taken a decade and dozens of dominance fights, some of which he lost early on. He'd taken to this life, but Sharon had never been happy, not as an *alter* wolf or living in Five Bridges. She'd basically endured a dozen years of disappointment before her death.

But theirs wasn't an unusual story. Few saw contentment in their world. The *alter* experience was like surviving a plane crash. Though you might still be alive, you had severe injuries and your life would never be the same again. New skills had to be learned and a new way of living adopted.

In addition, Savage had lived up to its name. Violence ruled the wolf territory more than it did any of the others. Harley, his number one beta wolf, had once told him that everyone who ended up in Five Bridges had a form of PTSD. He was probably right.

Mary's parents had both died during failed *alter* transformations.

Later, her sister, Alicia, an *alter* wolf, had been killed when a dominance battle got out of hand. She'd been an innocent bystander when several wolves in the spectator stands went berserk.

He honestly didn't know how Mary had succeeded in pulling her life together after Alicia's death, except that she loved her work. From the time she'd taken up residence in Revel, she'd focused most of her energies on her thriving small animal practice. All this he knew from their shared time in the dream-world.

He glanced around the combined family room and kitchen. He'd seen the space often in the dreamglide. But now the colors were real, the white of her couch, the purple of her pillows, the pale gold of her drapes.

He'd made love to her more than once on her couch, yet not exactly there, just what the dreamglide could manufacture.

His body heated up, and his gladiator briefs tightened.

Mary.

Jesus, what was he going to do with her now that they'd made contact in real-time? Would she finally remember what they'd been to each other? The sex and the dozens of conversations?

Fergus had wanted to date her, to bring her into Savage, to see where their relationship could go in real-time, but Mary had refused repeatedly. She'd never gotten past the differences between them and how he was an alpha wolf in need of a pack-mate and she was a Revel fae who enjoyed her solitary life. She couldn't see herself in a place as violent as Savage, and he couldn't leave his pack.

As his thoughts circled back to his wolves, he hated that he was in Revel. With the sun still up, his pack might as well be hundreds of miles away, instead of just a couple. He wouldn't be able to leave until full dark and in the middle of June, the sun didn't completely set until after eight in the evening.

He returned to the kitchen and finished his third glass of milk. He was cleaning up when he heard Mary's voice. "I see you're alive and kicking."

The sweet, gentle cadence to her words almost caused him to lose control of the empty glass. But he caught himself in time, setting it on the counter.

He turned in her direction, ready to thank her again for saving him, but all he could see was the woman he'd made love to in the dreamglide. His desire for her and what felt like a mountain of affection made him catch his breath. His rough voice came out on a whisper. "Mary."

She was across the room, her hair tousled. She wore her jeans and purple silk top. She looked weary yet so beautiful his heart ached.

She came toward him. "How are you feeling? Are you okay? I mean, are you really alive?"

He knew he smelled like ripe wolf and didn't want her near him until he showered. But the expression of concern and fatigue had him opening his arms.

The moment he did, she ran to him and landed hard against his chest. She slung her arms around his waist and held on tight. "I was so worried, Fergus. You couldn't have stepped closer to the cliff's edge if you'd tried."

He wrapped his arms around her and held on. Maybe she was finally remembering. "Thank you for saving me, Sweetheart." The word rolled easily off his tongue since that's what he called her in the dreamglide.

She drew back, staring at him from her light brown eyes. "Is that what you call me when we're together?" She pulled away from him in slow stages.

He looked at her, the arch of her brows and her beautiful high cheekbones. The wolf in him craved her, but he couldn't act on it; he didn't want to scare her. He nodded. "I do, but tell me you're okay after what I put you through. It must have been hell."

She frowned slightly, her eyes narrowing. "I've never been so scared. If I hadn't been able to sense you through my faeness, I would have believed you were already dead when I found you in the Graveyard." Her gaze dropped to his chest and she patted him above his sternum. "How's your heart?"

He couldn't help but smile. "Achy."

Her brows drew together. "In what way? Are you experiencing pain? What does it feel like?"

He chuckled. "Sorry, I forgot you were a vet. I was teasing you because I feel achy just looking at you. I'm in a constant state of need because of my annual alpha cycle."

Mary's brows drew together. "I'm at a real disadvantage because I'm only recalling bits and pieces of our time together in the dreamglide. But I know we've been close, haven't we? I mean that much I can feel as though you've become precious to me."

He drew a deep breath. "Yes, Sweetheart, we've been very close."

She tilted her head. "I'll be honest, I don't know what to do with all of this and you know about my sister, what happened to her, right?"

"Yes, I do. We've talked about it."

She chewed on her lower lip. "I'm drawn to you and there seems to be some part of me wanting to be a wolf, if that makes any sense at all. But Fergus, Savage?"

"I know. Listen, I have no expectations here. I respected the blocks you put in place. There's a lot against any real kind of relationship between us."

"Yes, there is." She frowned and glanced at the satchel on the floor. She waved at it. "Feel free to use the master bath to get cleaned up."

"The guest bath will be fine."

She met his gaze and for a moment looked confused, then said, "Oh, right. You've probably been through my home in the dreamglide."

He couldn't say the words but the truth was they'd made love in every room in her house. Even a couple of times in her surgery.

He moved past her and picked up the satchel. He felt he needed to say something about what she'd done for him. "Thanks for getting me out of the Graveyard."

Her frown dissipated. "You're welcome. I was happy to do it. I've heard terrible things about Sydon."

"He's the devil's own." He lifted the bag. "Thanks again and please don't worry about any of this."

He headed down the hall and made his way to the front bedroom. Opening the bag that Warren had brought over for him, he pulled out an oversized zipper-bag that held a pair of boots. They looked big enough to fit him. He laid out a pair of black leathers and a black tank, the basic uniform of the Savage Border Patrol.

He was just handling the Glock Warren had provided for him when Mary's voice entered his mind. *Fergus?*

Yes?

Warren put some ham steaks in the fridge for you. I'm cooking you up a solid meal, and I insist you eat before you head out. The milk isn't nearly enough to nourish you right now and that's your doctor speaking.

His doctor? His *vet,* because he wasn't a man anymore. He was a Goddamn animal. Still, he liked that she was looking out for him.

Okay. He fished out his shaving gear, but that's when he caught the aroma of the meat. He dropped the kit on the bed and was moving before he'd formed the thought.

The wolf in him knew what he needed and he levitated swiftly back to the kitchen.

Mary chuckled as she drew a plate down from the cupboard. She didn't offer a single comment as she slapped the fried ham down on the ceramic and handed it to him.

He felt like a freight train of must-eat-now.

He took the plate as well as the knife and fork she passed to him and moved to the table near the island. Some part of him was fully aware he was still in his gladiator briefs, but he didn't care. He could feel the skewer scar on his heart like a hard pebble reminding him he'd almost died.

He needed this meal because he had a job to do. He had to retake his pack before Sydon did any more damage. He glanced outside. Shit, at least an hour before the sun set.

He ate.

He ignored the rose-yarrow scent Mary exuded, the one that kept his cock twitching every other second.

Coffee came next, a large mug. He drank and didn't care that he burned his mouth a little. He sent healing to his tongue and fixed himself up.

Scrambled eggs were next. Then another ham steak. He ate, drank, and ate some more.

Mary didn't try to engage him in conversation. He was an *alter* wolf with a powerful need to take in sustenance that was more canine than human. His survival relied on the constant attention to his basic drives.

Protein kept him physically strong and ready to take on the enemy.

He thought back to the dominance battle. Where had Sydon concealed the skewer?

He already knew: At the seamline on the underside of his wrist guard. A small trigger-spring could have gotten the deed accomplished. The flurry of kicks and punches afterward that had cracked so many ribs had no doubt disguised a pinhole in his upper abdomen.

And of course, he shifted into his wolf form, further restricting a view of the wound.

Sydon had committed a perfectly executed illegal maneuver. If Fergus had died in the Graveyard, no one would have been the wiser.

~ ~ ~

Mary leaned her hip against the kitchen sink, one arm pressed over her stomach as though trying to hold back all that she was sensing and feeling.

Sometimes it was freaking hard to be a fae woman of some ability. In this case, she could sense Fergus's shift in focus, his almost desperate need for food, and that he was in an aroused state around her most of the time.

She just didn't know what to do with it all. And she really didn't understand why Fergus was even in her life. Of course part of her current predicament was completely her fault. Clearly lacking even a particle of self-control where Fergus was concerned, she'd taken him as her dreamglide lover. She still couldn't believe she'd engaged with him in that way.

Though who could blame her when Fergus was nothing short of a god among men. He stood six-five in his bare feet and his features were rugged yet handsome at the same time.

She stared at the back of his head. His long black hair excited her. The male wolves of Savage grew their hair out as a matter of course. She was pretty sure it had to do with the fur they produced when they shifted into wolves. Whatever the case, she found it absurdly sexy. She wanted to touch it even now. She also had a strong feeling she did that a lot when they made love.

A sudden dreamglide image shot through her head of Fergus face down on her bed. She was lying on top of him and kissing his broad shoulders and muscular back, one hand holding a thick sheaf of his hair as she bit and licked him. Was this really her?

Apparently, he'd loved what she did to him. 'More,' his gravelly wolf's voice had murmured. 'God, I can't get enough of what you're doing to me.'

'And I love your body.' How hoarse her voice sounded within the memory, almost more wolf than fae.

With some difficulty, Mary pulled herself out of the memory. Fergus finished his meal and rose from his chair. But he was scowling as he turned to face her.

She wasn't sure why until he asked, "What the hell have you been thinking about because your scent has suddenly flooded this room?"

She couldn't exactly speak. Her gaze fell to his thick pecs, then to his rippled beautiful abs and finally lower to the tan leather gladiator briefs. Yep, aroused. His erect cock was fully outlined, angling beneath the fabric.

More of the same memory returned. She knew his cock well. She'd taken him in her mouth. She'd licked up and down his stalk and played with him. She'd loved her time with him in the dreamglide.

Chills raced over her shoulders and her lips grew swollen with need. A deep ache formed between her legs. She could hardly breathe.

"You need to stop this." His growly voice was now hoarse, and his eyelids were low.

"I'm not sure I can, Fergus. I'm remembering more. I took my time with your body, didn't I?"

He lowered his chin. "Yes. You did." A soft low growl left his throat.

The sound got to her, causing her to clench. She gasped. She might not remember all that they'd done together, but her body apparently did.

She watched his nostrils flare several times. He took a deep breath and finally said, "I'm leaving right after dusk."

"Okay." He should leave. Whatever this was between them had no possible future.

"Thank you for the meal. For everything." He turned, moving in the direction of the hall once more.

"Fergus?"

He paused in his steps, but didn't look back at her.

She continued, "Why are you able to create a dreamglide when you're a wolf?"

He still didn't turn to look at her. "Because we're sharing powers, like Juliet and Brannick, though I have no idea why." He put his feet in motion again, then disappeared quickly down the hall.

She went to the table and gathered up his dishes. She was achy and badly confused. She felt a strong compulsion to follow after him, maybe jump on his back and bring him down to the floor.

Okay, she had to knock it off, or she'd go crazy.

She cleaned up the dishes and after a time, heard the guest shower running. The sound was unfortunate, however, because now Fergus wouldn't even be wearing his briefs. He'd be naked. All she had to do was open the door and she could take a good long look at him in the shower.

Once more, she told herself to get a grip. It helped to have a chore to do as she tidied up the kitchen.

When she was done, she made her way to the master bedroom. She stopped in the doorway and almost let out a scream since an unknown woman reclined on her bed. Well, not on her bed exactly, more like a few inches in the air above the covers. Mary had no idea who she was but she did know *what* she was.

"You're a ghost."

No shit, Sherlock. The ghost's telepathy went straight into Mary's mind.

The woman wore a red tank top, tight black leather pants, and matching boots that tied in front all the way to the knees. Though her form was mist-like, she seemed very real. She had short black hair and large, heavily made up blue eyes. The mist rippled as she moved.

Mary glanced around. "What are you doing in my bedroom?" It seemed a logical question.

The woman planted her hands on her hips and wagged her head. *And what are you doing with my husband?*

"Your husband?"

Fergus.

Mary put a hand to her chest as another memory surfaced, of talking with Fergus about his wife and what had happened to her. "Oh, my God. Of course. You're Sharon?"

Yup, the one with the torn up, broken neck. Her lips turned down. *What a stupid way to die. I'm still embarrassed that I let that bastard seduce me, then kill me. I should have known he was after the Gordion pack and didn't give a damn about me.*

Mary had no idea what she was talking about, but it sounded like Sharon had cheated on Fergus. "You had an affair?"

Several, but this one proved deeply unsatisfying.

"Did Fergus know?"

Didn't have a clue and you're not to tell him. She looked Mary up and down. *He's got the wolf-hots for you and by the odor in the air, I'm thinking your fae ass would like to be all over him. But in real-time, not this dreamglide shit. Oh, don't look so shocked. I'm here because I have a debt to pay and I'm supposed to help you out, or both of you, I still don't know. The full scope of my orders is as yet unclear.*

Mary blinked several times in a row. "What are you talking about?"

Sharon floated down to the floor then crossed to stand in front of Mary. *Well aren't you a tall one. Jesus, you could have been a model. Instead, you like cutting open small animals. You psychotic or something?*

Mary's nostrils flared. "I'm a vet."

Which war?

Mary got that a lot. "Do I look like a soldier?"

Sharon pursed her lips. *I guess not.*

Mary was out of her depth with this woman, this ghost. She needed a shower and some time alone. Moving into the master bath, she shook her head at the sight of herself in the mirror. Her hair stuck out in all directions.

Yeah, you look pretty grimy, yet still Fergus wants you.

Mary met Sharon's gaze in the mirror. "You're not going away anytime soon, are you?"

Nope. I've got a score to settle here in Five Bridges, among other things.

"I'm taking a shower. The night was long, the day longer, and I have a feeling things are about to get worse."

Sharon lifted her strong, arched brows. *Don't mind me. You do whatever you need to do.*

Mary didn't know what to make of a sudden ghost intrusion into her life, especially since she happened to be Fergus's deceased wife. It was too weird.

Mary ignored the fact that the woman remained leaning against the doorjamb and watching her. She stripped out of her silk tank, jeans and underwear. Her muscles ached from the night's activity and from sleeping on a way-too-firm surgical table. She needed to focus on her own self-healing.

She switched on the water and waited until it warmed. Stepping beneath the spray, she moaned softly, though it came out a little hoarse, the way a wolf might moan.

That's one of the things I miss, Sharon called out. *A good, hot shower.*

Mary ignored her.

But that didn't stop Sharon from continuing. *I miss all the tactile sensations, like warm water beating down on your shoulders and back. Lips touching lips. Oh, and Fergus's cock as deep as he can get it.*

"Sharon?"

Yes?

"Shut the fuck up."

She heard a ghostly laugh that sounded like wind through the trees. *So, you've got some grit. Good. You're going to need it.*

Mary glanced in Sharon's direction, ready to start yelling at her, but nothing was there. She could feel that the woman had left.

Had she offended her? Somehow, that seemed impossible since Sharon clearly had a pretty thick skin.

But why on earth was she even in her home?

She enjoyed the rest of her shower in peace as she washed her hair. Twice. She toweled off, then took her time drying her hair before she left the bathroom.

She wrapped herself up in another towel just in case Sharon was still hanging around. Sure enough, when she moved back into the bedroom, Sharon floated as though sitting on top of the headboard, her leather-clad legs crossed.

I changed when I became a wolf. I didn't used to be so crude or even so mean. When I look back, I can see that I was arrogant during my human and later my alter *life. I didn't appreciate what I had. Not even a little. Fergus put up with a lot.*

Mary sensed the shift in the woman's attitude and for that reason stopped to listen to what she had to say.

Sharon met her gaze but she remained on top of the tall, upholstered headboard. She shook her head, sighed a ghostly sound and turned her gaze toward the window. *I hated becoming an* alter *wolf. I mean I loathed it. I wished I'd become anything else, but turning into an animal? It still sickens me, and I think you might have felt the same way if it had happened to you. I can sense your disgust of wolves generally and that has to be hard on Fergus.*

"You're right. I am disgusted. But I'm not happy about being an *alter* fae either. I miss being human. I think everyone who lands here feels that way."

Sharon turned to meet Mary's gaze. *I disagree. Fergus took to life here pretty easily. And I think men like Sydon are thrilled to be whatever kind of beast they want to be. By the way, that man won't rest until he's secured the Gordion Pack."*

Mary frowned. "Haven't you heard? He's alpha right now."

Sharon floated off the headboard and dropped to stand in front of Mary. *I know what's going on and what Fergus intends to do. But one of the reasons I'm here is to tell you that Fergus won't succeed in reversing Sydon's rule without you. He needs your help, badly.*

At that, Mary laughed. "You're kidding. But what can I do? I'm a fae woman that likes taking caring of small animals. Which reminds me, I need to buy more bird seed."

Sharon made a disgusted, ghostly sound. *Wake up, Mary. Your life has changed forever, but you're not owning up to it. Listen to me. Fergus needs you and no, I don't get why that is. But he does. You've already saved his life once, and you may have to do it again. And again.*

Mary felt Sharon's sincerity, but she found it hard to process what she was saying. "It sounds like I'm supposed to be his bodyguard or something."

Yeah. Sharon nodded several times which caused the mist to float around and blur her features for a moment. When she pulled her ghostliness back together, once again she looked almost real. *I think that's exactly what I'm saying. Fergus is damn powerful, as you know. But Sydon will do everything he can to secure the pack. Gordion is his point-of-entrance for his larger plans to rule Savage. Fergus, thinking like a man of honor, won't be able to see the treachery Sydon intends to throw at him tonight.*

What treachery? Do you know what Sydon will do?

Sorry. I don't have the specifics.

Mary turned around and moved slowly to her dresser and pulled out fresh underwear.

No, not that. Sharon said. When Mary glanced at her over her shoulder, Sharon added, *This.* She then whipped across the room and with a profound show of kinetic ability for a ghost, pulled a long negligee from Mary's closet. It flew through the air, landing at Mary's feet.

"I don't get it. You want me to seduce Fergus?"

Sharon laughed, another windy sound. *Tell me you've been thinking anything else since you fed him a couple of ham steaks.*

Mary picked up the fairly sheer nightgown. It had a small leaf-pattern on a cream background. She'd bought it on impulse a couple of weeks ago. "How did you know?" She lifted the nightgown up. "About this, I mean. About how I'm feeling."

Sharon pinched her nose. *Like I told you earlier, you reek of wolf-lust.* Her gaze fell to the nightgown. *Fergus will love you in it.*

"I can't do this, Sharon. I'm not going to seduce Fergus, and I can't be his bodyguard."

Yes, you can and you have to. Otherwise, he'll be dead for real by morning.

Mary stared at her. "You're serious."

As hell. And now the ball's in your court. But don't take my word for it. Access your fae sense of the future and you'll know exactly what needs to be done.

She snapped her fingers and with a quirky smile disappeared.

Mary didn't move even an inch as she held the gown in both hands, her heart pounding in her ears. She could feel that the ghost was gone. A few minutes ago, she'd been planning her night, ready to take care of some sick pets and get on with her life. Maybe make a trip to the store to buy bird seed.

The problem was that the things Sharon had told her made way too much sense. Already her faeness was speaking to her, pointing her toward Savage and toward a very different immediate future.

Mary crossed the room to sit down on the far side of the bed, the negligee in hand. Glancing out the window, she saw that the sun still hovered in the west and wouldn't set for at least another forty minutes or so, which meant Fergus would be under her roof during that time. Wolves were as sensitive to sunlight as everyone else in Five Bridges. It was a terrible pay-off for a long life.

She could hear him in the guest room talking to someone. When Warren had dropped off the satchel with a change of clothes for Fergus, he'd included a cell phone.

Mary thought back to her fae friend, Juliet, and how she'd recently gotten swept up into a vampire's life. Brannick was a good, honorable man, just like Fergus and Juliet was a powerful fae woman who fell hard for the man. Fergus was right. The couple had definitely shared powers and still did. They were also deeply in love. In fact, Mary felt certain she'd learn of an engagement any day now.

Was this to be Mary's path as well, to hunger for a man outside her species, maybe to even be with him permanently?

She shuddered and shook her head. She'd shunned Savage because of how her sister had died and because there were more murders and uprisings in Savage than any other territory in Five Bridges. Wolves were violent.

Yet, she couldn't turn her back on Fergus. She would do what needed to be done, at least for right now. Sydon had a reputation as a man full of perverse, evil intentions. He ran a rogue pack, serving as their alpha, and had set his sights on taking over another pack.

Sydon had already tried to kill Fergus by puncturing his heart with a skewer. He'd do whatever he had to do until he accomplished all his goals.

Mary knew how the packs worked. Sydon, having defeated Fergus in the dominance battle, had a right to become the pack alpha. Even the Savage Pack Council would be forced to uphold his claim, regardless how many of his wolves he hurt in the process.

She cringed at the thought of any of the female wolves being forced to work the Savage Strip sex clubs. They'd be pumped full of amber flame first, of course, a drug that would make them more than willing to do what they were told.

Drawing a deep breath, Mary closed her eyes and took Sharon's suggestion. She used her fae senses to reach into the future. What came to her was a sensation of profound movement all around her. That's when she understood she was experiencing a wolf reaction, not fae at all. She stayed with it, holding the wolf energy close as she focused on the immediate future.

After a moment, images of Fergus came forward. She sensed that at least for the next night, she'd be heading into Savage, a place she'd never wanted to be. But her life right now appeared to be entwined with his, much like the intricate three braids he wore.

Opening her eyes, she glanced down at the nightgown in her hands. Maybe it was a fae instinct, or perhaps just a womanly one, but Sharon was right, Fergus would love her in it. She felt something else as well, that she would love wearing the silky gown for him.

He'd been her lover in the dreamglide. She could feel it now, how close they'd been and why she'd raced across the room and hugged him, why he'd called her 'Sweetheart'.

Knowing he would need her over the next few hours, and that she intended to accompany Fergus back to Savage whether he liked it or not, she stood up and let the towel fall to the floor. She knew this wouldn't just be about the pleasure of sex but about connection. In that sense, she was taking a huge forward step.

Slowly, she slipped the nightgown on.

CHAPTER THREE

SITTING ON THE side of the bed, Fergus stared at the cell Warren had provided for him. He'd just spoken to his fellow alpha and had learned the horrific state of his pack.

His ribs felt crushed all over again.

He had to challenge Sydon, the sooner the better. The bastard was planning on shipping off several of his female wolves to the Savage Strip sex clubs tonight.

Fergus knew Sydon. He wouldn't wait. It was clear he had big plans to rule the territory probably with the help of the cartels and the Gordion Pack was his jumping off point.

He sat on the edge of a wing chair, his towel still wrapped around his waist, damp hair down his back. He glanced out the window. Time was not on his side. He couldn't leave until full-dark. But as soon as he was able, he'd fly to Warren's compound. He and Warren would work together to oust Sydon.

Mary's voice entered his mind. *Fergus, I'm coming with you tonight.*

Fergus frowned. Her words made no sense and her voice, even telepathically, carried an edge. *What do you mean, you're coming with me? To Savage?* His territory was the last place Mary ever wanted to be.

You'll need me tonight. So, as soon as the sun drops below the horizon, you can fly me over. I assume you'll be meeting up with Warren and laying out your strategy for retaking the Gordion Pack.

Fergus stood up. He was thoroughly confused. What the hell had gotten into Mary that she was insisting on joining him? And why was she *telling* him what she planned to do instead of asking?

He left the guest room, headed down the hall and found the door to the master bedroom open. He moved straight in and laid out his thoughts. "You're not going to Savage. I'm planning on a coup and you'd be … in the … way." His voice trailed off as Mary emerged from the bathroom. She wore a sexy nightgown so sheer in places he could see her nipples. They were peaked, a sight that aroused him, to say the least.

His eyes widened. "What the hell are you doing?" He lifted his arm, gesturing to her nightgown. "I mean, what is all this?"

Mary's eyes glinted. "I'm supposed to be with you. I don't understand why and remember, you're the one who found me in your dreamglide so don't pretend for a second that you're an injured party here." Her lips quirked.

"I'm not injured, I'm confused. What's changed? I don't get it."

She moved a few steps closer to him, her scent riding him hard. He loved the way she smelled, her fae femaleness with a hint of rose and yarrow beneath. He could see that she was offering sex, but he needed to know what she meant by it. He didn't want any misunderstandings between them.

"Are you remembering our time together right now?" He asked.

She shook her head, her long blond hair floating around her shoulders. "No, well, maybe a little. A few memories have started leaking through. But I'm definitely sensing all that we did together. It's a fae thing."

"I don't want to take advantage of you. You saved me and maybe you're feeling something that's not real."

She put a fist to her chest. "What I feel is a powerful connection to you that I can't explain. I don't want it to be there, but it is. And I'll tell you something else. Though I'd blocked my dreamglide memories, each afternoon when I would wake up, I knew I'd been with you. I could smell your musky wolfness on my skin even though it was only a dreamgliding experience. I just never wanted to own the truth of what we'd been doing. Your territory represents what I hate most about the *alter* experience, that we live in such a violent place."

"I know. That's why I'm confused."

She took a few more steps so that she was only five feet away from him. Her brows were drawn tightly together. "Fergus, I don't want to hold back from you right now. I may not understand what's going on, but I'm relinquishing at least some of my fears about what your territory is like, what it would be like to truly be with you. But this isn't easy for me."

Fergus was stunned. "You know I've been wanting to date you, but you've refused and I've understood. You don't have to do this, Mary, not any of it. When I first came to you in the dreamglide, I promised myself I would never ask you to come to Savage. Even I knew it was too much. You're a sensitive fae woman. You have a right to despise my territory.

"But with that said, I know that you weren't having these thoughts even a half hour ago, so what changed?" He watched her swallow hard, but she remained silent as though debating what she should tell him.

He continued, "Please tell me. I need to know. You're talking about coming with me to Savage, that you're needed there, but we would be heading into a dangerous situation. At the very least, I need you to be honest with me."

At that, she drew a deep breath and lowered her shoulders. "I had a ghost come to me just a few minutes ago. She talked to me for some time and was very clear about what I should do."

"You're taking orders from a ghost?"

A hint of a smile curved her lips and an amused glimmer entered her light brown eyes, the Mary he knew. "When you put it that way, it does sound odd. But she was very persuasive. Besides, are you really going to reject the invitation? Maybe together we can figure out what's happening between us. It can't be an accident we've found each other or that you can build dreamglides and I can, at times, feel very wolfish."

When she put it that way, he didn't know how he could refuse her. Besides, she stood in front of him in an almost-sheer nightgown. What he wanted most was standing, in real-time, right in front of him. "I'm open."

She took another deep breath, this one punctuated with a huffing sound that was definitely more wolf than fae. "I also know that going into Savage I should be well-marked by you. Warren told me what's going on, about who I am in terms of your wolf-world. He said I was alpha-mate material and all the unbonded alphas would pursue me. If this is true, and I have no reason to doubt Warren, will you? Mark me, I mean?"

Fergus felt like a sledge-hammer had just hit him between the eyes. He couldn't think and he was suddenly dizzy with need as well. Mary was offering herself in real-time, Mary, who he'd lusted after so badly he'd somehow fabricated a dreamglide so he could seduce her while she was sleeping. This Mary, this beautiful woman who had saved his life.

He closed the remaining distance between them and took her arms gently in hand. "I've wanted you so much, just like this, in the flesh. You have no idea. I've craved being with you and now you're here and you're willing. But are you positive you want to do this, because I'm not sure there's any going back afterward."

"This is what I want. But what about you?"

Fergus felt all male in this moment. He might never understand what was going on with Mary, but right now he didn't care. He was at the top of his alpha-mate hunting cycle, and she had everything he needed.

He removed the towel from around his waist, let it fall to the floor, then took her in his arms. She moaned softly as he slanted his lips over hers. She parted immediately, the exact invitation he needed, and he drove his tongue inside with deep thrusts.

She leaned into him, sliding her arms around his neck. Nothing could have felt better to him than the surrender of these movements. Mary, at last, was his in real-time.

Thank God he was fully healed, because he would need to be at full-strength to mark Mary the way he needed to.

When he drew back from her, his jaw trembled. He pulled his lips back and bared his teeth.

He couldn't help what he was doing. It was a dominance signal.

She didn't seem distressed, either, as she brought her hand forward and rubbed her fingers over his incisors. Her touch sent a thrill straight to his cock. Then she kissed him.

You're shaking, Fergus. You need something from me right now, don't you? How about I stretch out on my belly?

He drew back and tilted his head, eyes closed. He released a long, low howl, but from years of training kept the volume turned down. He didn't want the Revel neighborhood to know there was a shifter at large.

~ ~ ~

Mary saw the angle of his throat and with an instinct that was more wolf than fae opened her mouth wide and took the front part of his neck in her mouth. She clamped down hard at the same time.

Mary, that's fucking hot.

She slowly started backing him up to the bed, while retaining her hold on him. She released his throat, but at the same time gave him a hard shove. He fell backward and she took half-a-second to strip out of the silky nightgown.

Leaping, she quickly straddled him, then settled her sex on his cock. She took her time moving up and back along his hard column so that he could feel how wet she was for him. She knew the marking would get very physical and she needed him to understand she wasn't afraid.

His neck arched, and he groaned. "I've wanted this with you so bad. The dreamglide was wonderful but this is incredible."

She leaned over him and looked into his eyes. The dark brown was lit with a familiar amber glow, very wolf. She loved it. She loved the physicality of his wolfness. His scent had started to rise as well, the deep heavy musk of the alpha that had her nipples tingling and her sex clenching.

She shouldn't even be with a wolf, not after how Alicia had died. In fact, she should hate everything about what he was. Yet she couldn't, because this was Fergus. He was a good man. And dammit if his wolf didn't turn her on.

She kissed his cheek and his lips, then moved lower to lick along his throat. His black fur had already formed a thin ring around his neck and his scent was thickest there, like warm summer grasses, sun-drenched rocks, and wolf combined. She nuzzled him, then licked his fur. *You smell like heaven, Fergus, and you taste so good.*

A low growl returned. She lifted her hand to touch his mouth then rubbed her finger over his wolf fangs again. She couldn't help the moan that rushed from her throat.

She lifted up so she could look at him again. She savored the strong shape of his brows, the amber in his dark eyes, the way he pulled his lips back to let her know he was very male.

She reached down low and caught the head of his cock in her hand. She held his gaze as she slowly positioned him at her sex.

As she eased onto him, he huffed out a series of wolf grunts. "Damn that feels good, Mary."

She released a long stream of pleasure-filled air. "And your cock feels amazing. I've wanted you like this as well, Fergus. In real-time." When another wave of his scent reached her, she shuddered. Her nostrils quivered, more wolf than fae. She drank in his musk, and it sent a ripple through her sex so that she clenched around him. He groaned heavily.

She leaned down and nipped at his throat along the line of his fur. His scent grew stronger, which sent another ripple and this time when she clenched it was like a melody she played with her internal muscles.

"How are you doing that? My God, Mary." He surrounded her with his arms, caressing her back.

"It's you, Fergus. It's how you smell. Your scent is making me do things I didn't know I could do. Give me more." She licked his throat. The fur tingled on her tongue and another wave of his musk hit her.

Only this time, the clenching caused a different kind of reaction in Fergus.

It all happened so fast that she was airborne before she knew what hit her. Fergus had pulled out of her and flipped her up, then over. She landed on the bed on her back.

He was poised above her on his knees. His cock stood upright and he held it in one hand as he stared down at her, his eyes at half-mast. A heavy V of black fur appeared on his chest angling well below his navel, pointing the way.

She arched on the bed, aching for him, needing him to get back inside her. She reached for his arms, but he leaned away from her. He seemed to have something else in mind as his gaze fell to the narrow landing patch of blond hair on her sex. Another growl left his throat.

Gliding backward, he moved farther down on the bed, then lowered his mouth to her sex and began to lap. But he wasn't gentle about it. Instead, it was as though he was feasting on her and the grunting, hungry sounds he made teased her into a frenzy.

She howled softly, a strange sound for a fae woman to make. Like Fergus, she kept the volume down as well.

He lifted up and howled with her.

In a quick, rolling motion, she turned on her stomach then lifted her hips into the air. It was blatant, animal-like and she loved doing it, knowing it would drive the wolf in him crazy.

She felt him grip her hips with his hands. At the same time, she rose up on all fours.

His howls transformed into a low guttural grunting sound. He pierced her sex with his cock and began to drive into her with deep thrusts.

Her breaths came in short gasps. She pulled her long hair away from her neck. She knew what was coming and the strange rippling inside her sex began to flow once more, repeating over and over.

Mary that feels amazing. He licked the back of her neck and the ripples increased in speed. *And you're showing a thin ridge of blond fur here.* He licked her neck.

He began to pump into her which strengthened the ripples. Her moans turned to a huffing kind of grunt. Pleasure built a fire inside her. His tongue on her neck kept the ripples moving even faster and her sex clenched around his stiff cock.

When she felt him bend over her with his chest pushing into her back, she knew what was coming. She felt saliva from his mouth first. He was grunting hard and pumping with equal force as his extended wolf teeth bit down on the back of her neck, clamping her into a submissive hold.

She released a high-pitched howl as pleasure flowed all down her body.

He held onto her chest, an arm across her breasts, and pumped faster.

She'd never experienced anything like it.

Deep within her abdomen, she felt a strong downward push, which she sensed was wolf in nature.

More, she sent telepathically.

He increased the speed of his thrusts until she was rocking hard on the bed. Ecstasy roared toward her. The inner push suddenly thinned out and an orgasm burst over her sex. The pleasure she felt exploded into a surge of heat so that she cried out in long, strained gasps.

At the same moment, Fergus released the hold on her neck, rose up, then slammed her from behind. He howled through clenched teeth. The sound of his wolf-cries brought another wave of orgasms flowing through her.

Ecstasy carried her into secret, hidden realms.

Her chest felt full and warm.

She joined his howls with a song of her own.

Knowing he was spending his seed inside her put a flush on her skin. She tingled all over and shivered as he began to slow down. She could also smell an unusual, heavy musk scent that rose off her skin. It smelled like animal but with a hint of mountain grasses.

Instinctively, she knew it was Fergus's mark, something every other wolf would be able to detect. The experience also wasn't the same as a true bonding, but for now it would help warn other wolves away from her.

She was breathing hard as she lowered herself onto the bed. He followed with her, remaining connected. She could feel that he was still hard inside her.

"You're still erect?"

"I'll be like this for a few minutes. It's the way of the wolf."

She moved her hips so that she could feel his girth deep inside. "I love it Fergus. All of it. Some of the blocks have weakened as well and I'm catching glimpses of how we were together, how many times we made love, the way we talked. It was beautiful.

"But there's something more. I can feel the wolf developing in me. The howls, the intensity of every scent. In the middle of everything, I even wrinkled my nose like I've seen you do and bared my teeth. She touched her throat. And I'm sprouting fur, how is that possible?"

"I don't know except like those before us, we seem to be sharing powers."

He lifted up enough to kiss her cheek and to keep the full weight of his body from compressing her chest.

It took a long time before her breathing evened out.

She turned her head toward the window and saw that the late afternoon was finally making its shift to night.

"We'll be heading out soon."

"Yes. We will."

~ ~ ~

Fergus felt like a man reborn. As much as he'd valued the dreamglide sex with Mary, real-time was so much better.

He drew out of her slowly and reached for the box of tissues on the nightstand. He pulled out several and tucked them between her legs.

"Thank you."

He leaned down and kissed her back over and over. He eased off the bed, careful not to catch one of her limbs or her hand with his movements.

He was satisfied in the best way, because he'd succeeded in marking her. His seed combined with her orgasm had released his wolf-musk through her skin, something other wolves would be able to detect.

For a moment, he'd almost felt as though he could bond with her, but it hadn't happened.

Nor should it have. Mary wasn't a wolf, yet somewhere deep within his soul he'd been hoping to cross that magical line and make her his alpha-mate.

He'd felt something low in his abdomen as well, a force that had reached for Mary. Maybe she'd experienced something similar. But as her climax soared, the sensation dissipated. The part of him exhibiting fae traits had actually sensed that the bond had tried to form, but couldn't.

The good news was that he'd felt anything at all. In the past, ever since Sharon died, his experiences with potential alpha-mates hadn't yielded the smallest bonding sensation.

He took a quick shower to clean up and when he returned to the bedroom, Mary was sitting on the side of the bed her gaze fixed to the floor. She looked shocked out.

Oh, God, had he been too rough with her?

"Mary, are you okay? Did I hurt you?"

She looked up at him and shook her head. "I'm fine. It was wonderful. It's just that I'm feeling as though something terrible has happened in Savage. Fergus, we need to get over there right away. Your pack is being hurt."

He drew close to her and instinctively put a hand on her shoulder. But as he made the connection, his back arched painfully. The same sensations pummeling Mary now afflicted him.

He felt pain.

Fear.

His people racing around wildly.

His mind became fixed on the outdoor communal area of the Gordion Compound. He felt the presence of several bodies and a lot of blood. He recognized one of his betas, now dead.

Jesus. What had Sydon done?

He stood up. "I have to call Warren and find out what happened. I'll let you know as soon as I reach him. Go ahead and shower, get dressed. Okay?"

She nodded, but tears were in her eyes.

He felt it as well, that some tragedy had happened. His throat was tight as he hurried to the guest bedroom.

Once there, he retrieved the phone Warren had given him to use, then called his fellow alpha. "What's going on with my pack?"

"How did you know?"

"It's hard to explain. Mary, as a fae, felt something and I did as well. Please, tell me what's happened."

"I just talked to Ryan. You have a young female wolf named Elena, new to your pack since she's only been an *alter* wolf for a few months, right?"

"Yes. Elena." She had dark brown hair, which she wore straight and cropped at her chin. The process of coming to Savage had been especially traumatic for her, since she'd lost the rest of her family through some tainted *alter* serum. She was a sweet girl still in high school. The women of his pack had worked hard to help her feel like they were her new family.

Fergus could feel what had happened to Elena at the same moment Warren spoke the words. "Sydon's rogue wolves raped her, then were forcing her into a van with a lot of other women destined for the Naked Wolf on Savage Strip where they'd be put to work for the night.

"Elena started battling the nearest rogue wolf. Apparently, she got hold of a knife from his belt sheath. But instead of attacking him, she cut her own throat. She bled out before anyone could save her.

"Some of your male wolves went insane and started attacking the rogue wolves. But Sydon had already stripped them of their weapons. Only his rogues were armed. Fergus, you've got ten dead, eleven including Elena."

Fergus dropped into the nearby chair and shaded his eyes with his free hand. Life in Savage was difficult at best. Wolf tempers ran on the fiery side and too many wolves lost their lives through hotheadedness.

Knowing Sydon's new policies had driven his wolves to madness strengthened his need to get back to Savage.

Warren continued, "Fergus, there's something else you should know. Though Sydon stopped the revolt almost as soon as it started, he's used it as an excuse to imprison your most powerful wolves, Harley and Ryan included."

"Fuck." They were both alphas-in-training who Fergus relied on.

"You've got to get over here. You can stay in my compound as long as you need to and I'll support your effort to get rid of this interloper. We'll do whatever it takes. Shit, if Sydon gets the cartels entrenched behind him, we'll have the devil of a time in the territory. I fear we'll end up with a war among all fifteen packs."

He knew what Warren meant, how a small portion of strife in one part of Savage could build easily into a full-scale nightmare. Mary was right to be concerned about an association with Savage. His land was a perpetual hot, dry wind headed for an already burning forest fire.

"Warren, listen to me. I've got a situation here, and I need you to go with the flow if you can. Mary is coming with me. I don't know why, but the pack won't survive without her. It's just something I'm sensing right now. Can you live with that?"

Warren said nothing for a long moment, then finally responded. "These are extraordinary times, Fergus. I was with Mary when she brought you back from the dead. And I can feel it, too. There's something about her that we need here in Savage. As much as either of us can comprehend what's going on, I get it. You're both welcome in my compound. Talk to you in a few."

Fergus hung up, relieved that Warren understood. He heard the shower running. A moment later, when the water shut off, Mary called out, "I won't be long."

Fergus stood up and put on the leathers and black tank Warren had sent over for him. Socks and the heavy leather boots came next. He and Warren were almost the same size though Warren was taller if only by an inch.

He added the belt and holster, then checked the Glock Warren had provided. Satisfied, he slid it into the holster.

Every death of a pack member hit him hard. He conducted funerals as a necessary way to console his pack. But he was furious that Sydon had succeeded in getting so many members of his pack killed within less than twenty-four hours of becoming the Gordion Pack alpha.

Sydon, however, wouldn't stay in that position for long, not if Fergus could help it.

As he thought the situation through, however, he knew he needed to talk to one other person. Sitting down on the side of the bed, he called the head of the Savage Pack Council, Andrew Dean, though he spoke with Dean's assistant first. The assistant sounded flustered as soon as Fergus mentioned his name.

He waited, wondering what Dean would make of hearing from a man he thought dead.

"Is this some kind of joke?" Dean's brusque voice hit Fergus's ear. "Because I don't think it's funny. Eric Fergus died last night, you sonofabitch."

"No, Dean, I didn't."

There was silence, then, "Fergus?"

"So, you recognize my voice?"

"Of course I do, but I was told by more than one reliable source that you'd been killed in a dominance battle with Sydon."

"You were only half informed. The fae, Mary Somers, found me in the Graveyard not far from Revel Territory and with Warren's help, she saved my ass."

The silence that returned disturbed Fergus more than anything else could have. "Sir?"

"You know of recent events at your compound?" Dean's voice was low and distressed.

"Yes, Warren just told me. But I can get proof in the form of an ultrasound picture that Mary took showing Sydon's use of an illegal skewer during the dominance challenge. He punctured my heart and that's how he almost killed me. Dean, I want my pack returned to me. Now. Call the council for an emergency meeting and get this done."

Dean let loose with a long string of invectives, ending with, "That fucking bastard. But listen Fergus, you can't tell anyone about the skewer."

Fergus didn't get it. "Why the hell not? I'll be able to reverse his takeover."

"I'm sorry, but it won't be that simple. Not anymore."

Fergus had expected some resistance, but not a flat refusal. He knew Dean. He was a good man. He was also frequently blocked by forces outside his control, some emanating from the cartels and others from the Five Bridges Tribunal itself.

Finally, Fergus asked, "What's happened since last night, that proof of an illegal weapon won't reverse Sydon's status with the Gordion Pack?" Something else had to be going on.

Dean huffed a heavy wolf sigh that carried a grunt at the end. "The cartels have gotten involved. They're backing Sydon. You know that there's a heavy demand for female wolves in the sex clubs, especially when they've been dosed with amber flame. Sydon has given the cartels the right to take any woman they want from the Gordion Pack, mated to another wolf or not. My sources tell me at least five are headed to Savage Strip as we speak."

"Warren told me Sydon was sending them to the Naked Wolf, but he didn't know about the cartels. So, what are you saying? Can I expect any help from the council?"

"No. I'm sorry Fergus. It wouldn't matter if you produced a thousand ultrasound photos. Though the council has to stand down, I won't block you if you want to retake your pack. But only a dominance battle will serve. In fact, this phone call never happened. Do you understand?"

"I do."

"Fergus, give him hell and I'm sorry."

When Fergus hung up, he turned his phone over and over in his hands. He felt a hand on his shoulder and looked up at Mary. She wore jeans again, a pair of running shoes, and a couple of tank tops, one over the other like he'd seen some of his wolves do. One of the tanks was white, the other lavender. She looked beautiful with her long blond hair loose around her shoulders and a concerned glint in her light brown eyes.

He covered her fingers with his palm.

"Tell me everything," she said. "Again, I'm supposed to help you, so use me."

As he spelled out the atrocities underway at his compound, he watched her jaw grow tighter and tighter. He'd half expected her to break down and weep, maybe even change her mind about joining him in Savage.

Instead, she dipped her chin. "I'm ready, Fergus. Let's go kick Sydon's ass to hell and beyond."

CHAPTER FOUR

MARY'S HEART POUNDED as Fergus held his arm wide for her. She stood with him on her back deck, the night sky showing a few stars despite Phoenix's light pollution.

She stepped onto his right boot, unable to believe she was actually going to fly with Fergus all the way to Savage.

His sawdust voice hit her ear and sent chills over her shoulders. "Now, slide your arm around my neck."

She felt dizzy as she lifted her arm and did what he told her to do. When he pulled her tight against his body and his wolf heat cascaded over her, she'd never felt more secure. "So, you're going to take me high into the air?"

"I won't go too far up, just enough to escape detection by the average eye."

She was close enough to smell his wolf scent, which had the effect of making certain parts of her shiver and ache all over again. Deep within her abdomen, she felt that same strange tug which didn't make sense to her. It felt sexual, yet not. It felt connected, oddly, to her heart, and she had no idea what it meant.

But it felt more wolf than fae, part of the sharing of inexplicable *alter* characteristics with Fergus that she doubted she'd ever comprehend.

As he rose into the air, she tightened her hold on his neck.

Fergus switched to telepathy. *Don't choke me now.* But she could see that his lips curved.

Despite how nervous she felt at flying for the first time, she eased back on her grip. He held her firmly around the waist so she knew she was safe.

She forced herself to relax and take in the view. Over a month ago, when he'd carried her to safety, she'd been unconscious. Now, she could have a good look at the western section of Five Bridges.

So much of our land, she said, staying mind-to-mind, *looks like we've been battling with tanks, mortars and grenades. There's one stretch of well-kept suburbia, then next to it a hundred feet of torn up cement and asphalt with weeds growing through.*

I think you've described it exactly.

He shifted direction slightly, easing more west than south. They'd soon reach Blackwater Bridge, one of the five main, tri-part bridges in their province, connecting the human part of Phoenix with both Revel Territory and Savage. Even at a distance of two miles, she could see the well-lit bridge and the searchlights indicating the border between the U.S. and Five Bridges.

I love the view from here.

Levitating is great, Fergus said. *And I'm wondering if that's something you'll be able to do soon. Juliet can. She gained the ability when she'd been working with Brannick to get you out of Roche's operation.*

Mary wondered the same thing. *She and I had a discussion about it. Nothing had shocked Juliet more than finding out she could take to the air.*

Two juxtaposed emotions ran through Mary at the same time. The first was a desire to fly just like Fergus. But the other, which seemed more profound, was knowing what she'd lose by not being wrapped up in his arms.

It was probably in this moment, more than at any other time in the past twenty-four hours, that she realized she was in trouble with Fergus. She felt a deep affection for the wolf and an accompanying desire to stick close to him despite the fact that he was an *alter* wolf living in a horribly violent territory.

She didn't respond to Fergus's observation about the potential for flight. Instead, she gestured with her free hand to the southwest. *I can see the tree-line of the Savage pine forest. The Gordion Compound is located the opposite direction, though, isn't it?*

Yes, near the eastern edge. Like your home, some of my pack residences border the Graveyard. Though we're not quite south enough to be close to Elegance Territory. Another pack rides the spellcaster border.

She sensed the sudden tension in him. She knew why. Wolves really didn't get along with witches or warlocks. The enmity ran deep.

Early on in Five Bridges's history, there'd been a series of wars between the two species that ended with mass casualties on both sides. These frequent, bloody conflicts had caused the U.S. Government to separate all five territories from each other with ditches and barbed wire. Some estimated the amount of wire used could stretch across the United States and back. She thought it was an exaggeration, though maybe not, because the province looked in many places like something from World War II newsreel footage.

She knew they were heading to the portion of Savage allotted to the Caldion Pack, led by Warren. The only thing she knew about his compound, however, was that he'd built in the densest part of the pine forest. Half his pack lived in cottages around the compound but with underground living spaces called dens. The other half resided in the compound itself in dozens of apartments, also belowground level. The Gordion Pack's compound had a similar set-up.

In more recent years, Savage Territory had become a quieter part of Five Bridges. But she'd learned enough of the history of the province to know that early howling issues had created enormous tensions between Savage and the rest of the territories.

Wolves howled.

They yipped, growled, barked and made all kinds of resonant grunting sounds. The noise just dozens of wolves could make together was overwhelming. But thousands residing in Savage had create a cacophony that had incited more than one inter-species war.

Mary had viewed several videos online featuring a multitude of howling wolves. She wasn't surprised that the noise level had driven other *alter* species into a battling frenzy.

Now Savage was quiet. Time and a lot of rules had established when, how and where wolves could let loose, mostly, underground.

She experienced a sudden sinking of her spirit. She recalled what it had been like earlier to be making love with Fergus and ready to open up her throat and howl like a wolf. She'd restrained the sound, knowing it was necessary. But it had been like having a pair of reins in her hands and pulling with all her might.

The part of her that was sharing Fergus's wolfness knew a powerful impulse to really let go, yet an equally strong instinct to keep silent. The result, however, was an ache in her soul.

Because of her faeness, she sensed how hard it was for wolves to remain in one place and to repress their needs to howl. The pervasive discontent in Savage was the primary reason why wolves like Fergus and Warren worked hard lobbying for National Forest terrain in the White Mountains of Northern Arizona where wolves could be wolves.

As they drew closer to Warren's compound, she began to see scattered, small cottages through the tops of the pine trees. They appeared to be laid out in an arc so that each residence faced the compound dead on. Fergus didn't approach from the north, however. Instead, he flew slowly along the eastern border of the lodge-like stone structure.

The trees opened up to a fairly wide street on the southern property boundary. Though most of the forest roads were made of dirt, this main thoroughfare was paved.

Fergus's rough wolf voice touched her mind. *In case you weren't sure, this is the Caldion Compound. I'm contacting Warren now telepathically.*

Good to know, she responded, aware suddenly that her fear of levitating had disappeared completely.

Her gaze was fixed on the compound below, taking it all in as Fergus began to descend. She saw that the visible portion of the complex looked to be at least five-thousand square feet and was made of stone with a dark gray slate roof. Most of the landscaping was traditional desert rock, hardy plants, and stone walkways.

At the north end of the complex was a large cement area free of trees. A bonfire burned there despite that it was June and hot during the day. Wolves loved fire.

Warren's expecting us at the front entrance, Fergus said. *He'll meet us there. He said he has a dozen wolves standing guard with AR-15s.*

Did you see all the men around the bonfire? Also armed? Fergus, there had to be at least a hundred.

I know. We've got a bad situation brewing because of Sydon and his determination to work with the cartels. If we're not careful, tonight's events could launch another massive war in Savage.

Why a war?

He snorted. *You were right to be worried about the violence in Savage. When our blood gets up, sometimes we forget who the enemy is. Wolves get hurt inadvertently, which causes a pack to rise up and call for revenge. It can be a real domino effect in our territory.*

Mary wasn't surprised. Her sister had died because a few wolves near Alicia had lost it and ended up killing her and several more bystanders. As Fergus had put it, they'd gotten their blood up.

He flew in a wide arc, passing well beyond the paved road to the tree-line opposite Warren's home. He swung back toward the road and crossed it, descending slowly, which served to make his presence known to Warren's guards.

But Mary's fae senses told her he didn't need to be concerned. Though the wolves held automatic rifles in their hands, not one of them raised a weapon in their direction.

Warren was there as well and had his hands on his hips. He was a big man, and frightening to look at especially with his lips compressed into a grim line.

Her gaze was drawn to the scarring on the left side of his face and head. While Fergus drew them close, she allowed herself a few seconds to accustom herself to his disfigurement. That way, she'd be more likely to see the man rather than his scars.

He wore a black tank and leathers, the typical uniform of any of the Five Bridges border patrols. His militarized force wore similar clothes but their tanks bore the Caldion Pack emerald green logo patch. She knew that each pack's force could be identified by their logos and specific colors. Having searched the web several times about Savage, she knew that the Gordion pack wore amber logo patches. If braids were worn, they were also tied up with narrow leather cords in the matching pack color.

Fergus dropped them down to the long, stone front walkway, five feet from Warren. Mary stepped off Fergus's boot and unwrapped her arm from around his neck.

Warren lowered his chin and inclined his head in Mary's direction, but didn't at first make eye-contact with her. Instead, he kept his head bowed for several seconds.

Finally, he stood upright and met her gaze. "Welcome to the Caldion Pack, Mary Somers. We are forever indebted to you for saving our brother's life."

Mary knew the packs often spoke formally, especially during an initial greeting. But his words surprised her and at first she didn't know how to respond. Finally, she said, "And I'll always feel thankful for the part you and your men played in bringing Fergus to my surgery."

Warren appeared to sniff the air, his nostrils fluttering. Afterward, he nodded solemnly. Her fae instincts told her he'd just caught Fergus's marking scent on her. She felt his approval.

He then shifted his attention to Fergus. "We're more grateful than we can say that you've survived."

Mary glanced at Fergus, wondering what his formal response would be. Instead, he smiled and moved swiftly in Warren's direction. He took Warren's outstretched hand in a typical handshake, but slung his free arm around his shoulders and offered up a bro-hug, their clasped hands between. "Thanks for getting my ass out of the Graveyard." Yup, much less formal than Warren.

Mary couldn't see Fergus's face, but the sudden sheen in Warren's eyes told her more about the relationship between the two alphas than anything else could have.

Warren finally pushed away. "All right, you ugly bastard, come into the compound. We've got a lot to discuss and not much time."

Fergus pivoted toward Mary and held his hand out to her. She joined him swiftly, but at the same time glanced at the warriors nearest her.

They each remained on guard, and she could feel their high level of tension. Sydon's actions had definitely stirred up the wolf community.

As she moved through the massive doorway, she saw that the same pavers on the front walk continued into a large, two story foyer. No ornaments were there, no paintings or even a table. In that moment, she felt the absence of a woman not just in Warren's house, but in his life and in his pack as well. It seemed to her that the entire structure was waiting for the right woman to arrive.

The house proper was two-story with a broad curved staircase off to the left. She supposed Warren's private rooms were up there.

A bank of windows covered the back of the house so that she could see the bonfire and the pines in the distance.

Warren led them down a hall to the right of the foyer and into a smaller room with a leather-topped table in the center. "I've been in continuous contact with the Gordion Pack wolves but we've got to move fast. Sydon's just issued orders to kill the men he's holding in the dungeon prison."

Mary felt a wave of wolf-energy blast from Fergus's body. "What the fuck is he doing? A mass execution could ignite another all-pack war in Savage."

She knew this was Fergus's biggest concern, that all the packs would suddenly start attacking each other, igniting a full-scale conflict throughout Savage.

~ ~ ~

Fergus paced Warren's strategy room. After he'd walked off some of his rage, he returned to the table. Warren was spreading out a broad map that he soon realized was a detailed and very professional rendering of Fergus's compound. "Holy fuck, I had no idea you had something like this."

"I confess that I have one of each of the fifteen main compounds, including my own. I wanted to get one of Sydon's house, but no spy I've ever sent out to investigate has come back with useful information. Sydon conducts his rogue pack business entirely in secret."

Fergus moved to the side and as Warren weighted each corner, Fergus examined the map. The scale was perfect, every room detailed.

Warren slapped his hand over the belowground, third level area on the east that served as a series of several large dungeon jail cells. "He's keeping your men here."

Fergus knew every inch of his pack's compound, including a few secret passages not on the map.

"There's only one entrance to the row of dungeon cells," Fergus said. "It's along this corridor that leads back to the central stairwell." He used two fingers to trace the path as he spoke. "Even if we could get a team down there, we'd be trapped between Sydon's guards working this area and the ones sure to follow us in."

Next, he ran his fingers along the edge of the ground floor, on the same side of the compound as the cells. "However, what you probably don't know is that there's a door here that leads down two flights of stairs and into a hidden hall that runs the entire length of this wall behind the dungeon area."

Warren smiled. "A secret passage. I like it."

"But even with that advantage, this would be a difficult rescue."

Mary, who stood at the foot of the table, said, "I could use my dreamglide and scout everything for you. And I can keep scouting the whole time. I'd be able to see where the guards come from, let you know when they arrive, and how many in each team. Would that help?"

Warren, who was at least ten feet away from her, took another step backward. Fergus had seen him do this before and he understood. Alpha-mate hunting during the peak of a cycle was like a series of knives in a man's hide. Despite the fact that Mary now carried Fergus's mark, she would still be highly attractive to an alpha.

He contacted Mary telepathically. *I need to do something right now for Warren's sake. Will you allow it?*

Of course, but what?

He headed in her direction, but he was smiling. *A kiss should work.*

Wasn't the mark enough?

He's near the peak of his annual cycle. You know about that, right?

I do. So, I guess you'd better kiss me because I can sense his distress as well. Her beautiful full lips curved as he descended on her.

He took her in his arms, surrounded her fully, then pulled her close. He rubbed her face with each cheek in turn, releasing more of his wolf scent. Finally, he kissed her.

Fergus, my God. That scent. You could probably throw me on my back right now and do whatever you wanted, and I wouldn't raise a whisper in protest.

Those words did not help his groin at all. But he was feeling it, too, an overwhelming need to get inside her again. He'd kissed her to strengthen his bonding scent for Warren's sake. But as he drew back, he had to work at re-learning how to breathe while at the same time doing math-sums in his head.

Mary didn't look in much better shape. Her cheeks were flushed where he'd marked her, and she held both hands away from her body as though trying to regain her balance. Her lips were swollen, her eyes glittering.

That's when he caught her scent as well, part fae and now, yup, part wolf. It still shocked him that he and Mary were caught in a strange sharing of *alter* abilities. What the hell was happening between them?

Sure, he'd seen this first-hand between Brannick and Juliet, but now the same phenomenon was making him question everything he knew about living in Five Bridges.

"You're sharing powers, aren't you?" Warren's voice had a good effect since it drew Fergus's attention away from Mary.

He turned slightly to meet Warren's gaze. "We are. It's strange as hell."

He heard Mary take a shuddering breath as he left her. He then moved back to the side of the map table.

Warren murmured, "Thank you for that. I suggest you do it a few more times throughout the night. It helps."

Fergus caught Warren's almost tortured gaze, then slid into telepathy. *But it's Mary, isn't it? I'm not just imagining that she's alpha-mate material?*

She is. I felt it the moment I arrived in the Graveyard last night. It shocked the hell out of me.

Against his will, Fergus stiffened. "Did you hit on her?" He asked aloud. The question was completely out of line, but again his mate-hunting cycle had also reached its peak and he had to know.

Warren pressed his fist against his own chest. "On my honor, no, Fergus. I knew even then she was yours. Besides, we were a little busy getting your ass into a sling for transport, if you recall."

Fergus squeezed his eyes shut for a long moment. He breathed through a powerful need to pound the shit out of Warren for being so close to Mary during the shared ordeal. "I know this is wrong, but I wish you hadn't been anywhere near her."

At that, Warren appeared to relax. "Well, I'll say this. I'm glad I was there, because if I hadn't been, you'd be worm-fodder."

Fergus chuckled. "You're right. I would."

Fergus? Mary's telepathic voice pulled his attention away from Warren, but she wasn't standing at end of the table anymore. In fact, he couldn't see her at all.

He rushed toward the door, but found her unconscious on the floor where she'd last been standing.

What the hell?

She was stretched out on the woven carpet, her blond hair laying in a thick wave off to the side. He didn't know what was wrong with her.

He picked up her hand and patted it. *Mary? What's going on? What happened? Are you okay?*

Fergus, relax, I'm in the dreamglide. Warren said we didn't have time to mess around and there you both were sparring with each other. Anyway, I'm in the foyer of your compound. I focused on Sydon and found him. He's getting his rogue wolves worked up. In a few minutes, he's planning to send them to the dungeon to slaughter your men. But it won't be anything tidy and neat like a few bullets; he's ordering his men to use their swords.

I'm safe here for now in Warren's strategy room, but you've only got a few minutes to save your wolves. I'll stick close to Sydon's team in the dreamglide to keep you informed.

As Fergus stood up, he realized how much he trusted Mary. He'd stake his life on the truth of everything she'd just told him.

He waved Warren forward and told him what was going on. Warren was right with him.

Fergus led the way back to the entrance area.

Once there, Warren ordered two of his troops to stand guard in front of the closed door of the strategy room. No one was to go inside. They were to guard the door and the Revel woman, Mary, with their lives.

The men lined up, somber as hell.

Warren then levitated swiftly in the direction of the back patio. He stood on the threshold of the doorway and barked a series of orders that separated a number of his wolves from the rest. This team levitated into the air. Not all wolves could levitate, only those with enough essential power

Once they moved into position, Warren turned to Fergus. "Lead the way. My team is yours."

Fergus levitated in their direction. They were ten wolves strong, each armed to the hilt as Fergus shot into the night air and headed east. As fast as he flew, Warren and his men kept up with him.

He arced well to the north of the Gordion Compound then circled back to come in from the east. To his surprise, he saw that though several of Sydon's men milled around the front porch, most of these carried bottles of beer and no weapons. There wasn't a single guard posted outside the actual structure, which meant that Sydon's arrogance had left his flank exposed.

Fergus contacted Mary. *We're on the east side of my compound. Can you get us in unseen?* He explained about the lack of exterior guards.

I'll head in your direction, but you've got to move fast and do as I tell you each step of the way.

Understood.

He counted the five seconds it took Mary to get back to him. Each one felt like an eternity.

All right, Fergus. The foyer is swarming with wolves, though half of them are drunk. I don't see Sydon anywhere, but his execution team has levitated down to the lower levels. Can you arrange for one of your Gordion wolves, maybe a female carrying cleaning gear, to let you in through the east window of the living room?

I'll get on it. He knew of one female wolf, Brynna, whom he could trust and who would have the presence of mind to perform this small act of subterfuge. It took a moment to contact her telepathically, but once he did, she said she was on it. He warned her about Sydon's unruly bunch by the front entrance.

Don't worry, Brynna telepathed. *I can handle them and I'll take the route through the kitchen. It shouldn't be a problem getting the east window open.*

But as soon as you're done, Brynna, I want you of there.

You'd better believe I won't stick around. Several of us are in hiding. I take it you've got a plan to get rid of this monster?

I do. And thanks.

My pleasure. And by the way, we're so happy you're alive. Warren let both Harley and Ryan know. The word spread fast. All right, I'm gathering supplies now.

Fergus kept his team hidden in the forest to the east of the compound. He relayed to them what Brynna was planning to do.

As soon as he saw Brynna pretending to wipe down the window, then open it, he checked the immediate area once more. He still couldn't believe Sydon didn't have a single wolf patrolling the exterior of the compound. Unbelievable.

Fergus moved swiftly to the window that led into the long living room. He rarely used this space and fortunately the thirty yards to the foyer, where Sydon's wolves had gathered, would make it easier to sneak in.

By now, Brynna had already left the room. He lifted the lower portion of the window up and leaped inside, waving for Warren and his team to follow.

He moved toward the door leading to the hall and waited there. Though he could hear Sydon's men in the foyer, he was stunned by how quiet the rest of the compound felt. Then again, he wasn't.

By now, a good number of his people had probably escaped into the forest seeking shelter in several places he'd set up just for this contingency. The rest would be hiding out in their apartments, trying to fly below Sydon's radar.

Mary's voice hit his mind. *I can see you're in the house, but the crew near the front door has a direct line of sight to your doorway. Can you create a diversion outside? Otherwise you'll never be able to get to the secret door.*

I'm on it.

Fergus contacted Warren telepathically and let him know what needed to be done. Warren in turn sent one of his men outside into the nearby pine trees.

Mary, I've sent a man into the forest to make some noise. Let me know when we can head into the hall.

I'm watching the foyer now.

As directed, a sudden burst of automatic gunfire sounded to the east of the compound.

They're heading out, Mary said. *Hold. Hold. All right, you're clear. Move!*

Fergus didn't hesitate, but levitated through the doorway and felt Warren and his men follow swiftly behind. He turned to the right, away from the foyer and flew swiftly to the end of the hall. Once there, he found the latch that opened the hidden door. Because a tall cabinet was attached, he moved it carefully.

The moment he had access to the secret passage, the well-trained warriors darted through the opening, each levitating to keep from making a sound on the stone floor.

Fergus went in last and closed the panel. To Mary, he said, *We're in.*

No one saw you and I can keep up with you, so get moving, wolf.

Fergus loved the way she talked to him.

Inside, the wolves were lined up, waiting for him.

He levitated swiftly past them. There were no lights in the stairwell, but his *alter* wolf vision enabled him to see in the dark as though a warm glow lit the space.

He descended to the dungeon area on the third level. Once there, he flew as fast as he could along the hallway. Through the adjoining wall, he heard his wolves howling, more than one in pain.

When he arrived at the end, he drew up. *Mary, we're in position.*

I can see you, and I've got my eyes on the hallway outside the dungeon cell. Timing will be important if you stand a chance. Some of the rogue wolves have already gone into the cell, but there are at least eight outside, waiting. They're all focused on the wolves getting hurt, though it wouldn't take much to divert their attention.

Fergus knew they couldn't risk getting discovered or they'd never even make it into the hall.

Fergus, you've got to be really careful at this point.

I understand. At the same time, he could hear the shouts of the rogues. One of the captives cried out in pain. He had to do something.

Warren was right behind him. Fergus told him the situation, then added, *Let me see if I can set up another diversion. I'll have Mary get me out with the least possibility of detection, fly above the guards, then hopefully get them headed away from you.*

Sounds like a smart move. Warren responded.

He contacted Mary and relayed the plan. She agreed that it was the best strategy, but added, *Just wait for my signal.* She was cool as hell.

He felt for the mechanism that would open the hidden door enough to allow him to slip through. He held his hand above it, waiting for Mary's command.

Hold, Fergus. Hold. On my command. Hold. And … now!

The snap of her last word had him pulling the mechanism, and the door slid open about ten inches. Like the arrangement on the ground floor, this door also held an attached shelving unit, which made it heavy. He gave it another push, slipped through, then closed it. He rose into the air.

About thirty feet away, Sydon's rogues were clustered around the doorway of the dungeon just as Mary had said they were. They jeered at the prisoners inside.

In order to continue avoiding detection, he levitated to a horizontal position close to the ceiling and began gliding down the passageway. He held his breath as he flew above Sydon's men.

His movement must have caught the eye of one of the men since he started shouting about an intruder.

Fergus put on some speed and called back, "Come on, motherfuckers." He bolted down the long hall, away from the secret door and the rogue warriors.

Mary's voice entered his mind. *It worked. Four of Sydon's wolves are flying after you. The rest are shouting all kinds of things. Let Warren know he's clear to move.*

He shifted his telepathy to Warren. *The ruse worked. Mary says you're good to go.*

Fergus knew the rogue wolves would start firing, so as he reached the top of the corridor, he whipped to the right, into the intersecting hall. A hail of bullets followed. He'd just escaped getting hit.

He dropped to the stone floor to stand his ground and wait. *How we doin', Mary?*

Warren and his team are leaving the secret passage. The four who followed you have slowed their pursuit. They're ten feet away from the upper hall. Warren has part of his team engaging with the wolves by the door. He and the rest are heading toward the four near you.

Everything happened fast.

He heard Warren give a battle shout and guns being fired. He didn't dare engage yet or he'd get caught in the crossfire.

Mary, give me a blow-by-blow. What's going on with Warren?

He's brought three down, the other is rounding the corner in your direction now!

At the same time the last words hit his mind, the fourth rogue appeared. Fergus fired point blank into his chest.

The wolf flew backward, landing in a heap in the corner.

Mary spoke quickly. *All four of the nearest wolves are down. Warren is heading back in the direction of the original cell. The rest of the team has subdued the others who were outside the cell. I think a couple of them are dead. Warren just got there. He's issuing some orders. I think your team has secured Sydon's force in the cell.*

Fergus turned the opposite direction. He stood twenty feet from a broad, ascending staircase leading to the second belowground level. With all the gunfire, someone must have heard. *Mary, is anyone coming down the stairs to this level? Do you see anyone?*

No, there's no one. Wait. I'm seeing movement from the ground floor. Let me check it out. A few seconds passed, before Mary continued, *It's Sydon. I see him now. He's already reached the second level. He's heading in your direction toward the third level.*

I can hear him, heavy boots on stone. But he didn't hear any other sounds. *Mary, doesn't he have a guard with him?*

He's alone.

More arrogance. *That's good news. Thanks.*

For a split-second, Fergus thought about taking Sydon down with a single bullet. But he knew in order to regain his pack, he'd have to battle Sydon again in another dominance fight.

The Savage Pack Council didn't have a lot of rules, but assassination would have removed Fergus from ever becoming alpha to the Gordion Pack again. Though for a few seconds, he actually considered doing Savage a favor and getting rid of Sydon for good anyway.

Living as an *alter* wolf had forced Fergus over the years to develop his own creed. In the chaos of their world, the values he upheld kept him sane.

So, instead of killing Sydon flat out, he moved back into the long hall again, just a few feet, so Sydon wouldn't be able to see him. He waited.

What Fergus couldn't believe was Sydon's arrogance that he would come down to the dungeon level alone, without back-up, when by now he would have learned or possibly even heard that shots had been fired.

What weapon is Sydon carrying?

A sword, right hand.

Okay. I've got this.

Fergus rounded the corner and Sydon came into view as he reached the bottom step.

Fergus took several steps in Sydon's direction, his Glock pointed at chest level.

Sydon stopped in his tracks. "Impossible."

His black brows rose as he stared at Fergus. His hair was as oily-looking as ever and hung in long curls past his shoulders. He had an emaciated look and coal eyes which had always made Fergus wonder if Sydon took witch herbs.

For one of the first times ever, Sydon actually looked surprised. "You're supposed to be dead."

"Not quite. Drop your sword."

The weapon clattered on the stone.

Sydon sneered. "You were flat-lined in the Goddamn Graveyard."

"I had some help." To Mary, he telepathed, *How we doin'? How's Warren? Anyone else coming up the hall?*

No bad guys in any of the nearby halls. I'm moving the dreamglide closer to the dungeon. Okay, I'm here. I can see you at one end and Warren is issuing orders at the entrance to the dungeon cell. Whatever happened in there appears to be over.

Good.

Fergus shifted his attention back to Sydon. As he stared at the wolf who consistently caused misery in Savage, he wanted nothing more than to put a bullet through his heart. But the best he could do was make the situation clear to Sydon. "We'll be battling again soon. Though, for now I'll be keeping you in a cell down here."

He wasn't taking any chances, however. He lowered the angle of his Glock and fired. The bullet pierced Sydon's thigh.

Sydon shouted his pain as he fell, then shifted into his wolf state and lay trembling on the floor. He was a black wolf with a stripe of silver down his back.

Fergus moved to stand over him. "You should be able to heal yourself by tomorrow night, then we'll have a real battle, you sonofabitch."

He contacted Warren. *I just shot Sydon in the leg to incapacitate him. Do you have his rogue wolves contained?*

Most of Sydon's team are dead. Yours are still with us, though a couple are beaten and cut up, but they'll survive.

Fergus breathed a sigh of relief. *Good. How about sending a couple of men down here. I want to move Sydon into a cell and lock him up. But we'll need a muzzle.*

I'll bring help myself.

A half minute later, Warren arrived with three of his men. Each had wild, triumphant battle eyes. They'd engaged Sydon's forces and prevailed.

Fergus directed them to shove Sydon's ass into the nearest cell and lock him up.

During the next few seconds, Warren's team muzzled Sydon, hauled him to the cell, then threw him inside. Sydon thrashed and whimpered because of the pain, but Fergus had no sympathy for him. With the door shut and locked, Warren ordered his men to remove the corpse at the top of the hall.

Fergus joined Warren near Sydon's cell. From there, he had a view of the clean-up in progress all down the hall.

Warren waved his arm off to the side. "I'm having the dead moved into the adjacent cell until we can get them taken to the morgue."

Fergus nodded, then looked inside Sydon's cell. He lay shaking.

Warren crossed his arms over his chest, a hard expression on his face. "I'm glad you shot him. He can't do much harm in this condition. But are you sure you don't want to finish him off?" He growled his anger and added a disgusted grunting sound.

Fergus understood where Warren was coming from. "Believe me, I'd like nothing better. But he's pack-bonded. If I kill him straight out, I'll lose the pack forever. Given what Dean said about the cartels, the council would probably be forced to assign a drug-friendly alpha instead. Besides, I want to defeat Sydon in a legitimate dominance battle. Nothing else will do."

Warren shook his head, his lips turned down. "Something isn't right with this wolf."

"I know. I feel it, too."

Fergus stepped away from the cell a few feet.

Warren followed, then said, "Let me bring some of my men over here to take care of Sydon's rogue wolves. The team we have down here might be able to do it themselves, but a larger force will subdue the wolves faster with less chance for hurting your pack once the battle engages."

Fergus was relieved. He could sense that the pack-bond had already started to form between Sydon and the rest of the Gordion wolves. It was a peculiar, amazing process, one that he'd experienced and loved.

But the bond was neutral, without discernment, which meant there were good men at the head of packs and several bad ones like Sydon. The close pack ties were the best and the worst of Savage. The bonding process in the hands of strong, ethical leadership could create a harmonious supportive community. In the wrongs hands, death always followed, reminding Fergus he had eleven funerals to plan.

"I won't refuse that offer."

Warren got out his phone and contacted his beta in charge of the Caldion compound. "Alessandro, I want a hundred of our best warriors over here ASAP. And I want them armed, swords, handguns and AR-15s."

Fergus watched Warren for a long moment as he added a few other pertinent directives. Warren had been a good friend for several years. He'd battled drug-runners alongside Fergus while serving on the Savage Border Patrol. He'd been one of several wolves to demand tighter regulations for dominance fights so they could never be used to kill wolves of significantly lesser power. Warren was the kind of man you laid down your life for.

When Warren hung up, he said, "My men will be here in less than a minute. They're ready to take on Sydon's rogue wolves. So, how do you want to handle this?"

Fergus thought for a moment. "Let's ask Mary what's going on out front. We can start there. Keep Alessandro on the com."

Warren held up his phone. "He's right here."

"Good." He pivoted away from Warren slightly, turning in the direction of the stairs. "Mary, you there?"

Her voice entered Fergus's mind. *I'm here.*

Can you bring Warren in on this conversation? He had no idea if Mary had that kind of capacity, but they were both experiencing new abilities. Maybe it was possible.

Let me try. He felt her telepathy expand to include Warren as she drew him into the conversation. *Warren, are you reading me?*

Warren met Fergus's gaze, his unscarred right brow high on his forehead. *Yes, I am, Mary.* He looked startled. Fergus didn't blame him. He'd had the same reaction several times during events of the past few hours. *And I appreciate what you've done for us.*

My pleasure, Mary said. *Now, how can I help?*

Can you get to the front entrance? Warren asked. *My men are headed in, and I want to relay the positions of the enemy before they arrive.*

I'll get right on it, Mary said. *But I'll need to head back to the foyer.* Two beats later, her telepathic voice sounded agitated. *Fergus, Warren, something's happening outside the compound.*

What do you mean? Fergus asked. His whole body tensed up and he drew his Glock. He started to head to the stairs, then decided to wait. He needed to know everything that was going on before he left the third level.

Mary continued, *I'm watching dozens of rogue wolves launch into the air, while some are shifting to wolf form and running hard. All are heading due south. They're wearing gray logo patches and they keep streaming out of the complex. I can see Warren's men in the distance off to the west, but by the time they arrive, Sydon's force will be gone.*

Fergus finally holstered his Glock. He turned in the direction of Sydon's cell. The part of him that was sharing Mary's fae abilities sensed a powerful energy emanating from Sydon.

Fergus got it. *Sydon heard Warren's orders to Alessandro and he contacted his men. He's sent them away.*

Mary said, *That's what it looks like from here.*

Fergus looked around. *Mary, would you reenter the compound and check out our location again? I need to know if there are any more of Sydon's wolves on the lower two levels.*

Will do.

He turned to Warren. "Did you get all that?"

Even Warren smiled. "I sure as hell did. I would have been happy to battle Sydon's wolves, but that would have meant a lot of bloodshed all over your compound. This is much better."

Fergus had to agree. But it also meant a future reckoning with Sydon's force. For now, he focused on securing the safety of his pack.

Mary's voice sounded once more. *There's no one on the third or second levels that look like rogues. I see a lot of shifters hunkered down in odd rooms here and there. Some are hiding. Others I can tell have been hurt.*

Okay. Thanks. But stay put. In real-time, I mean, over at Warren's house. I'll come and get you in a few minutes.

I'm not going anywhere. And right now I'm hovering above you. The halls on the third level are clear as well as the stairs.

Fergus addressed Warren. "I want to do a room-by-room search of the compound. Why don't you and your men hunt through the grounds and the surrounding forest for any of Sydon's wolves and I'll round up my team and do the same for the compound."

"You got it and by the way, we couldn't have done this without Mary."

Fergus nodded slowly. "I know."

Warren called to his team in the dungeon cell and soon had them flying up the stairs, with Warren in the lead. Fergus headed back down the hall and went into the cell that held his men.

Harley came up to him immediately. He was limping with a severe gash on his leg. He had long thick auburn hair and his blue eyes were pinched from pain. His face was bruised as well. "We thought you were dead. But Warren filled us in. Did Sydon really use a skewer during the battle?"

"He did. We can go over the details later, but right now, I want to know what happened in here."

Harley gave a quick report, which confirmed what Warren had told him.

Fergus planted his hand on Harley's shoulder. "You're all alive and that's what matters."

Harley's eyes filled with tears. "Fergus, we lost men tonight and our youngest female wolf. Sydon and his men … vicious … without souls. We didn't have any weapons. We couldn't do anything." He shaded his eyes with his hand.

"I know you, Harley. You did what you could. This is on Sydon, no one else. But I need you to focus right now. We've got to secure the compound."

Harley nodded and worked to compose himself. He stared at the stone floor for a long moment and took several deep breaths, releasing each one with a hoarse wolf sound. When he'd come back to himself, he said, "Tell me what you need me to do."

Fergus took a moment to adjust as well. He wasn't used to feeling so separated from the pack. Because Sydon had begun the bonding process, Fergus felt the distance between himself and the men in the cell like a chasm difficult to cross. But it was just one more reason to make sure the dominance battle happened as soon as possible.

As he glanced around at the wolves, he knew one thing for certain. They might not be bonded right now, but these men would follow his lead. He updated them on the departure of Sydon's wolves and that he'd wounded Sydon to make sure the bastard didn't do any more harm tonight.

A cheer went up that made Fergus smile. This was a beginning.

But there was work to be done to make sure all the Gordion wolves were safe. He instructed his team to make a room-by-room search of each level. "And let our people know that Sydon has been contained and that I'm calling for another dominance battle for tomorrow night."

With his men hunting through the halls, Fergus waited in the central broad hallway of the third level, which housed a long oval running track. Any of the wolves could use it when they needed to take off on all fours.

At least forty Gordion wolves, male and female, were found on the third level, all in hiding. Fergus told them to be very quiet, though most of the women had tears running down their cheeks and at least half reached out and physically touched him.

He examined every person. He found bruises on many of them and healing cuts on quite a few. It was clear Sydon and his men had brutalized the entire pack.

Those who had previously served in guard capacity for Fergus were given weapons that came from Sydon's men. With his team's number now at nearly thirty, he instructed them to do a dedicated search of the second and ground levels.

He knew Warren's team would scour the exterior of the compound and the nearby pine trees.

Fergus stayed on the second level while his men did the search. More wolves emerged from hiding places. At least a hundred of his pack of six hundred were now gathered on the second level.

He did the same as before. Despite the fact he could feel Sydon's bond on his pack, more wolves wept and touched him. He searched the faces of everyone present and comforted those he could.

What surprised Fergus was that there was no sign of any of the rogue wolves. Somehow each had been given the order to retreat and they'd taken off. Which meant Sydon had power, not a good sign. No matter what happened in the coming dominance battle, Sydon wasn't going away anytime soon.

Warren contacted him soon after. *We found no sign of Sydon's men on the outside of the compound. We're combing the forest now.*

Make sure you go cottage-by-cottage carefully.

You know we will. Warren's deep voice had never sounded more serious.

Many of the pack homes had intricate dens belowground, but Warren knew that. His pack was similar, wolves being wolves.

Fergus contacted Mary and updated her. *My team will be heading to the ground level in a few minutes. How are you doing?*

I'm fine. I'm still in the dreamglide. I'm searching your private rooms right now.

He heard her gasp suddenly, an odd telepathic sound.

Oh, dear God. Fergus, you need to get to your master bedroom immediately, but bring medical personnel with you. Several female wolves have been hurt. Bad.

FIVE

MARY REMAINED HOVERING in her dreamglide above Fergus's bed. She felt sick at heart at the sight before her, yet not surprised. Sydon was the monster who had skewered Fergus's heart and sent wolf females to work in the cartel-run Naked Wolf club.

Why wouldn't he have three women chained to Fergus's bed?

They'd been beaten and the sight of amber flame markings on their cheeks, necks and wrists told its own tale. In addition, each wolf had an unusual amount of fur showing on her breasts and all down the insides of her thighs. Amber flame had a terrible quality of forcing a partial shift and creating a pseudo-animal experience.

During sex, the women would exhibit a wolf-like need to be on all fours and to be dominated. They would howl and thrash. The men who liked rough sex enjoyed taking advantage of the women further *altered,* if temporarily, by the drug.

She heard the door open and watched from above as Fergus entered the room. He'd done as she'd suggested and brought a medical team with him, including two women who offered soft wolf-grunts as they approached the bed. Even Mary could feel how comforting these sounds were to the injured women.

The wolves cowered at first as each was released from her shackles.

Fergus wisely remained near the door, though she felt his fury rising.

Fergus?

I'm here.

Can you dial it down? She asked.

What do you mean?

Your rage, Sweetheart. The women can feel it. Earlier he'd called her 'Sweetheart', but until she'd entered the dreamglide she hadn't realized she'd used the endearment as well.

She hadn't said anything earlier, not when the only critical issue was saving Fergus's men from slaughter. But the moment she'd entered the dreamglide, as before, all the memories of her time with him had returned, the way he'd made love to her, the wolfness of him that turned her on, his strength yet endless capacity for tenderness.

Her heart was full just looking at him through the dreamglide.

She felt his rage fall away at her words, reminding him that how he felt wasn't the priority right now. He spoke to one of the nurses and excused himself, adding quietly, "When the women have been taken away and tended, I want this bed burned."

She watched Fergus leave the room. Knowing the abused women were being cared for, she followed after him in the dreamglide.

He didn't return to his men, but walked farther down the same hall and went into his library. He closed the pocket doors behind him, then sat down in a chair angled next to the fireplace. *You're remembering more,* he said.

Because I'm in the dreamglide, she said, *I remember everything.*

Fergus leaned forward in the chair and put his head in his hands. She knew he was upset and she valued his compassion for his people more than anything else about him.

You okay?

He leaned back in his chair and huffed a heavy sigh that ended in a typical wolf grunt. *I will be.*

From the moment she'd entered the dreamglide, and the memories of their times together had come back to her, she'd felt confused. Not about what she could recall, but about what she ought to do with their relationship. She'd been making love with Fergus for the past several weeks. They were intense lovers and he'd satisfied her as no man ever had.

But it was more than just sex, that much she knew. She felt a profound affection for Fergus, something she couldn't easily dismiss.

Where do we go from here, Fergus, you and me?

He shook his head. *I don't know. More than anything, I'm feeling the need for an alpha-mate, for a woman in the pack, but you're fae.*

I know. And though I've come to appreciate who you are in this world, and wolves like Warren as well, the constant level of violence hurts me. It's like a pain in my heart that I can't shake. At least you have Sydon locked up. Are you planning to turn him over to the Tribunal? Five Bridges had a court system run by the Tribunal, though more often than not the cartels' reach extended well into its halls of justice.

I'll leave his fate up to the Savage Pack Council, but only after I engage him in a dominance battle, without wrist guards. My primary goal is to re-bond with my pack. Nothing else matters.

Mary grew very still. She knew this was the necessary order of events, but her fae senses were screaming at her that it would be a mistake to let Sydon go free. He was an abusive, ambitious monster. *He should be put down, Fergus. Right now.*

It's not the way we do things. And if I killed him straight out, the Council would be within its rights to prevent me from ever taking the reins again.

But Sydon doesn't play by the rules.

He rose from his chair. *I'm not going to argue with you, Mary. It's important to me that I battle him according to rules I believe in.*

She thought for a moment. *Okay. Then just make sure it's a final battle. If you don't believe in the necessity of eliminating Sydon as a future threat, then I suggest you check your newly acquired fae senses. You'll see what I mean. He's more dangerous than you or any of your fellow alphas know.*

He spoke aloud. "Mary, I've heard you. I want you to know that. But I will do what I believe is right and best for my pack as well as for the future of Savage. I'm heading your direction right now. You can leave the dreamglide if you want. I won't be long."

I'll be waiting for you.

With that, Mary left the dreamglide and with it her blocks fell into place once more. She was back in Warren's map room and realized to her surprise that she was in a partially conscious state and had been the whole time. Always in previous instances, she was asleep or unconscious in order to be in the dreamglide. But not right now.

She rubbed her arms, feeling a wolfish kind of power invading her, strengthening her. She'd been part of a rescue operation that had saved the lives of decent wolves and she'd loved every second of it. Yup, very wolf.

Rising to her feet, she thought back to being in the dreamglide. She could recall everything about the experience, of breaking into the compound, of getting Fergus all the way through the hidden passage, and even helping to capture Sydon.

She remembered the women in Fergus's master bedroom as well.

But she couldn't recall the blocked portion, the several weeks with Fergus as his lover in the dreamglide. Her blocks held. Yet she knew that anytime she headed back into the dreamglide, she'd be able to remember everything about their time together. It was a bizarre disconnection.

For a moment she wondered if she should disable the blocks, but that would mean accepting more about her relationship with Fergus than she wanted to right now. There was a part of her that kept hoping what she was going through was only temporary, that maybe she was on a mission that would soon end and she could return to Revel and resume her life.

So, the blocks stayed.

She stretched a few times, angling her arm over her head and bending sideways one direction, then the other. She ached in a few places. The stone floor had a carpet, but it was fairly thin and she'd remained in one position way too long.

She didn't disturb the guards outside the door but waited for Fergus.

He arrived barely a minute later. When he came into the room, he closed the doors behind him. She could feel the connection to him, even though she couldn't recall the details of their time together.

"You're back."

"I am." His deep voice, full of male resonance, swamped her senses.

He held her gaze for a moment and his strong wolf energy quickly permeated the room. She wasn't surprised when he crossed to her and pulled her into his arms.

The kiss that followed was full, warm and moist. His wolf musk scent rose as well and took away her remaining restraint. She wrapped her arms around his neck and kissed him back, her whole body moving against his. She might not remember all that they'd done, but the part of her becoming wolf was into him.

She'd never had this kind of experience with a man before, needing him the way she craved Fergus. In fact, if she was honest with herself, she'd never even been in love before.

She drew back from Fergus and couldn't repress a sharp intake of breath.

In love.

She was in love with Fergus.

He held her loosely, his arms still wrapped around her. "What's wrong?"

She didn't know what to say to him. She could hardly proclaim her love, not when the concept had just marched into her head.

She settled her hands on his chest, then chuckled softly. "You're a big man." She spread her hands over his pecs. A memory returned to her, of doing this with him, of touching and fondling him.

"Do you want me to take you home? Back to Revel?"

She lifted her gaze to his gorgeous dark eyes. She could see the amber rings emerging, the ones that always formed when he was aroused. His brows were drawn together in concern.

"No. I don't want to leave."

He released a sigh of relief. "Good. I've thought about where we should go. I have a place."

"What do you mean?" She glanced around. "In Warren's compound?"

He shook his head. "No, but I also don't mean the Gordion Compound either. I have a home, not far from here, my first with a belowground private den. Will you be with me tonight and afterward through the day?"

Her head was nodding before she'd even formed the thought. Everything about her situation with Fergus felt as though it had an internal drive she couldn't resist or even slow down. She couldn't *not* be with him.

"Is that a yes?"

She slid her arms around his neck and kissed him. *That's an I-can't-say-no.*

He drew back and smiled at her. "I know exactly what you mean. And I swear to you that I won't make demands. I just want and need to be with you right now. Once my mate-hunting cycle ends, we can go back to, I don't know, where we were before. I just don't know what the future holds or what commitments I can make."

She shrugged slightly. "Me neither."

She stared into his eyes, mesmerized by him, by what was happening between them. "I loved helping out tonight. It was one of the most satisfying experiences of my life."

"You made everything possible. You played a critical role in saving my men and we captured Sydon because of you. I'll never forget what you've done for my pack."

She leaned close and dragged her nose over his jaw and cheek, taking in his scent, loving it, wanting more. "Who do you need to tell about where you're taking me?"

"Warren. I'll take care of that now." He looked away from her and she could feel his telepathic frequency light up. When he was done, he shared the details. "Harley and Ryan will hold the fort at the Gordion Compound until the dominance battle has taken place. Warren's there for a few more minutes to make sure the compound is secure. He'll be sending a security squad over to the den-home once we head over there."

She felt a blush warm up her cheeks. "What if we both get to howling, I mean if we get caught up in things?"

His lips curved. "I took precautions early on and soundproofed the den."

She remembered how hard it had been to hold back her howls the last time she'd been with him. "I'm glad."

She thought of something else as well; she wanted to hear him in full voice. The possibility of listening to his deep, resonant howls sent shivers all the way to her toes.

"We'll be free to do whatever we want this time. But there's one thing you should know. My wife, Sharon, lived there with me. I go back every once in a while, but her touch is in the space. Will that be a problem?"

Mary thought about the moment when Sharon had told her she'd be needed tonight. Sharon had been right. "No problem at all."

Fergus finally released her and led her to the door.

Mary loved the feel of Fergus's hand on her waist. She was in tune with the wolf. Even walking beside him, she fell easily into step, matching his long stride. Of course it helped to be as tall as she was, just short of six foot.

She glanced up at Fergus as he took her out onto the front stone walkway. The more she was with him, the stronger her wolf-like qualities became. Right now her nostrils quivered as she took in his alpha-mating scent. She swore she could separate out three different scents, one like grasses, the other a rich layered musk and finally the smell of stone. The latter seemed an impossibility, yet earth had a smell, everything did. Wolves could detect subtle variations, like dogs and other forest predators.

When he stopped and held his arm out for her, this time on his left side, she lifted her nose to the air in front of her. In a slow arc, she sniffed moving from the eastern portion of the front landscaping all the way to the west.

She smelled something in the air she couldn't define. Because Warren's guards were still in the front area, AR-15s in hand, she switched to telepathy. *What is it I'm smelling? It's metallic yet has an odd odor that reminds me of the Graveyard.*

When he lifted his nose into the air as well, she watched his nostrils elongate slightly, one of the fairly common attributes of shifting *alter* wolves.

She couldn't do that, because her body was fae. But she understood the sensation.

He repeated her former action of smelling the air left to right in an arc. *I see what you mean. I wouldn't have picked up on it except that you mentioned it. Must be your fae sensitivity combined with your growing wolf.*

So, what is it?

He shook his head, yet his nostrils kept elongating, then returning, back-and-forth.

Uneasiness crept through her though she didn't know why. She held him tighter. Her heart started pounding. The strange odor in the air intensified and her fae senses lit on fire. "Fergus, get down!"

She pulled him with her, falling onto the pavers. Within the same split-second, automatic rifle fire sounded from the forest opposite. She'd hit the stone hard and her cheek felt bruised as well as her knees.

The guard-wolves all started shouting. Still on her stomach on the stone pavers, she lifted her head enough to see four of the wolves fly swiftly into the air, angling southwest.

When Fergus started to get up she held him down. *That smell is still there.*

Can you locate the source?

Mary lifted her nose. *It's straight out front.*

The remaining guard wolves crouched behind stone planters.

We need protection, she said. Glancing to her left, she saw that a large planter, housing a tightly pruned tree was her best bet. *Move it, wolf,* she all but shouted telepathically.

She tugged on him as she levitated in a horizontal pattern and landed behind the planter. Just as Fergus followed, another layer of automatic fire kicked up stone shrapnel off the pavers right where they'd been.

He covered her body protectively with his own.

She had so much adrenaline in her system, she shook all over. He rubbed her arms. "You saved us both, Mary. Jesus, it's as though you've become my bodyguard."

She twisted her head to look at him. Given the angle, she craned her neck hard. *I think that's funny when you're this powerful Savage wolf.*

But you've got some badass wolf-senses developing as though you're combining both your fae abilities and my wolf skillset. His eyes widened suddenly. *Holy fuck Mary, did you just levitate horizontally to this position?*

Mary glanced back at the stone. *Oh, my God. I did.* He was so close she felt his breath on her cheek. *Fergus, what's happening here is extraordinary. I'm experiencing your levitation ability as though I've always been able to do it. I could do somersaults in the air if I wanted to.*

He kissed her cheek. *I think it's great. But more than that, I'm glad you're alive right now.*

One of the guards called out. "Warren and his team are on the way."

"Thanks," Fergus responded.

Mary swallowed hard. *What do you think is going on out there? Is it a rogue sniper, pissed off and shooting at us, or what?*

Worse. I think it's Sydon's illegal pack. The initial attack was designed to lead off a portion of the protection squad. They were gunning for me.

A few seconds later, the air was filled with Warren and his men flying above the forest. One thing about wolves, as *alter* predators, they could see extremely well in the dark.

It wasn't long before two single shots hit the air followed by a yelp. Two more, shots, then nothing.

Mary stayed where she was, but the reality of what had probably just happened sunk in hard. A rogue sniper wolf, possibly two, had just been killed.

She couldn't regret it because this was a war against Sydon now. The loyalty of his rogue pack had grown increasingly clear. They would do whatever their alpha wanted.

Reality struck hard. She'd been comfortable in Revel with no pack wars and dominance battles to worry about. Revel had other issues, of course, as each of the Territories did. But the level of conflict in Savage always hit Mary square on the chin.

She rested her forehead on the pavers and huffed a sigh that carried a slight wolf grunt. She couldn't deny what was happening to her, that she was definitely taking on wolf characteristics, but this wasn't the life she'd planned for herself.

She'd hoped one day, even as a mere *alter* fae, that a Revel man would find her, they'd date, fall in love and live quiet lives together. She'd treat parakeets and horribly obese lap cats. Together, they'd binge-watch TV, maybe develop a taste for specialty beers.

Instead, she was face down on a stone walkway in front of an alpha's compound, waiting for an all-clear to avoid getting her head shot off.

She heard Warren's voice. "We're good. My men cleared the forest."

When she felt Fergus lean back and rise to his feet, she joined him. He and Warren were immediately laying out plans to set-up blinds in the forest to watch for Sydon's followers.

"The real problem," Warren said, arms folded over his massive chest, "is that the snipers weren't after me or my men. This was about you and the Gordion Pack."

"I know."

Mary wondered just how smart she was being in sticking around Savage. Yet, the thought of returning to her very safe life grated in a way it never had before.

Was this what her sister had felt? Why Alicia had spent half her time in Savage? She'd dated several wolves, each one a little more dangerous than the next. She'd talked about the sex being amazing with a creature that could sprout fur.

Mary definitely agreed with the last bit. As she looked up at Fergus, a mating warmth flowed over every inch of her skin. He glanced at her, then took her hand in his and squeezed. He was feeling it, too.

She understood something in that moment; she couldn't go back. She couldn't return to her old way of life. But it also didn't mean that she had to stay with Fergus long-term. His pack was his priority and it seemed unlikely she could ever truly fit in.

Also, on some level she questioned if any of the wolves in Savage would actually live out the same long-life that other species could. Savage had the lowest overall population because of the frequent pack wars that sometimes involved every pack in the territory.

A woman's voice whispered in her ear. *How's it going?*

Mary gasped softly as Sharon appeared off to her left, away from Fergus and Warren.

Fergus was still speaking with his fellow pack alpha and didn't seem to notice Mary's gasp. *What are you doing here?*

Oh, just hangin' around. You did good earlier.

Thanks. I think. You could see all that?

I could.

Mary glanced at Fergus, then back to Sharon, *And he can't see you, right? He doesn't know you're here?* For a ghost, the woman's expression grew solemn as she stared at her husband.

He wouldn't want to know. I didn't leave him on the best of terms.

Because you cheated on him.

Sharon's ghost-mist floated around unevenly as she nodded. *I did, more than once. But the last time was with one of the worst men in Savage, the same man that killed me.*

Before Mary even asked the question, she knew the answer. *Holy shit, you were with Sydon and he killed you during sex.*

How do you know it was during sex?

Mary pursed her lips. *When you were murdered, the details were all over the web, that your neck had been ravaged by wolf teeth and broken in what I have no doubt was a hard, killing shake. He had you from behind, didn't he?*

Yes, but it was more rape than consensual. Sharon huffed a sigh. *A broken neck ended my consciousness with a gray-white explosion through my head. I was dead before I could even form the thought, 'oh, the bastard is killing me'.*

I remained by my body for a long time, staring down at my glassy eyes. Sydon rose up over me, smiling. I didn't understand why he would have done this to me until I realized he'd planned this from the beginning. Getting rid of an alpha-mate opens a pack up to takeover. A pack is strongest when a woman's energy aligns with her wolf. Loyalty doesn't just double within the community, it becomes an exponential increase and a solid layer of protection for all the wolves. I know I brought that to the Gordion pack, even if I was ill-suited to the role.

Sharon's face wrinkled up. Mist trailed down her cheeks like tears.

Mary considered her for a long moment, all that she'd lost when she'd become an *alter* wolf and that she'd never taken to Savage. *You should know something. Fergus has never said an unkind word about you.*

That's just him. His code of honor.

Mary shifted on her feet. She could hear Warren and Fergus conversing, but her attention remained fixed on Sharon. *What if I don't want this? Being here in Savage, I mean?*

Sharon laughed. *You're already in so deep, you don't even know it. You're holding an alpha's hand. Do you have any idea how significant that is?*

Mary sighed. *Well, it doesn't have to be permanent. Neither of us thinks it can be.*

Like hell. But your relationship isn't even the biggest problem here. There's some impediment to Fergus bonding with another woman. Several of his female wolves have tried and failed and each had alpha-mate potential. You may not be able to forge a real wolf-bond with Fergus even if you wanted to.

Then, what's the point of all this?

I know this may be hard to hear, and I don't have all the answers, but the survival of the Gordion Pack will one day hinge on you and your role in Fergus's life.

But why is this on me?

How the hell should I know? I'm just here relaying information. I think what it boils down to is that the path isn't clear, only the objective. So stick close to him, keep him alive, and if you can do it, forge the damn bond. But now I have to go. My supervisor seems displeased with my attitude.

Mary felt Sharon vanish. She was relieved. Sharon seemed to be dumping an awful lot of responsibility on Mary's shoulders. Worse still, every fae instinct in her body told her that Sharon was right. For reasons she still didn't understand, everything that was happening right now was a serious turning point for Savage Territory. Sydon wasn't finished with his bid for a takeover.

The Gordion Pack needed a bonded alpha. Even she had felt the desperate lack of it while in Fergus's compound. Which meant that all this time, Fergus had born the weight of the leadership alone.

Yet Sharon seemed to think Fergus might never be able to complete the necessary bond. And if a real wolf couldn't bond with Fergus, then there was no way she could. Not that she even wanted to.

Her frustration mounted all over again, about being drawn into a situation that seemed so juxtaposed to her life as a fae woman.

"Are you okay?" Fergus's wonderful resonant voice pulled her out of her reverie.

She turned and lifted her gaze to meet his. And there it was, the profound attraction she felt for him. "Just thinking about some things."

"Are you ready to go?"

"I am." Was she ready for everything else her relationship with Fergus appeared to be demanding, she had no idea.

He released her hand but slid his arm around her waist and led her closer to Warren. He spoke quietly. "Mary and I are still headed to my cabin. You can reach me through my cell or telepathically anytime you want."

"Good deal. And I'll be sending a security team to guard the property through the rest of the night."

Fergus dipped his chin to Warren, then turned toward Mary. He held his arm wide, a signal he was ready to fly her to their destination. But she looked down at her own feet and lifted off, rising a foot, then two. Fergus tracked with her, sticking close.

When she was well above the compound, she switched to telepathy. *Lead the way and in case you didn't know it, I love levitation.*

~ ~ ~

Fergus had been talking things over with Warren while making use of telepathy half the time. Warren had asked if Fergus intended to attempt an alpha-mate bond with Mary. His response of 'we seem to be headed that way' had left him feeling unsettled.

How could a fae woman possibly serve his pack and provide the profound level of communal bonding even his most powerful female wolves couldn't achieve?

The whole situation made no sense. But then it hadn't from the beginning, from the time he'd first held Mary in his arms and had howled like he'd discovered air for the first time.

While talking to Warren, telepathically or aloud, the whole time he'd sensed something was going on with Mary. The part of him growing in fae powers knew she was distressed, but he didn't know by what. He'd glanced at her several times and had felt a series of emotional shocks hit her, but he didn't know their content or source.

Now he flew with her slowly in a southeasterly direction while she worked her levitation sea-legs.

"You're flying beautifully," he said.

"I can go faster if you need me to, but I'm entranced by the way the forest looks below us. All these pines. Who would have thought they could grow in the desert."

"Reclaimed water has made it possible." He flew a little faster, adding, "We're almost there. I'll guide you in."

He slowly dropped down to the narrow opening in the trees. He sensed that someone had been in his home and he would have drawn his Glock, but the fae part of him could tell he wasn't in danger. Focusing his attention on the cabin, he soon realized that several women of his pack had gone in to tidy up. He could also smell a fresh-baked apple pie with tons of cinnamon. His mouth watered.

He levitated straight down in front of the stone path.

He watched Mary glide in and land easily next to him. Her face was glowing and she grinned as she held her hands wide and said, "Tah-dah!"

He laughed. "You did great."

She smiled. "Thanks."

As he walked her up the path, she asked, "Not that I'm complaining, but I thought we'd be heading to the Gordion Compound."

"I have to get rid of Sydon first. The fact is, I won't be able to stay there until the dominance battle has taken place and that won't be until tomorrow night. It's pack law."

"I didn't know." She glanced up at the steeply pitched roofline of the cabin. "I'm glad we're here, then."

"Me, too. It seems like a better transition for you and me, for whatever is going on between us."

"I think you're right."

He released her and pushed the front door open. This had been his first home with Sharon, the place given to them by the Gordion Pack when they'd first moved to Savage Territory as new wolves.

As he entered the house, an entire host of memories rushed at him, beginning with what it had been like to realize that his human life had come to an end and he could never go back. His life had been the Sedona resort they'd built together, now it was gone. Later, there'd been a time of growing acceptance and an exploration of powers. He remembered being stunned by what he'd become and all that he possessed as a wolf.

He'd learned early on that he had alpha potential and the next few years had been a long yet exciting climb up the rungs of pack life. He fought a series of dominance fights that he could still remember as one of the best string of events he'd ever experienced.

What he hadn't expected was the night he fought the alpha for the position as top wolf. He'd expected to be more torn up about unseating the man, but he soon realized that the true alpha accepted dominance as a way of life. He suspected one day he'd be supplanted as well.

A sense of sadness returned as he recalled how the alpha, Mark, had been killed in one of the ensuing violent outbreaks in Savage. He'd died honorably while protecting several Gordion female wolves from another pack's onslaught.

Sydon's attempt to become alpha of the Gordion Pack, however, had been a different matter. He'd challenged Fergus as an outsider. It wasn't unheard of and the Savage Pack Council had ruled that dominance was dominance. Anyone could demand a dominance fight with an alpha.

Fergus had known for a long time that Sydon wanted the Gordion Pack. He hadn't been surprised at all when the official challenge came through, signed by Dean himself. But the last thing he'd expected was a skewer into his heart in the middle of the fight.

Now he was here, with Mary, and Sydon was in a dungeon cell, a bullet in his thigh.

Once inside the living room, Mary turned in a circle. "This must have seemed so small to you. I mean, you're a big man."

"True, but I joined the Savage Border Patrol soon after landing here. I didn't spend much time indoors except to sleep."

When she headed into the kitchen area, he remained by the dining table.

"Look," she said, "Someone brought over a meatloaf and an apple pie."

"They're from my pack. The women have always taken care of me."

She glanced at him. "You're smiling."

"I suppose I am."

"You love the Gordion Pack, don't you?"

"I do. I care about every member. They're family to me."

"I'm getting that." She reached for the meatloaf. "It's still warm. I don't think we'll even need to heat this up. You hungry?"

He extended his nostrils. "That smells fantastic. And yes, I'm starved."

"Me, too."

He followed her into the kitchen. The small woodsy cabin still had the same earthy smell that he remembered, even though he hadn't been here in over a year.

Mary moved around the small space that had an undersized butcher block island and pots hanging overhead. Sharon had been gone three years now. He was appalled by how little he missed her. But things hadn't been right between them the entire time they'd lived in Five Bridges. She hadn't adjusted to wolf life as well as he had. She'd hated the dominance fights, but they'd been a form of sustenance for him.

He'd known she'd cheated on him, but he honestly couldn't blame her. He'd become obsessed with caring for the pack and had little time for her.

He'd been faithful to her, but he'd been unable to help her create a satisfying life for herself in Savage. She'd loved the resort they'd built together in Sedona and despite that she'd lived over a decade in Savage, he knew she'd never stopped resenting that his business partner had sabotaged their meal with the *alter* serum.

With her resentment, her dislike of wolfness generally, and his own focus fixed so completely on the pack, he couldn't think badly of her if she'd taken pleasure in the arms of other men. He was enough of a man to admit he'd failed as a husband.

Then there was Mary in her jeans and double tank tops in white and lavender. She was hunting through the cupboards and her ass looked gorgeous in the snug denim. She'd found a bottle of wine and now pulled two glasses off the shelf.

Desire for her heated up. He was drawn to her like water to a river and he almost reached for her when his cell rang.

Warren's voice hit his ear. "My security detail should be there by now."

"I'll check." He moved to the window and saw the lead man at the end of the front walk, AR-15 in hand, his back to the cabin. "They've arrived. Thanks Warren."

"You bet. I also wanted to invite you and Mary to my compound for first meal tomorrow night. I'll see that we grill some steaks."

Fergus smiled. "Sounds perfect. See you then."

When he hung up, he told Mary what Warren had done for them.

Mary glanced at him over her shoulder as she screwed the old-fashioned cork-remover into the cork. "That's wonderful. Knowing the cabin will be well-guarded, I think I'll be able to sleep really well."

He'd make sure she got some good sleep.

But not for a while.

CHAPTER SIX

NOW THAT FERGUS was in a cabin with a strong security team outside, he settled his gaze on Mary's ass. She wore tight blue jeans and her tank tops rode up just enough that he could see the exact shape of each bun. He already knew what she looked like naked, which meant his leathers had started to shrink.

Rather than encourage an erection he couldn't do a damn thing about until after dinner, he turned his attention to a necessary chore. He went around the cabin and shuttered the windows. Given the small size of the space, light could reach the center of any of the rooms once the sun rose. He knew it occasionally happened that a wolf wasn't completely sun-intolerant, but it was rare.

Fergus, especially, hated sunlight.

With the windows covered, he went to the stairs leading down into the den. From where he stood, he could see the short hall to the right that led to an adjacent bathroom. The bed was visible the opposite direction, as well as flowers sitting on the nightstand. No doubt the women of his pack had brought the bouquet in.

Mary would love them. She'd planted flowers all around her backyard.

"Ready," Mary called out.

He returned to the kitchen and she handed him a plate. He took it along with a glass of wine she passed his way. "Mary, are you happy? I mean here in Five Bridges. Not Savage, necessarily, but as an *alter* fae?"

Picking up her plate and wine glass, she cocked her head slightly. "I suppose I am. I mean I still wish for my old life in the human part of Phoenix. I think most of us do." He let her move past him.

He followed her into the living area, set his plate and goblet down on the table, then pulled her chair out for her.

She seemed surprised, but smiled up at him as she sat down. "Thank you. I guess I didn't expect—" She broke off.

He chuckled. "You can't offend me. But I could probably finish that sentence a dozen different ways. Say, you didn't expect a wolf to have manners, politeness, consideration, or any of the above. Am I close?"

She spoke quietly. "This is Savage. The territory is well-named."

He sat down and sipped his wine. "I admit I was more civilized before coming to Five Bridges. For one thing, I never thought I'd serve as a border patrol officer or any kind of peacekeeper armed with a gun." He set his goblet down, considering. "But I'll bet you're also thinking about your sister, Alicia, and how she died."

"Her death is rarely far from my thoughts."

As he took a bite of meatloaf, he couldn't help but wonder about Mary. Could a sensitive woman like her ever fit into Savage? If not, why was she here? Why had she become part of his wild, Savage life?

The rich smell of the meatloaf, however, called strongly to him suddenly and his stomach rumbled. He needed food, both to recover and to prepare for his upcoming dominance battle with Sydon.

He tried not to eat too fast, but given that he was still healing up from the heart-skewering, he had a hard time checking his speed. He wasn't even aware he'd stopped making conversation, until Mary set another slab of the savory ground beef on his plate.

He chuckled as he looked up from his plate. "Sorry."

"You don't have to apologize. I'm on my second portion as well, though I think I'm getting full."

By the time he was done, Mary was already leaning back in her chair. She held her glass in one hand as she glanced around the room. "This is nice," she said. "Restful. Let me know when you're ready for some pie. There's vanilla ice cream in the freezer, too."

Now that his pressing need for food was taken care of, the other demanding aspect of his alpha nature rose like a rocket. He was pretty sure he'd even forgo pie for what he wanted next.

She leaned toward him, her nose sniffing the air. "What am I smelling?"

He lowered his chin. "Me."

~ ~ ~

Mary had actually been thinking about having Fergus start a fire in the pot-belly stove. Though it was early June in the Arizona desert, and hot during the day, the middle of the night was still cool enough to fire up some logs. Maybe they could sit and talk, get to know each other in real-time. But apparently, the wolf was already burning hot because the smell of his musk meant only one thing.

Besides, his scent had already started teasing her between her legs. As desire built, her gaze fell to his long, thick hair. She wanted her hands buried in it, feeling the texture through her fingers. She longed for his mouth pressed against hers. He had wonderful lips and his kisses were like heaven.

She thought back to the reality that they'd been serious lovers for at least four weeks. She even questioned again whether she should keep the dreamglide blocks in place anymore.

As she considered the possibility of having full possession of all her memories of their time together, another series of images leaked through to her conscious mind. In this dreamglide experience, she'd practiced making the unique braid sequence Sharon had created for him. The whole time, he'd had two of his fingers buried inside her, slowly working her sex until she was writhing. She'd kissed him often, savoring his lips and the way he would drive his tongue into her mouth.

Ecstasy had finally torn her away from the braiding task, but she'd held onto his hair as he'd entered her. He'd planted his mouth on hers and quickly brought her to a powerful climax.

Watching him rise from his chair now, his dark eyes glinting, she set aside her tidy-up-after-every-meal habit and joined him. She set her glass down firmly, then headed to the stairs. He was right behind her and looped his arm around her waist. She squealed when he lifted her off her feet, swooped her down the stairs and into the den.

When he set her down, he turned to close the soundproof door, then locked it up.

They were finally alone.

He wheeled back to her, grabbed her in a quick embrace, and kissed her once on the lips. "Shower first." She understood. He'd been flying and battling. He needed to get cleaned up.

He said nothing more, but sprinted toward the bathroom. She would have joined him if he'd extended the invitation, but her faeness sensed he didn't want to heat things up until they were in bed together. She also knew that he'd bite her again, a thought that sent shivers of anticipation pouring in hot waves over her body.

With the shower running, she glanced around the small room. She was locked up with a wolf and the idea of it created the familiar tugging sensation deep in the center of her lower abdomen, the same way she'd felt when he'd made love to her earlier.

Something was happening to her that felt very un-fae. She wondered if she was experiencing the early stages of the mysterious mate-bonding of an alpha wolf to his woman.

She took deep breaths, but they came out like a wolf's growl. She huffed through her nostrils in quick bursts. She began to travel the room, sniffing the chest of drawers. She smelled Fergus's complex wolf scent, then Sharon's scent, though much fainter. Farther back were the smells of other *alters* and humans that no doubt owned the furniture even before Fergus.

On the dresser was a photograph of him with Sharon in what must have been their human lives. They looked young, in love, happy. Behind them were the red cliffs of Sedona, the photo probably taken near their resort. Though Mary had transferred her veterinarian practice to Five Bridges, both Fergus and Sharon had been forced to relinquish an extraordinary life.

She could understand Sharon's profound disappointment in her *alter* existence.

She wondered suddenly if Sharon was here. Would she watch them having sex? She didn't seem like a woman who cared too much about boundaries.

Mary moved to the nightstand and slowly stripped off her double tanks. She folded them and set them on a nearby rocking chair. The wolf in her felt strong, demanding. She wanted different things from Fergus this time. Would he give them to her?

She growled again, the sound vibrating along her throat. She loved the feel of it. She liked the idea of being very physical with the wolf tonight. Savage troubled her and maybe it always would. But the part of her slowly becoming wolf gave her an unexpected thrill. She'd even begun to understand why Alicia had been so drawn to the wolves of Savage.

On the nightstand was an old brass compass and a trio of antique books. Had Sharon brought these here? Probably, because each carried her scent.

A vase of flowers brightened the entire room. She leaned close and breathed in the fragrance. Her nostrils flared as she tipped her head back. She lost track of how many lines of redolence she detected, a dozen, two dozen, a hundred?

The human nose could only smell one; this was a rose, that was a carnation. But her wolf senses caught layers and layers of odors and fragrances. She smelled fields alive with growth, the rich earth, the freshness of the rain, even the way the scents changed as the sun rose and fell.

She felt alive in ways she'd never been before. Her body hummed with her need for Fergus and glancing at her wrists, she saw a thin dusting of light wolf fur.

The queen size bed, with a black wrought iron headboard, was almost pressed up to the far side of the small space. Sleeping with Fergus through the day, as big as he was, would be close and intimate.

A quilt lay on top. Again, she leaned down and smelled all the fingers that had once labored over the antique patchwork made up of small two-inch squares. Dozens of hands through the distance of time. She could hear the women talking about love, life and their children.

Reverently, she began folding the quilt back in careful panels until she could slide it over the wood chest at the end of the bed. Other wolves had lived here. She could smell them, those who had preceded Fergus and Sharon. They were gone now, each and every one, lost in pack wars or dominance fights that had ended tragically many years ago. All this she could detect or maybe it was the fae part of her that sensed the past, she wasn't sure.

When Fergus rose to serve as alpha, he'd kept the cabin, maybe for unexpected times like this, like losing a dominance battle with a murderous wolf like Sydon.

With her fae senses combined with her wolf abilities, she knew Savage was riddled with dens just like this one, cool, closed off, and dark. Only a single lamp lit the space and the bulb had a low wattage. The wolf in her loved it, loved the solitude, the sense that being here with Fergus was private and belonged only to them.

Across from the foot of the bed was a beautiful wood paneling, like nothing she'd scene. She was pretty sure the wood was called burl. How odd to see it here, but the grain looked as though an ocean wave had washed up on the seashore, leaving foamy patterns in the sand behind.

She decided she loved this room, the simple beauty of it, the warmth, the presence of others who'd come before. No other rooms were in the wolf-den, just a bathroom and a bedroom. The space was for sleeping, love-making, maybe healing after a battle and a lot of nothing-held-back howling.

Fergus could let loose now.

So could she.

Having examined every part of the space, she began stripping out of her shoes and jeans. She removed her bra and her panties and folded everything up, setting her shoes on the floor and her clothes on the tank tops already on the rocker.

Standing naked on the rag-rug carpet, she closed her eyes and listened intently to Fergus in the shower. She could hear the pleasure he felt as the warm water beat on his body. He wolf-moaned softly, the sound just shy of a howl.

A half-minute more, and the water shut off.

She waited for him, her body tingling in anticipation. She touched the soft fur on her wrists and took deep breaths.

When he finally stepped into the small hall between the stairs and the bathroom, he wore only a towel around his waist.

His chin was low, and he growled as his gaze skated over her body.

But she held up a hand. When she spoke, she sounded hoarse, very wolf, very different from her more human-like fae voice. "This is my time with you, Fergus. It doesn't belong to you, but to me."

His nose wrinkled, and he bared his teeth. "You're taking control?"

She smiled as his demanding wolf scent swirled around her. "Right now I am," she said. She pointed to the bed. "I want you there, waiting for me, because when I'm done with my shower, I'm taking you into the dreamglide."

At that, at the mention of something so essentially fae, his wolf retreated and his eyes flared. He made a huffing sound at the back of his throat. "You'll remember all the times we've been together."

She nodded slowly. "And I'm ready to remove the blocks so that I can keep remembering in real-time."

He dipped his chin in acquiescence. "If you want to take charge, I'm game."

He passed by her slowly, but didn't do more than take her hand briefly and offer a single squeeze as he moved in the direction of the bed. His long black hair was damp. When he reached the bed, he unbound the towel at his hips and tossed it to her.

She caught it, then watched as he stretched out on his back.

She didn't head to the shower right away. Instead, she allowed herself to take in the pure animal beauty of his body, the heaviness of his muscles, his leanness, the size and shape of his cock and testicles.

He reclined at an angle which meant his feet were only a few inches off the bed. He shoved a pillow behind his neck. She drew close and put her hand on his leg.

She felt both connected to him yet distant in a way she didn't understand, perhaps because they weren't bonded.

Her needs felt paramount as though what would happen tonight would be deeply important to her life. "I won't be long."

With one hand gripping the black wrought iron of the headboard, he inclined his head with an almost imperceptible movement. He looked as solemn as she felt.

She moved into the bathroom and took her time showering. She felt caught up in something sacred and which felt extremely *alter* wolf.

She washed using a black tar soap. It had a clean, rock smell that seemed fitting. She used the same soap on her hair and between her legs.

As she looked down at her ankles, she noticed more fur had appeared similar to what rimmed her wrists. She marveled at the physical changes, wondering how it was possible for a fae to produce fur.

She knew in her bones she couldn't truly transform into a wolf as Fergus could. She'd never be able to shift and become a creature that pounded the dirt roads of Savage on all fours. But she was definitely part wolf now with no going back.

When she dried off, she used a blow dryer to take most of the moisture out of her long thick hair. She glanced in the mirror and saw that the same dusting of fur now encircled her neck as well as each nipple. Her cheekbones looked sharper and as she stared into the mirror, she saw a narrow amber ring of light glowing in her brown eyes. Incredible.

Very wolf.

Like Fergus.

This time was hers, in her wolf-fae form.

It belonged to her.

Whatever this hybrid-creature was, the wolf would enjoy Fergus's body and the fae part of her would take him within the dreamglide. She would open herself up to what they'd been doing together for the past few weeks. She wanted to know everything.

Even now, she let the blocks fall away. The memories slid toward her as though falling from the sky and dropping into her mind.

She gasped.

She'd been so wild with Fergus in the dreamglide, nothing held back. He'd ridden her hard, and she'd loved it. With no one to hear, he'd howled in a dozen resonances and pitches. The sounds had become a music that had eased her soul.

She turned the light out and left the bathroom.

She walked as if in a dream. The memories blew through her like an exotic wind from distant worlds. Fergus lay where she'd left him but now he was fully erect as he waited for her.

His deep voice rolled toward her. "I could smell you, your desire, your need." He wrapped his hand around his cock and stroked slowly, his hips arching. A thick V of fur angled from his shoulders well past his navel, almost to his trimmed pubic hair.

The light from the lamp cast shadows on his muscles, showing off their size, ripples and veined cords. She'd spent at least one time in the dreamglide licking and sucking on every muscle he possessed. The memory sent pleasure flowing between her legs.

She moved to the side of the bed and stared down at him. "I'm remembering."

His gaze fell to her breasts, then her wrists. "You're displaying like a female wolf."

"Not as much as a real wolf, but yes, I am." He had thick black bands of fur around his ankles. She leaned down and rubbed her nose along the line of fur, flaring her nostrils to capture the depth of his scent. She rubbed her hands over his legs, taking her time to feel the muscles along the way. His skin had a golden hue and the earthy layers of his scent floated in the air above him, beckoning her on, of stone, musk and grass.

He took deep breaths as though in pain. She understood. Whatever scent he released that had her sex swollen and ready, she was doing the same for him. It was a magical kind of agony.

She rubbed his thighs and spread his legs. His testicles were cloaked in thickly ribbed protective skin. She felt them, caressing and savoring. His seed would come from this place and she wanted his essence inside her, causing the ripples he'd created before, the strange sensation that had added so much extraordinary pleasure during the peak of ecstasy.

A new line of black fur formed suddenly on the insides of his thighs, drawing her close. She bent and nuzzled the fur, then his testicles and finally licked a long line up his cock all the way to the dip in the crown.

He groaned heavily, a low almost grunting sound.

She placed her hands on his abdomen and traced the deep lines that angled away from his cock, leading to his pelvic bones. He was pure animal and so beautiful she felt turned inside out.

Because he fisted the wrought iron of the headboard, his abs were taut. She spent time slowly palming each rise and fall. She buried her nose in the erotic V of fur as well.

Her nipples were hard and she was wet between her legs. Everything about Fergus turned her on.

She shifted slightly and played with his pecs, taking his left nipple in her mouth. She sucked heavily, wanting him to release a wolf flavor into her mouth.

When he did, she drew away from his nipple, arched her back and a low, sexy howl left her throat. It was punctuated with three successive, but very soft, barks.

Fergus groaned and growled deep in his throat, adding to her arousal.

She did the same with his other nipple, sucking hard. He continued to growl the entire time and made wolf huffing noises with his throat. When he once more released the flavor she needed, she howled again, and kept howling.

She couldn't move. She was so full of need, she felt frozen, yet waiting, her throat open, her voice singing.

Her eyes were closed as she felt the bed move slightly. A moment later, his warm palm caressed her stomach just below her navel. Slowly, he slid his hand up her abdomen and fondled her breasts. She remained in the same position, her back arched.

As he leaned close and suckled her breasts in turn, her howls finally ceased. This was what she'd been calling for. She needed Fergus touching and using her body.

She felt as though she was floating when he picked her up in his arms and laid her out on the bed beneath him.

Using his hands, he stroked her arms, her chest, her fingers, her hips.

Lower he went, caressing her between her legs. She felt lost in a place of bliss more profound than she'd ever known.

"Fergus." She spoke his name, but only to warn him she intended to move things along. Without saying anything else, she gave shape to her dreamglide and pulled him inside.

Within the identical space, though hovering above the real-time bed, he stopped touching her and looked at her.

The memories of all their times together once more flowed through her.

She looked at him, then down at the bed beneath the dreamglide. He lay stretched out beside her in real-time.

She felt Fergus's power begin to move and something magical happened as she watched him become one with the Fergus on the bed. "Fergus, do you see that? This is all happening at the same time. And we're fully conscious in both places."

"You're right, I can feel you in real-time and in the dream-glide." His movements were in tandem. He touched her on the bed and in the dreamy state of the glide at the same time.

"The air feels charged." His power radiated over her body. Something locked into place and she knew she was one with herself on the bed in real-time as well. She didn't know something like this could happen, but she sensed it was because of how they were together, the power they created between them.

It was an extraordinary doubling of sensations as he leaned down to her and took her breast in his mouth once more. The suckling arched her back all over again.

What she knew to be a dreamglide wind began to blow, moving her and rolling her yet keeping her in one position at the same time. Pleasure grew as she tumbled through time and space, as he suckled harder. Using his fingers, he pierced her between her legs and began a strong, erotic thrust.

She began to howl again, a high, keening sound that prompted him to move his fingers more swiftly. The ripples returned, intensifying every sensation.

Suddenly, the orgasm barreled down on her, throwing her around in the dreamglide until ecstasy peaked. Her howl sounded like a cry in the wild. On and on the orgasm rolled, pleasure flooding her abdomen, her chest, her mind.

The tugging sensation in her abdomen returned, pushing low as though trying to reach the internal part of her sex.

She flew over the pinnacle, howling, then began the slow delicious slide down the other side. As the wind of the dreamglide ceased, her arms slid away from him to rest outstretched on either side of her. In both realities, she was barely able to move. He withdrew his fingers and his lips.

This is incredible, he said, reclining on his elbow next to her. *Combining the dreamglide with real-time.*

It is. She lifted an arm and using her hand caressed his shoulders, one of her favorite parts of his body. He placed gentle kisses on her breasts, nuzzling the small circlets of fur around her nipples. At the same time, he stretched out on top of her, then kissed her.

As she spread her legs for him, he planted himself firmly between her knees. He rubbed his cock over her sex, then kissed her on the lips. When she parted, he drove his tongue inside and began to pulse within her mouth.

She rocked beneath him and surrounded his hips with her legs, drawing his cock toward her opening.

I need you Fergus. All of you.

He used his hand to position the head of his cock. She whimpered, but it was a hoarse wolf sound.

He began to push, easing his way inside, deeper and deeper.

The more he pushed, the stronger the internal tug became as though a hand inside her was reaching for his cock. She couldn't explain it. Yet in a burst of fae insight, she knew this was the alpha-bonding mechanism by which she could become his alpha-mate.

The idea thrilled her yet repelled her at the same time. She was fae, and he belonged in the most violent territory in Five Bridges.

But her body responded against her will, with a flow of shivers and chills that traveled from her shoulders, down her torso and all the way to her toes. She trembled with pleasure and need.

She'd never felt anything like it.

He kissed her again, driving his tongue and matching his movements between her legs.

She arched with each thrust, pushing back into him, pulling away, then returning. He kissed her cheeks and drifted his lips down her neck until he was licking her throat repeatedly and huffing against her skin.

She took her breaths in long slow crawls of air. She knew what he wanted and her sex tightened in anticipation. *Do it, Fergus. Take hold and don't let go.*

She felt him open his mouth. She sensed that the wolf part of him had elongated his jaw. He gripped her throat in a clamp of his teeth that sent a drive of pleasure straight through her body and into her sex. She couldn't move, except to rock her pelvis against his. Yet in no way did he injure her throat. She was safe, but he kept her firmly in his control. He thrust heavily now, curling his hips and slamming against her sex.

In that moment, the dreamglide began to move once more, only this time it raced through Savage Territory. In the dream-world, she shifted fully and became a wolf as did Fergus and suddenly she was running beside him, all four paws hitting the dreamglide streets and dirt roads of his land.

In real-time, she felt Fergus as he made love to her as a man, alive and dynamic, his hips pumping into her, his cock thrusting in and out. Ecstasy began to build. He released her throat in real-time and rose up howling.

Yet in the dreamglide she ran beside him as her climax roared through her. Pleasure cascaded in a series of intense waves as their wolves ran and ran.

She joined her voice with his and howled.

But the pleasure didn't stop. Instead, the sound of Fergus's wolf-cries, so beautifully loud in the small room, drove her quickly toward the pinnacle all over again. He pumped into her hard and fast. The bonding sensation pushed on her sex again, driving her into another profound orgasm so that she howled with him once more.

The sounds blended and became a thrill that added to the pleasure now pouring in hot waves over her sex.

Fergus's voice pierced her mind. *Look at me, Mary.*

When she met his gaze, she could feel him release into her. He slowed his rhythm but angled his hips in hard, exquisite thrusts. He continued to pump until every drop had pulsed through his cock, filling her full of his seed. The whole time, he stared into her eyes until finally he slowed his hips, then stopped.

She howled softly and appreciatively in response.

Within the dreamglide, she shifted from wolf to woman as did Fergus. Gradually, she let the dreamglide go and felt herself sinking back into herself as it vanished.

It would take some time before she caught her breath completely.

He breathed heavily, too, but he'd closed his eyes. His back was arched, his hands planted next to her shoulders, his arms stiff. He was still connected low and his cock felt firm inside her. A soft wolf sound, very guttural, came out of his throat in small jabs, fading and slowing until at last he fell silent.

Mary lay beneath him, waiting for him to come down from the heights completely. She felt as though Fergus somehow held the moment with his body and the force of his wolfness. She couldn't have moved if she'd wanted to.

Finally, his hips relaxed against hers, then his eyes opened, and he looked down at her. He searched her face and lowered himself enough to kiss her right cheek, her forehead, then her other cheek.

He placed more kisses on her lips.

The tenderness of these actions made her eyes burn.

She'd never known a man like Fergus before, so strong and powerful, yet careful with her at the same time.

"You're beautiful, Mary, every bit of you. Not just your lovely light brown eyes, or your perfect features, but your soul and your thoughts. Thank you for the dreamglide. When I was racing through Savage, I'd never felt so sexual in my life. It was an amazing experience. You're amazing."

She caressed his face and ran her thumb over his lips. "I remember it all now, how many times we had dreamglide sex together. You're a powerful lover, but so tender. I can recall all the times we talked as well. There's no one like you in the entire world. I'm sure of it. I want to stay like this with you forever, to remain in this den until the world folds up and disappears."

He kissed her again. And again. Until it really did feel as though the world vanished and it was just the two of them.

~ ~ ~

Fergus felt changed in the depth of his soul. He loved Mary's spirit. She was all in, nothing held back and the dreamglide had been an incredible experience.

He'd savored all the previous dreamglide sex, but this was a thousand times better because he'd taken her in real-time as well.

He wanted more and the alpha wolf in him almost felt appeased. He knew then this was the closest he'd come to finally having an alpha-mate since Sharon's death.

When at last he pulled out of her, he left the bed, then returned with a washcloth. He'd released so much of his seed inside her that a few tissues wasn't going to cut it. His wolf loved that he'd covered her so thoroughly.

He returned to the shower and cleaned up.

He looked forward to crawling into bed beside her and sleeping for several solid hours. He still wasn't a hundred percent after his near-death. Rest would be welcome besides the fact he had a dominance battle to face at nightfall.

As he left the bedroom, he opened the soundproof door to let fresh air flow into the room.

He turned out the light and finally stretched out next to her.

When she shifted to lie on her side, her back to him, he spooned her, then settled his arm over her waist and held her tight against him. He felt her sigh deeply and knew she was drifting off to sleep.

He wasn't far behind.

His last thought was a measure of relief that tomorrow night he'd take Sydon down in a legal dominance battle and kick him out of the Gordion Compound for good.

He didn't sleep well, however, and woke up several times throughout the day. His dreams were full of Savage Territory and wolves moving back and forth restlessly from one end to the next, hungry, growling, anxious.

It wasn't good for wolves to live outside their packs, ever.

Each individual community grounded them, gave them purpose and eased the constant unresolved need to run through the forest for tens of miles on end.

He finally awoke sweating. He'd been running through the Arizona White Mountains, free, his tongue lolling, his heart pounding hard with each stretch of his forearms, reaching for another mile and another and another.

He leaned up on his elbow and used the pillowcase to wipe his forehead.

The room was still dark, though a dim light flowed down from the upper ground level living area. He checked his internal clock, that odd gift of a long-lived life, and knew it was late afternoon. He might have awakened from a series of disturbing dreams, but he'd still slept through most of the day—a good thing.

Though Mary wasn't in bed, he touched the sheet next to him anyway. His heart swelled. He'd loved sharing a bed with her. He wanted more of this, more of being with her.

He listened to the house and could hear her moving around upstairs. He could smell coffee brewing.

He went into the bathroom and pulled out his shaving gear. He lathered up and took care of his stubble. He showered afterward, but as the hot water beat down on his shoulders, his thoughts kept circling back to Savage, and to his dreams of wolves moving restlessly through the pine forest and through all the neighborhoods of his territory.

He accessed the part of him becoming fae. He extended his senses, reaching beyond himself and into the immediate future. Mary had said something to him recently, about the future in Savage. He could feel it now, as though a dark cloud lay suspended over the entire territory.

What was coming felt evil as though Savage was in for a world of hurt. If he wasn't careful, he'd lose not just his pack, but his life and Mary's as well.

CHAPTER SEVEN

AFTER HIS SHOWER, Fergus dried his hair and with years of experience created the three-part braid Sharon had once designed for him. He then tied the end with a narrow strip of amber leather. In previous dreamglides, long before last night, Mary had enjoyed taking the braids apart and running her hands through his hair.

He heard Mary coming down the stairs and wasn't surprised when she came into the bathroom. "I brought you coffee."

He met her gaze in the mirror. "Thank you. Much appreciated."

When he turned to her, she smiled at the braid. "I remember now. You told me in one of the dreamglides that Sharon had experimented for the longest time on this particular design and that it took you a solid month to get it right."

Wearing only a towel around his hips, he pivoted a little more to face her. "You look beautiful, Mary. And I'm grateful you're here with me tonight."

"I never thought I'd be in Savage like this, but last night was incredible."

He smiled. "Yeah, it was." He held her gaze for a long moment, then sipped his coffee.

She returned the smile. "I have a favor to ask. I know we're meeting up at Warren's for steaks, but I'd really like some fresh clothes. Could we zip back to my house so that I could pack up some things?"

"Of course." He glanced toward the stairs. "But it's not quite dusk, is it?"

"No, not yet." She frowned slightly. "Fergus, is anything wrong? I mean, you don't look very rested. Were your wounds bothering you while you slept?"

He looked away from her and took another sip of coffee. "I had disturbing dreams. They weren't violent, but I felt as though all the wolves of Savage had become desperate and restless. The territory verged on something, but I couldn't pinpoint what it was."

"You mean like a pack war?"

He shook his head. "This felt different to me. Bigger. Broader. We need more physical room in Savage and not just the extra couple of miles we've recently acquired to the south."

"Is this something you're detecting with your fae senses or your wolf abilities?"

He looked at her again, settling his gaze on her light brown eyes. "Both, I think. You know, ever since I held you in my arms in Roche's jail cell, things have been changing. With you. With me. And here." With his free hand he covered his chest. "You've changed everything, Mary."

"I feel the same about you, yet I still don't know where all this is leading."

"I know."

"I mean, you're an alpha in one of the strongest packs in Savage. How can I ever have a place beside you? I don't belong here, not by a longshot. Yet, I don't want to leave, either." She chuckled. "Can't see myself returning to Revel just to treat dogs for hives and cats for molting fur. But how can you and I truly build a life together? I guess that's what I don't see."

"I understand. We're both mystified. But I'm sure time will settle things soon enough."

She smiled. "So, is that the wolf or the fae?"

He laughed, then suggested he get dressed and they finish the conversation upstairs.

After he put on a clean black tank and leathers, he climbed the stairs to the living room. She refilled his mug, then sat chatting with him easily, the same way she had in the dreamglide for the past several weeks. He had a third mug of coffee while waiting for darkness to fall.

When the sun disappeared completely, he armed himself with his Glock. He then left the cabin with Mary, rising into the air beside her. The trip to her house only took a few minutes after which he waited in the living room while she packed. The cats milled around his ankles, encouraging him into the kitchen just like they'd done the last time. As though he'd been doing it for months, he picked up the dishes, washed them and refilled each one with fresh canned food.

He contacted Mary telepathically. *I'm feeding your cats, but what about later?*

I've already made arrangements. My assistant will be here shortly. She's going to take over the practice as well as a few household chores until the whole situation with Sydon and your pack is resolved. I told her I didn't know how long it would take. I trust her, but thanks for taking care of the felines.

You're welcome. He looked down at Mary's five cats, all lined up and hunkered over each bowl. He smiled. Once again, he thought how strange it was for a wolf to be caring for cats.

Leaving the kitchen, he called Warren who said all was well at the Caldion Compound and that he'd be grilling steaks soon.

When he hung up with Warren, his thoughts turned to Sydon. He'd gotten word from his lead beta, Harley, that Sydon was all healed and ready to fight.

Reports of Sydon's behavior however, disturbed Fergus. The incarcerated wolf hadn't paced or howled or exhibited any of the usual reactions to confinement. Instead, he'd soon shifted back to his human form and had sat in a corner with his back to the wall the entire time. He'd refused to answer questions put to him, his attention focused inward.

Fergus wanted more information and got Harley on his cell. "What's he doing now?"

"He's just sitting there," Harley responded, with a wolf grunt. "Like a fucking statue. And he won't talk, not a single word."

"Which is odd for Sydon who loves to flap his gums."

Sydon was a powerful mix of educated and fucked-up. Any wolf who would rig up a skewer for a dominance match, then use it on a powerful alpha, worked on a different plane than everybody else. Fergus felt in his gut the man was psychotic.

But along with Sydon's twisted view of the world came a kind of charisma that drew dozens of loyal rogues to his service.

Instinctively, Fergus knew Sydon was up to something. He'd already coordinated the sniper-attack in the forest opposite Warren's house, which meant he was communicating with his troops. He probably had been from the time Fergus had locked him up.

"Thanks, Harley. Keep a close watch on him."

"Will do."

When Mary returned to the living room, she wore a fresh pair of jeans, though a darker blue this time, and a black top with a narrow silver belt at the waist. She'd pulled back a portion of her long, blond hair, setting off her full cheekbones.

His chest expanded at the sight of her, and his feet were in motion before she'd taken five steps into the room.

He took her rolling flight bag from her, which made her brows lift. "That's not necessary. Honest, it's not heavy."

"I know. But let me do it for you anyway."

She stared at him for a long moment, then smiled. "I'm so used to doing things for myself that your offer took me by surprise. But, thanks. I appreciate it."

"You're welcome. Are you ready to head back to Warren's?"

"I am. I heard you talking earlier. Was that Warren?"

"No. It was Harley, my number one. He'll be an alpha soon."

She got a funny look on her face. "Which one is he?"

Fergus had to remind himself that she'd been in the dreamglide the night prior, hovering over his entire compound. She'd probably seen Harley, but didn't know who he was. "He's a couple inches shorter than me, has light blue eyes and long auburn hair. He wears a double braid on the left side of his head."

"I remember him now."

When she got very quiet, he asked, "Can you pick him out of the crowd as you review your memories?"

"He was imprisoned when we arrived, wasn't he?"

"That's right."

When she still remained quiet, he turned to her. "What gives?"

He was surprised by the shocked-out look on her face. "I don't know. Would it be fair to say he's your most trusted wolf?"

"Yes." Fergus felt irritated by Mary's current state, as though she knew something she didn't want to say. "Mary, tell me what's going on."

"And you trust Harley?"

"Yes. I have no reason not to, but I take it you have a concern?"

She blinked several times in a row and he could feel her distress. "Fergus, I know two things right now: How much you trust him even to the marrow of your wolf bones. But I also know you need to be careful. Something isn't right with him."

Her words angered him. She didn't even know Harley, yet somehow she'd judged him.

He needed her to know the truth. "Do you have any idea how many times Harley has saved my ass? A dozen, at least. Maybe two. He's been my right arm from the beginning. My guards told me he tried to protect the Gordion wolf who got hurt in the dungeon cell? Then he'd been knocked unconscious for interfering, his leg sliced up. He would have been the next to fall to their swords except that my appearance in the hall distracted Sydon's men. You can ask any of the men what happened."

Her expression grew grave, her cheeks smoothing out as she held her lips together firmly. Finally, she responded, "I can see that what I've said has caused you tremendous distress and for that I'm sorry. I also won't argue with you about the accuracy of my fae senses; you must judge that for yourself. I only ask that you consider the possibility that something isn't right."

He drew a harsh breath through rippling nostrils. "You're wrong. And if I can't trust this wolf, then Savage has no chance at all."

She looked as though she wanted to say more. Her lips parted, then closed several times. Finally, she nodded. "I understand, and I won't bring it up again. Did you speak with Warren? How is everything else at his compound?"

Fergus was grateful for the abrupt shift in subject. "He'll be putting steaks on the grill as soon as it's full dark." His anger started diminishing in stages. On a rational level, he knew he shouldn't be so defensive about Harley, but any kind of accusation seemed unthinkable.

However, Mary had powerful fae abilities and he had to respect her concerns.

Mentally setting aside the subject of his second-in-command, he continued, "Warren is worried, of course, and thinks that Sydon is planning to take control of Savage. At this point, we all have reason to be concerned well beyond his attempted takeover of my pack."

Mary didn't look any less grim, but her features had started to soften and with a slight curve of her lips, she offered, "And where would we be without some madman making a push to take over the world?"

He chuckled. "You're right. Some things never change." He then glanced around. "Are you ready?"

"Yes."

"Then we should go."

~ ~ ~

Mary wasn't much of an eat-a-big-meal-first kind of person. But she did appreciate the necessity for wolves, especially of the male variety, to chow down. And the smell of steaks charring on the grill actually brought a couple of rumbles shaking her stomach as well.

By the time Fergus brought her a small ribeye with a side of potato salad, she had no hesitation accepting the plate. She was definitely embracing her wolf-side.

She stuck to her coffee, though. Most of the pack was drinking beer, though she'd heard wolves could metabolize alcohol better than most species.

Coffee, a steak and potatoes. Not exactly a fae first-meal. She usually had yogurt and fruit. But the wolf in her salivated, and she dug in.

A lot of laughter rang around the belowground communal eating area. At least a hundred sat down to share the meal. Though this was Warren's compound, she'd noticed a similar set-up at the Gordion second level when she'd cruised through in her dream-glide.

She watched another group of wolves serve and do clean-up. "Does the pack have hired help?"

Fergus glanced toward the area where wolves moved in and out of the large commercial kitchen. "No, we all take turns on clean up."

"Even you?"

He grinned. "All right, most of us work the kitchens. Those of us who serve on the border patrol are allowed to skip our turns, as well as the warriors who guard the compound."

She held his gaze. "But that makes sense to me. If you lay down your life every night for the good of your territory, you should be given a pass on regular chores."

Though the tension between herself and Fergus had passed, she still worked hard to restrain the deep anxiety she felt about Harley. She knew something was terribly wrong with the wolf; every fae sense she possessed had gone into overdrive the moment Fergus had mentioned his name. Yet she had no idea what it could be. Harley sounded like a good man.

She'd completely understood Fergus's anger. He didn't want to believe anything bad about his most trusted wolf. And if treachery existed with someone so close to him, then who could he ever rely on? But with so much at stake, she knew she couldn't let her fae instincts rest idle. She could only hope that if Harley was a traitor, his actions would reveal themselves long before she had to confront Fergus again.

For now, she enjoyed her meal as well as the sight of Warren taking care of his pack.

At first, she'd thought Warren would join them. But from the time they'd arrived and he'd shown them to their table, he'd never once sat down. Instead, he moved through the room, and it seemed to her he made an effort to talk to everyone. He had excellent eye-contact. She supposed his pack was used to the scars on his head and face, as well as the partial-baldness and the tattoos.

He was an excellent leader, attentive to his people the way Fergus was with the Gordion Pack. She watched several of the female wolves track him as he moved. She understood. He was powerful, a lot of man to watch.

She felt Fergus's hand suddenly on her knee, squeezing gently. But it felt more like a warning than a sign of affection.

She glanced at him. By now she'd finished her steak and a server had carried her plate away. With a fresh cup of coffee, she sat with her elbows on the table, the way many wolves did, and supported the mug with both hands.

What is it? she asked.

Stop looking at him.

She was surprised. *You mean Warren?*

That's exactly what I mean.

She shifted slightly in her seat so she could meet his gaze fully. *Do you do the same thing at meals with your pack?*

He glanced back at Warren. *Make the rounds?*

She smiled. *Is that what you call talking to everyone?*

Yes. Most of the alphas I know use a communal meal as much for chowing down as for staying in close contact with each pack member.

Mary sighed heavily. This was as different from Revel and her life as a fae as anything could be. *Would your alpha female be expected to do the same?* Mary wasn't naïve. She knew that unusual forces were at work in her life, and there was a chance she could make the cut as Fergus's mate. She needed to know what would be expected of her.

I think I know what's going on in your head. You're trying to guess what your duties would be if this fell to you. But try not to think of it that way. Instead, use your fae senses. What does the situation tell you? He chuckled softly, a low hoarse wolf sound. *Because I think you're too much wolf right now and not enough fae.*

The comment surprised her. But as she glanced out at the wolves dining together, she focused on her fae ability to sense things. What came back was a strange rush of speed and oneness, as though the pack had a strong central unity definitely not found in Revel.

She also saw that the ease with which Warren performed his task wasn't because of his natural abilities, but because the pack carried him from one person to the next. She found it hard to fathom, but there it was. Warren wasn't doing this alone in the same way Fergus didn't care for his pack on his own.

It also explained why, until Fergus defeated Sydon in a dominance battle, the pack wouldn't be able to accept him as their alpha. The

Gordion wolves had already started forging a bond with Sydon, however unwanted.

She turned back to Fergus once more. *I'm amazed.*

It's very different, isn't it?

There's a oneness of thought that I didn't see before.

It's also the reason I can't be with my pack. They're in the middle of a bonding process with Sydon.

I know. I sense that as well. Her shoulders sank. *Fergus, this must be terrible for them because of who Sydon is?*

Pain flashed through his eyes. *I think the suffering is as much mine as theirs. But the bond is also different from what you might think. It's hard to explain, but bonding doesn't require approval or appreciation. It's very wolf and one of the reasons packs can be as strong as they are, even if there's an absence of morality in the alpha himself. Bonding is chemical, not personal.*

He pushed his plate away and swigged his beer, then continued. *It doesn't help that Sydon is a charismatic entity because not everyone knows how bad he is. His rogue following is proof of the support he can garner.*

This time, she put her hand on his knee. *This must be killing you.*

Waiting is hard. My first impulse when I woke up, was to go straight to the Gordion Compound and kill the bastard. I might have, if I hadn't already discussed everything with the head of the pack council.

With Andrew Dean? You never told me this, Fergus. What did he say?

He held her gaze, one hand on his beer bottle. *Because Sydon already made a deal with the cartels, Dean believes that if Sydon was killed outright, the cartels would take revenge. And the last thing we want is a war with the drug lords.*

She shook her head. *But what if it comes to that despite your efforts? The cartels are always looking for a way to make inroads into a territory and Sydon was definitely holding that door wide. I can't imagine, even if you bested him in a dominance fight, that the drug lords would give up such a powerful advantage.*

Fergus shrugged, but his jaw had grown tight and his nostrils elongated. *I can't possibly predict what the cartels might or might not do. So, I'm moving forward by the book because it will give me the best advantage legally.*

She remembered his distress over his dreams. *You're worried the whole territory is headed for war.*

He held her gaze. *I am.* His dark eyes glinted with both fear and determination.

Mary sighed deeply, though it carried an odd wolf-grunt that had several nearby wolves turning to stare at her. She didn't mind. She was an oddity to herself right now so of course she'd be the same to everyone else.

She wasn't sure if the situation could get much worse than the idea that Savage was headed for a cataclysmic event. She thought back to hauling Fergus out of the Graveyard, but to what purpose? To lead the charge in a war? To mate with him? To become a fae-wolf? Would his pack ever accept a woman like her?

There was a larger question, however, one she struggled to ask given the bizarre and swift way events had moved over the past forty-eight hours. But she needed to ask it because it went to basic mental health, something even an *alter* person had to honor: *Did she even want this, any of it?*

Somehow, though, she knew she'd already answered the question the moment she'd agreed to come to Savage in the first place. Yes, Sharon had persuaded her and yes, she'd felt it in her bones as well that she would be needed here. But it had been her choice, one she'd made willingly.

She calculated the number of times she'd played a part in either saving Fergus's life or keeping him safe. The numbers kept stacking up. Would this be her role even beyond the last few encounters?

As Warren reached the final few tables, Mary saw that he looked solemn. But the color of his eyes had deepened to a lustrous emerald. She glanced past him to his wolves and knew that the way he'd just connected with them had added to the beauty of his eyes.

Something inside her leaped with pleasure and joy combined. The fae part of her could appreciate what she knew he'd just experienced. She turned to Fergus and marveled at him as well.

At the exact same moment, she realized how much pain the severed bond had cost Fergus. The alpha responsibility of leading came with a deep emotional connection to those in his care. Where Sydon would abuse and torture his pack, men like Warren and Fergus would serve and protect, the same way they performed their jobs on the border patrol.

Without giving it too much thought, she slid her arm around Fergus's neck. When he turned to her, his eyes lit with surprise, she kissed him on the lips. The wolf in her knew it would be acceptable in any pack setting. She also knew everyone present was aware she was a female with the ability to become Fergus's alpha-mate. Little was hidden in pack life.

Fergus's eyes glowed amber in the same way Warren's had shown with a more intense emerald light. She saw the pleasure in his eyes, and not just because theirs was a sexual relationship.

You honor me, he said.

I admire the hell out of you, Fergus. She felt dizzy suddenly and could detect the nature of his dreams. *And you're right. Savage will need men like you and Warren.*

You're feeling it as well.

Like a distant rumbling and nothing good.

At last, Warren moved in the direction of Mary's table. He sat down opposite Fergus and immediately two wolves brought him his meal, which included a large tankard of beer and a steak two inches thick.

He made no apologies as he picked up knife and fork and settled in.

Between bites and a large swallow of beer, he addressed Fergus. "What time is the dominance fight set for?"

"We're on in an hour."

Mary drew in a long, slow breath. Her gaze skittered away from both men. In an hour, Fergus would battle to regain his pack. She felt confident Fergus could beat Sydon, no question about that. From what she'd heard about the initial match, Fergus had been well on his way to taking Sydon down when the skewer struck home.

This time Sydon wouldn't be wearing his wrist guards. But would he have some other nefarious trick up his sleeve?

~ ~ ~

The nearest underground sand pit arena was big enough to house the leaders of the Gordion Pack, Sydon's rogue pack, and Warren's Caldion Pack. Named the Sand Boulder for the massive boulders left intact at the southern and northern entrance-exit points, the arena pit sat halfway between Warren and Fergus's compounds.

Fergus had already changed into his tan leather gladiator briefs. He wore an amber cloak over his shoulders that hung to the floor, but nothing else, not even shoes.

He left the pre-battle room and levitated down the tunnel that led into the arena. Mary was on his right, Warren on his left. His wolf blood flowed hot, and his muscles in his arms and legs contracted and released, ready for a fight.

The last time he'd traveled this tunnel was just before his first dominance battle against Sydon. At the time, Fergus had felt equal to the task of taking Sydon down. He knew his strength, and Sydon, despite his power level, couldn't compete with him. Sydon's confidence, however, should have been a warning to Fergus that the wolf was up to something. Yet even now, Fergus was shocked that any wolf would have resorted to using a blade in a dominance match. When it came to honor and ethics, clearly Sydon wasn't interested.

At the very least, Sydon wouldn't be allowed to wear wrist guards. He'd only have on his dark gray gladiator briefs and nothing else. He'd be weapon-free and the match should be equal. Because the fae part of Fergus felt uneasy, however, his focus became fixed as much on Sydon's nature as his batting skills.

When he reached the tunnel opening, he dropped down from levitation to walk along the stone pavers. He had a limited view of the arena, but he wanted a good look around before he headed to his staging platform.

In the center, a full sixty feet down from the top row of seats, was the pit. It was filled with sand two feet deep and smoothed with the back of a rake. During a dominance battle, limited levitation was allowed and a combatant could only shift into his wolf form when he surrendered the field.

Punching, kicking and wrestling moves were all allowed, but no biting and no weapons of any kind.

The seats were already filled, the bulk with the members of the

Gordion Pack, who would be most affected by the outcome. He sensed the partial bond his wolves had already forged with Sydon. He wasn't surprised by it, but it fired up his blood even more.

Fergus recognized the gray logo patches of Sydon's force since the wolves hovered near the south entrance-exit.

As he began to walk out from the tunnel, along the path that led to his platform, his gaze moved in a strong arc, watching for any sign of trouble. Warren's pack drew close from the sides of the path, guarding him. Wolves were volatile and the presence of Sydon's loyal rogue pack was a bad sign. Sydon had no fear and neither did his wolves. The air was charged with wolf adrenaline, which had his heart pumping.

When he turned and began to mount the stairs leading up to his platform, the Gordion wolves began a rousing applause that soon thundered through the space. As the howling started, his throat closed up with emotion. He loved every single one of the men and women present and he knew each by name. He'd worked hard for years to do right by his pack.

No one in his pack lacked food, shelter or the opportunity to move up in the ranks as powers emerged. No one was made to feel small or insignificant. Not everyone was born with muscle power and some of his top people, though lowest in pack rank, served as accountants and job placement staffers that kept his people happy.

To see how much he was valued meant more to him than he could possibly say. He'd do everything he could to win this battle. His wounds were healed, and he was ready.

He pressed a fist to his chest, then lifted his arm high. His wolves shouted, howled and stamped their feet all over again until the noise was deafening. Both Warren and Mary waited discreetly at the bottom of the platform stairs.

Opposite him, beyond the blank canvas of sand, was Sydon's still empty platform.

When the applause began to abate, he shifted his arm, holding it out to Mary and Warren, gesturing to each in turn. Warren started to ascend, but stopped when Mary didn't join him.

Fergus sensed Mary's hesitation. *What is it?*

Her eyes were wide. *I'm not sure where I should be. Maybe I should take a seat nearby.*

Her voice in his head caused him to pivot fully in her direction. He waved her forward. *I want you beside me. I might even need you here. But I also want the Gordion Pack to know my intentions toward you, though I suspect they already do.*

She nodded. He could feel her nerves, and he understood why she was uncertain of her role. For one thing, she'd never been in a dominance sand pit before. The size of it, compared to anything else in Five Bridges, was staggering and the wolves made a lot of noise.

I'm not afraid, if that's what you're thinking, Fergus. But I don't want to intrude where I shouldn't.

Again, you're too many steps ahead of this process. If nothing else, I want your fae senses at full bore while I'm battling Sydon. I don't know if he has anything planned, but it's possible he might. You're the one person here, without the single-minded focus of the wolf nature, who can be a second pair of eyes for me. So, besides the fact that I want you close to me, I'm also looking out for my own ass.

He felt her relax at these last words, and she mounted the few steps to his platform. A tall stone wall backed the space protectively, but Warren's toughest wolves had already filled in the seats beyond the wall.

She took Fergus's hand as she drew near, and he squeezed it to reassure her. *For now, stick close.*

She gripped his hand harder in response. *I will.*

A commotion on the opposite side of the arena drew his attention. Sydon appeared at the end of his tunnel, to which Fergus had a direct view. Several Gordion wolves escorted him. He wore a charcoal gray cloak, his hair had the usual oily appearance, and his lips were pulled back in a sneer.

Maybe it was the obvious disdain in his expression, but a profound booing started up and rose in volume as he began his ascent up to his platform. Despite the pack's semi-bond with Sydon, Fergus was proud of his wolves for expressing their disapproval of the man.

Sydon flipped his cape back and lifted an arm, theatrically acknowledging the boos of a large portion of the audience.

At the same time that Sydon took center-stage on his platform, his rogue pack marched in and filled in the seats directly behind Sydon's protective wall. The number staggered Fergus since that area alone could hold up to two hundred wolves.

Mary's voice entered his mind. *I can't believe the council allowed Sydon's rogues to support him like this.*

Fergus kept his gaze fixed on Sydon, who now continued to wave intermittently at the hostile crowd.

Without a legal challenge in the Tribunal court, he's the Gordion Pack alpha. In a technical sense, he can add as many wolves to the pack as he wants. According to pack law, once I shifted into my wolf state, it meant I quit the field of battle.

She offered a scoffing snort, very wolf. *You were stuck with a skewer, your heart severely damaged. Then you were hauled out of here and dumped in the Graveyard. How is that considered 'quitting the field'?*

Her words lightened his spirit, and he smiled. *I guess I have to agree.*

When another heavy round of boos slid through the crowd, Mary leaned close. *Do you think word has gotten out about the skewer?*

I'm sure it has, Fergus said. *And this is one of the few opportunities when a pack can express its disdain for an alpha's conduct.*

Well, if there was ever anyone who deserved to be castigated by a large number of people, it's that asshole.

Fergus chuckled and turned to Mary. *Asshole, huh?*

At the very least. A lot of other words come to mind, but I'm not saying them as a matter of courtesy.

He squeezed her hand again. *I'm glad you're here.*

Me, too. But is it wrong to say I'm nervous as hell? Though just to be clear, she added, *I'm not worried about the dominance battle.*

I know. I'm not either. I can take Sydon. But there's a current in the air more troubling than anything I've experienced since I arrived in Five Bridges.

She nodded. *I can feel it as well, as though the entire territory is about to be turned on its head.*

CHAPTER EIGHT

MARY FORCED HER wolf to calm down. The atmosphere in the arena hit every nerve in her body and kept her heart beating hard. But she had to think. Her wolf was second in her *alter* being, despite its love of the energy in the air.

Her fae, which relied more on instinct than raw animal power and quick reactions, needed to have skin in the game as well. *Fergus, do you want me to do a quick dreamglide? See if we missed anything? All I would need is for you to hold me close and let me rest my head on your shoulder.*

You think you can create one in this noisy gathering?

Yes. I just need to be supported.

Go ahead then. He slid his arm tightly around her waist, drawing her close.

She leaned her head against his shoulder and dropped quickly into a deep meditation. What surprised her was that she didn't fall unconscious, but instead remained upright. When they'd made love, she'd been fully awake in both realities. The same seemed to be true here. But being supported by Fergus gave her a sense of security.

The moment she was in her dreamglide, she telepathed, *I'm in.*

And you're not unconscious?

No, I'm not, but it helps to have you support me since I'm on my feet.

This is changing too, isn't it? Fergus asked.

Everything is. Within the dreamglide, she gained her bearings. She was directly above Fergus. *All right, let me find out what's going on.*

She piloted the craft over the sand pit and headed immediately toward

Sydon and his crew. When she was directly overhead, she moved slowly up the rows, but nothing seemed to be out of place. With the seats made of stone, little could be hidden.

Where are you now, Mary?

I'm over Sydon's rogue troops but I'm not finding anything. They're clean. I'm going to make a pass over the rest of the spectators.

Okay. Detail it for me.

She gave him a blow-by-blow as she made her way first around all the seats then outside at the north entrance, then the south. She made a quick trip over the surrounding pines as well. *The forest looks clear.*

Okay. Then get back here because the referee is heading down into the pit right now. The dominance challenge is about to start, and he'll announce me first.

She smiled at the 'get back here' part. She could move the dreamglide to China, but she didn't have to make the return trip to come back to herself. All she had to do was let the dreamglide go, which she did. She lifted her head. "I'm back," she said aloud.

"That was fast."

"I might have been over the forest, but in terms of distance, it doesn't really exist. As real as the dreamglide is, it's still a product of a dream sequence."

The referee began his introduction of Fergus, listing his former rank as alpha of the Gordion Pack and his challenge to Sydon. No mention was made of the skewer, however.

She felt a tremor of pure excitement run through Fergus. She instinctively stepped away from him and as she did, he withdrew his arm from around her waist. She could sense how focused he became, intent on the battle ahead.

As Fergus dropped his cloak, then levitated off the platform and into the sand pit, Mary resisted the urge to reach for him, to pull him back. It was an odd impulse since she was fully on board with what needed to happen here. But she felt protective of him at the same time, as though her job had become to ensure his safety no matter what. Was that part of the role of an alpha-female?

So much was at stake. Mostly, Fergus needed to bring the Gordion

Pack under his care once more. No one in their right mind would argue this wasn't the priority.

The crowd fell silent. That alone was an extraordinary circumstance given the general noise the wolves had been making the entire time. Yet the bite to the air remained.

Another round of boos sounded as the referee began his introduction of Sydon. The referee continued to state Sydon's stats despite the ruckus and hissing. Mary thought all the noise appropriate given Sydon's heinous conduct against Fergus and the Gordion Pack.

When the wolves grew quiet again, everyone's attention became focused on the men now standing in the middle of the sand pit not ten feet apart. By her best visual calculation, the pit area was an oval twenty yards long and about fifteen yards wide. With limited levitation allowed, the space didn't need to be bigger.

The referee wore the Savage Pack Council's dark blue-and-white striped long sleeved shirt and quickly called out the rules. So far the event was unfolding just as Mary had been told it would. She could see Fergus's muscles twitch. The wolf was ready.

Another wave of dread, however, passed through her. Something wasn't right. Sydon and his men were too relaxed, too confident. Yet, she'd checked their seats, she'd made a circuit of the arena and she'd even gone into the forest. But she'd found nothing unusual or troubling.

Yet a powerful concern remained.

The referee shouted, "Let the battle begin!"

A roar rose up from the crowd and at the same moment, Fergus lowered his shoulders and headed straight for Sydon. He looked like he meant to slam into his chest, but instead at the last second threw a right punch that caught Sydon off guard. Sydon flew back. He ended up sitting in the sand and rubbing his jaw.

A howling cheer went up so loud, it was all Mary could do to keep from joining the wolves herself.

A split-second later, Sydon was on his feet. He came at Fergus hard and caught Fergus in the ribs with his foot. Fergus doubled over, then spun on his heel. Sand sprayed.

Sydon missed a second kick, but that allowed Fergus to catch his foot. He did a back-flip which turned Sydon's leg and sent him once more into the sand.

Fergus didn't stay put long. He levitated, pivoted horizontally, then plowed into Sydon's stomach. Fergus drew up, gathered his strength and headed straight back for him.

But Sydon retreated quickly, spun in the sand at the same time then levitated off at an angle. Fergus missed him by an inch and his momentum caused him to tumble forward into the sand.

Turning in the air, Sydon aimed straight at him. It seemed to Mary that Fergus looked dazed, but it was a ruse. The moment Sydon drew close, Fergus flipped over, putting himself out of Sydon's reach. But at the last moment, he caught Sydon's ankle.

With a slick levitation move, he swung Sydon around in a complete circle twice, then launched him into the air, sending him twenty feet away. The crowd roared its approval.

Mary's gaze went to Sydon, who rolled in the sand as he landed. He lifted up slowly, one hand at his waist as though injured.

Mary felt it again, a fae sense of dread so profound that she knew Sydon was up to something and Fergus was in trouble. She didn't know how since there was no way Sydon had a weapon on him this time.

But Mary knew what she knew.

She had to dreamglide.

She moved close to Warren and slid into his mind. *Listen, Warren, my fae instincts tell me our boy is in trouble. Something's not right, and I need to dreamglide. Will you support my body while I do it, because I'll be vulnerable while I see what's going on.*

Warren, however, stared at her as though she'd lost her mind.

She understood the problem instantly. Warren didn't want to touch her because she belonged to Fergus. Being physically close to her would cause all kinds of problems, for Warren personally and alpha-to-alpha. *Mary, I can't do this. I won't do this to Fergus. Touching you is beyond inappropriate.*

She lowered her chin and held his gaze, then growled softly. *If you don't get on board right now Fergus will die, and that's my fae speaking. Get with the program. Now!* She all but shouted the last part into his head.

Her posture, and maybe her wolf-growl, had an effect.

He nodded, then opened his arm for her. By the time she was wrapped up, she felt him shaking from head-to-foot. He was fast reaching the peak of his own alpha-mating cycle as well. Being this close to a female with alpha-mate bonding potential had to be agony for him, but it couldn't be helped.

The moment she felt secure, Mary dropped quickly into her deepest meditation and slipped into her dreamglide. She flew directly over the battle. No one could see her of course and even if one of the men struck in her direction, they wouldn't actually touch her. She could fly through both men as they battled and wouldn't feel a thing. She was, in that sense, a ghost.

The men fought wildly until Fergus landed Sydon on his back, jumped on him and pinned him in the sand. He punched Sydon's face repeatedly.

Mary knew this was the moment she was meant to watch, because the dread she felt had become a torture over every inch of her skin.

She brought the dreamglide right down next to the men. Fergus's face was flushed red as he continued to hit Sydon with his bare fist.

She shifted her gaze to Sydon. Why wasn't he fighting back?

That's when she saw it. Sydon's hand had slipped just inside his gray leather gladiator briefs. When he pulled his fingers back, he had something small pinched between his thumb and index finger.

She sniffed the air. Even in the dreamglide, she could catch odors and whatever Sydon had in his possession smelled like something the dark witches could create.

She knew then that Sydon had a potent, deadly spell between his fingers.

From the dreamglide, she shouted inside Fergus's head, *Sydon has a witch powder in his hand. Get away from him, now! Now! Move, now!* If she could have pulled on his shoulders, she would have.

~ ~ ~

Fergus heard Mary's words through the thrill of beating his opponent. But it took him a moment to register what she'd said.

Witch's spell.

Shit.

Move! Mary's voice once more struck his head.

He flew backward just as Sydon released a blue powdery substance. Fergus had escaped immediate impact, but a vapor the color of cobalt kept moving in Fergus's direction as though designed for him.

Holy hell! It was a witch's concoction.

Time slowed down and as the powder began to reach Fergus, panic took hold of Sydon's face. Sydon hadn't thought he'd get caught, which meant that if Fergus hadn't moved as he did, the powder-based spell would have made contact with his skin, and disappeared as it penetrated his body. The spell would have been undetectable.

The referee immediately shouted, "Foul! I can see the witch's spell. This dominance battle is at an end!"

Fergus wanted to say something, to call for Sydon's imprisonment, but he suddenly felt dizzy and sick as hell. As he dropped to his knees, he watched helplessly as Sydon and his wolves raced for the south exit.

The crowd howled its rage at what Sydon had attempted.

The referee again called out. "Because a witch's spell has been cast here, I find in favor of Fergus, and reinstate him as alpha of the Gordion Pack."

Fergus sensed Mary's presence just before she put her arm around his shoulders and knelt beside him. His eyes rolled, he felt profoundly sick to his stomach. "I'm going to throw up."

"Let it out. It's poison."

Fergus threw up all over the sand and what came out of him was dark blue, like the vapor he'd witnessed.

"We need water here," Mary shouted. "Lots of it."

Within a few seconds, he felt movement around him as others came to his aid. Mary thrust a bottle beneath his nose and commanded, "Drink as much as you can and drink it fast."

With a profound thirst setting in, he guzzled. He went through the first bottle, then a second one before he started feeling a little better. He was still dizzy as hell, but worked to gain his feet anyway.

Warren was right there beside him and caught him around his waist, holding him upright. Mary was on his other side, took the empty bottle from his hand and shoved a third one at him. He drank some more.

His head was spinning. The spell had been powerful and he knew if Sydon had put it anywhere on his skin he would have died within seconds with no one the wiser.

He leaned into Warren. "Get a witch over here to clean this up. Don't let any of our wolves near the sand."

He then heard Warren shouting commands to that effect.

Though Warren supported him, he wanted Mary close. "Stay next to me while I drink. I need you right now." It was an odd thing to feel and to say. But she'd saved his life. Again.

Mary settled her hand on his shoulder and didn't let go no matter how many times he lifted the same arm to drink.

Taking another swig, he then looked at her, frowning slightly. "What did you see? I mean, how did you know something was going to happen?"

Mary nodded as tears started to her eyes. "I experienced a terrible feeling of dread that became focused on Sydon." She explained how she'd positioned the dreamglide close to their battling bodies and had watched Sydon's hand go to the waistband of his briefs. "I'm just glad you listened to me when I told you to get away from him."

"The moment you spoke into my head, I knew you'd drawn close and I could feel you in the dreamglide. But where did he get the spell?"

"Someone must have given it to him, one of his wolves, maybe?"

"That had to be it. He must have been planning this since I shot him in the thigh and jailed him in the dungeon cell. I'm convinced the whole time he was there he was communicating telepathically with his rogue wolves, setting this up. Still, I can't believe he brought a dark witch's spell into a dominance match, although since the skewer incident, I shouldn't be surprised."

He glanced around and saw that most of Warren's pack had already left the arena. With the exception of Warren's close-knit security force, only the Gordion wolves remained. He asked Warren to get him over to the seats so he could sit down.

Once there, not far from his platform, he sat down on a stone bench and sent his self-healing into his bloodstream where the remnants of the spell were still working on him. How strange his life had become as an *alter* species, that he could feel the dark witch spell trying to cause more damage.

A wolf came near and put Fergus's amber cloak around his shoulders.

Mary sat down beside him. He slid his arm around her and pulled her close. Her presence comforted him, but not because she'd yet again saved his life. It was just her, the goodness of her soul, her kindness.

He checked his self-healing and felt the last of the potion leave his body. "It's gone."

"Thank God."

He kissed the top of her head and affection swelled his heart. "Thank you," he whispered.

She drew back enough to meet his gaze and smiled faintly in return. "You're very welcome."

At that, he kissed her, though afterward, he heard a soft howling move through the arena.

Glancing up, he saw that the Gordion wolves were all moving in his direction and seemed to be responding to his relationship with Mary. He could also tell that the bond had already started to form. The pack was his again and with so much general good will, it wouldn't take long.

Warren, standing nearby, patted him on his shoulder and said, "Congratulations. The pack is yours again."

He wasn't sure he'd heard better words in his life. Sydon's brief but violent reign was over and the wave of appreciation that he felt from those Gordion wolves present, brought him to his feet once more.

A smattering of applause turned into a roll of thunder, one that made him smile. Slowly, his wolves drew close until they filled all the nearby aisles, then began to pass by him in a long procession. He took his time and greeted each one, accepting their love and well-wishes.

Mary and Warren moved in behind him as the pack continued to stream by. Within a few minutes, he felt fully restored and knew his pack was the reason.

As the arena emptied, he thanked Warren for his help.

Warren nodded, but his nostrils elongated and flared. "We have an enemy out there, and I don't think he's finished with us yet."

"As long as Sydon has breath, he'll keep trying for a takeover," Fergus said. "Which means I need to return to my compound and you should get back to yours."

He glanced past Warren and saw the green-trimmed black tanks of his security force, standing guard. Fergus nodded in their direction. "Your men are waiting for you."

Warren held Fergus's gaze and a crooked smile touched his lips. "Glad to have you back."

"Thanks again, for everything."

Warren dipped his chin a couple of times, then turned up the aisle and headed in the direction of his men. Fergus watched until Warren and his large contingent flew out the south entrance.

As for the Gordion wolves, Fergus's lead wolves had formed an arc near him and several levitated in the air on either side of the aisle. The rest of his team stood all along the path at the top of the seats.

Harley was nearby.

Fergus stiffened slightly, remembering what Mary had said about him. He wanted to ignore her warning, but she'd just saved his life again. He had to take her concerns seriously even if they made no sense.

He wasn't sure what to think, but for now he needed to give Harley the benefit of the doubt, if not for Harley's sake, then for his own. Harley had been his right hand man for years now.

Fergus slowed his steps and contacted Mary telepathically. *Do you see how beat up Harley is? He got that way battling Sydon's men. I know for a fact he worked hard to save the wolf Sydon's force tried to kill in the dungeon cell. I can't believe he's anything but loyal to me and to his pack.*

He felt Mary's stillness and the part of him that was fae reached toward her, silently begging her to recant.

She turned to him and caressed his face. Looking up at him, she telepathed, *My worries about Harley aren't important right now. All that matters is that you bond with your pack. Okay?*

It wasn't the response he wanted, but it gave him enough space to shift gears and head with her in Harley's direction.

Fergus kept his arm around Mary as they drew close to Harley. In a low voice, Fergus asked, "How the hell did Sydon conceal a witch's spell in his gladiator briefs and who brought it to him?"

"We don't know yet. I have Ryan and a couple of his men working on it, but the best we can figure is that Sydon had someone on the inside."

"Which means we have a traitor."

"It looks that way, but I know all our wolves and not one comes to mind who isn't loyal to you."

He felt Mary tremble next to him, but he ignored her reaction. Harley couldn't be the one. Even his newly forming fae senses told him that Harley was speaking the truth. So, how could Mary be right about him? It didn't make sense.

Harley continued, "We're interviewing every wolf who had contact with Sydon since he was locked up last night. I'll let you know when we find something."

"Good. Stay on it."

Harley stared at Fergus for a long moment, then his lips curved.

"What?" Fergus asked.

"You're back." Harley nodded several times. "Dammit, you're back." He patted Fergus once on the shoulder, then whirled and took off with several of the Gordion security force, levitating to the north entrance.

Fergus glanced around at the remaining guards and those members of his pack who hadn't left yet. "Thank you, all of you. How about we head back to the compound?"

A cheer went up.

Fergus drew Mary tighter to his side. *Let me fly you back, okay?*

She smiled, leaned up and kissed him. "Whatever you want."

~ ~ ~

Mary felt relieved and exhilarated at the same time. Though she was a little overwhelmed that Fergus had come within a leaf's width of getting struck down again, she reveled in the fact that Sydon was gone and the pack had been legally restored to Fergus.

Being that close to Harley had caused her to stumble mentally, however. The moment she'd seen him, the same terrible sensation returned, that his loyalty was completely divided and had been for a long time. Yet she'd felt no dissimulation in Harley as he'd spoken to Fergus, something she couldn't explain.

Harley exuded a solid, even unshakeable alignment with Fergus. Yet she knew something was terribly wrong. Was it possible a witch was involved and somehow interfering with the Gordion Pack? It seemed unlikely, since dark witches loathed the wolves of Savage. Their enmity was one of the most intense in Five Bridges. And yet Sydon had employed a dark witch spell which meant there might be a connection.

But she couldn't have said anything to Fergus about Harley when he was greeting everyone, even when he spoke with Harley. His priority right now was reestablishing himself as alpha to his pack. So, she'd held back and kept her difficult fae reactions to herself. The trembling, however, she'd been unable to help.

She felt Fergus's focus move outward, and knew he was embracing his pack. His scent bore a layer of tenderness not there before because he'd been severed from the Gordion wolves for the past two nights. But the subtle smell was there, like the wind in the pine trees: Fergus's alpha wolfness to his pack.

He'd also wanted to fly her to the Gordion Compound, even though she was fully capable now of taking herself into the air. Truth? She wanted to be physically close to him.

Once secured against his side and poised on his bare foot, he took her high above the pine forest, heading east. He still wore the amber cloak wrapped around him, with his arm pinned to her waist.

His voice penetrated her mind. *I wouldn't be here but for you. Thank you, again, Mary. A thousand times. I'm overwhelmed by what you've done for me and for my pack.*

She leaned her head against his shoulder, her hand pressed to his chest. *I wish Sydon was gone for good.*

I know. I don't think any of the alphas will have peace until he's been run to earth. He's dangerous. What I don't know is the price he paid for that dark spell.

I hadn't thought of that, Mary said. *He must have made a promise of some kind because I've never seen that level of spell-craft before, at least not in Revel. Have you seen anything like it here in Savage?*

No, I haven't. But I'm aware of the prices paid for spells of that kind. Exorbitant. How could Sydon have afforded it?

Has to be the cartels. They gain if he moves into power. He's already made it clear he'll sacrifice everyone in his pack to do the bidding of the drug lords. Even hearing these words telepathically distressed Mary. She knew the cartels had been involved in Sydon's attempted takeover. And Sydon had already shown what his ambitions would mean for any pack he tried to engulf.

As Fergus made his descent toward the Gordion Compound, Mary was surprised to see dozens of wolves lined up at the entrance, many levitating.

"They're welcoming you home. Fergus, are you sure I should even be with you right now? Because this is for you, their alpha."

He squeezed her waist. "That's where you're wrong. Can't you feel it, the pack's desire to thank you for all that you've done? By now, they know it was you who kept me from receiving a killing portion of the dark spell. This greeting is as much for you as for me. So, embrace it."

He flew lower toward his people so that soon he was within handshaking distance, even while levitating.

Applause resounded into the warm June night air. Mary's cheeks warmed up as she saw the appreciation on many of the wolves' faces. Several reached out and touched her as she moved by. Each time contact was made, she felt a warmth flow through her that was all wolf and very much a pack sensation.

Fergus dropped them slowly down to the stone entrance to walk the rest of the way. More of the pack was lined up to welcome Fergus home.

As soon as she crossed the threshold into the main entrance, like Warren's compound, she could see through to the back gathering area.

Hundreds were assembled for Fergus's return, maybe the entire pack, starting out front, then ranging along both sides of the massive entry hall, and finally grouped in the large patio area out back.

Harley and his team were in the center of the large foyer where a three-tiered fountain flowed. One of Harley's team, Ryan, called out, "We have a celebration planned in the communal area. There will be three shifts so we can include everyone. We have champagne on ice and plenty of beer. We're firing up the barbecues as we speak and two of the Savage packs are sending extra meat over to help us celebrate. And, best of all, Councilor Dean called to let you know the council has approved your default dominance win."

Another cheer went up, traveling through all the wolves present.

Mary worked hard to avoid eye-contact with Harley and instead focused her attention on Fergus. But the pull was there, a concern Harley was a linchpin for Sydon in some inexplicable way.

She stuck close to Fergus, which wasn't hard to do since his arm never left her waist. Though, after the first shift was called down to the second level dining area, Harley made sure Fergus was given some time to shower and dress.

Mary went with him to his master bedroom, where she found her flight bag. She suspected Fergus's wolves, who had provided meatloaf and wine the night before, must have packed up her things from the den and brought them to the compound.

She was about to pick it up, when she realized Fergus had grown very quiet. Reaching out with her fae senses and seeing that he was staring at his bed, she realized he was remembering what Sydon had done here.

Fergus's wolves, thank God, had already cleaned up the space.

"Even though this is a different bed, I don't want to be in this room," he said. "Sydon shot up all three of those women with amber flame."

Mary knew what it meant to have a flame drug forced into her system. The withdrawal process had required days in order to completely get the highly addictive substance out of her body. And even then, she'd had regular treatments for residual reactions to the drug.

His voice was low as he said, "They'll need therapy as well."

She drew close and took his hand. "Do you have another place where we can stay?"

He inclined his head in a northerly direction. "A guest suite just down the hall. We'll go there now to get cleaned up because I don't want either of us in this room as it is. I'll want it gutted before I return."

She understood completely. She could recall the horror she'd felt when she'd first seen the three female wolves chained to the bed. She remembered Fergus's order to burn the bed, which she suspected had already been done. But the space felt evil to her as well.

When he gathered up his clothes, and picked up Mary's flight bag, she left the room with him.

He immediately summoned his housekeeper and issued orders that after he and Mary had used the guest suite to change clothes, he wanted the rest of his belongings moved temporarily to the guest bedroom.

His housekeeper wore a solemn expression as she said, "I'll put everything in motion right away."

A half hour later, Mary still wore her jeans, black t-shirt and the thin silver belt, but Fergus had showered and changed into a new set of leathers and a t-shirt bearing the amber logo patch of the Gordion pack. With his arm once more around her waist, he led her to the soundproof communal dining area where the first shift of wolves was howling, noisy and exuberant with celebration. They'd finished their meal, but had waited to greet their alpha before turning the space over to the second shift.

He took her first to the head table where she sat while he made a speech, thanking everyone for their support. Afterward, she watched him do the same thing Warren had done at his compound. Fergus made his way from table-to-table and wolf-to-wolf, making contact with each person in his pack.

Much later and well into the third-shift celebration, Mary was woozy from too much champagne. She sat in the same place, at the head table and had been visited by most all of the Gordion wolves. She was pretty sure it would take a full day of self-healing for her fingers to recover from so much hand-shaking.

How did you know about the spell?

The sound of Sharon's voice in her head forced Mary to sit up a little straighter and look around.

Sharon floated in the air off to Mary's left as though reclining on her side. Her elbow appeared to be resting on something solid as she supported her head in her palm. It was all posturing of course. A ghost didn't exactly have a head to put anywhere.

But Mary gave her credit for attitude.

She rose from her chair and moved to stand beside Sharon. *So, you're back. Are you here to celebrate Fergus's reinstatement?*

When Sharon didn't answer her, Mary turned to look at her, but Sharon didn't seem happy. *What's wrong?* Mary asked. *I thought you'd be pleased.*

Sharon shifted to look at her, then moved to a sitting position. She now appeared as though perched on top of a wall, her legs dangling over. *How did you know about the spell, Mary?*

Of all the things Sharon could have addressed, Mary was surprised she would want to talk about the spell. *For whatever reason, my fae senses were on high alert. The moment we left the tunnel, I knew something was wrong.*

Well, what you did was brilliant. I followed you in the dreamglide and saw what you saw. Sydon is a real piece of work, isn't he?

Undoubtedly a psychopath.

Sharon grew quiet. Mary turned to watch her, wondering why she was back this time. Sharon's gaze followed Fergus almost exclusively.

What you are thinking about? Mary asked.

Sharon released a ghostly sigh. *I never knew how to love this man. He was always a mystery to me even when we were human. But it seems so easy for you, and that makes me a little sad, even pissed off.*

How can you possibly be mad about something like that? Mary asked. *I always had the impression, especially by way of a few dead-talkers I know, that the afterlife is meant for letting go, for different kinds of atonement, but mostly for moving on. So, what are you here for, Sharon?*

She huffed another ghostly sigh. *To help you and Fergus make this transition.*

Mary's faeness fired up once more. *Wait a minute,* she said. *This is about Sydon, isn't it? He's why you're here.*

To some degree, yes, Sharon responded. *And also about the witch who gave him the spell. You're on the right track there, which is what I came to tell you. But Mary, things are going to get rough. You'll need to be brave, I mean really brave. And now, I have to go.*

As quickly as she'd come, Sharon was gone.

Mary felt deeply unsettled by what Sharon had just told her. She'd confirmed her suspicions that a witch was involved more extensively than just selling a dark spell to Sydon. But she had no idea what to do about it.

She needed more information and though she tried to call Sharon back, the ghost remained stubbornly unreachable.

Fergus greeted the last of his pack members and finally headed in her direction. His leathers and snug black t-shirt were a great look for him. The fabric showed off his thick pecs and trim waist. His hair hung in a mass as it always did, and as was his habit, he'd created Sharon's intricate braid after he'd showered.

CHAPTER NINE

MARY PUT HER hand over her mouth and giggled just as Lydia had. The room was full of flowers and lit candles, at least a dozen. The fragrances had her wolf-nose wrinkling and she loved it. The bed had been turned down with pink rose petals scattered over white sheets. Champagne sat chilling in an ice bucket beside a pair of flutes.

"They did this for us?" she asked, moving into the room and turning in a full circle to take it all in.

"The women wanted to show their appreciation for all that you've done. This is for you, Mary, which is the least you deserve."

She shook her head and couldn't quite blink. "There have to be a hundred pink and yellow roses in here." There were four large bouquets and several smaller ones. She glanced toward the other side of the room. "And lavender ones as well."

Her nostrils flared and once again she embraced the rich scent. As had happened before, she could detect layers of fragrance and took her time exploring each one. It was like having a feast for her senses.

Fergus headed in the direction of the bathroom. Once by the doorway, he turned back to her, smiling. "There's more in here."

She followed after him, then stepped inside. She gasped faintly at the sight of three full-length negligees hanging from one of the above-the-sink light fixtures. The gowns were made of beautiful lace, one each in black, cream and purple. "I wouldn't know how to choose."

But that's when she saw the oversized bathtub full of bubbles. Steam rose from within. Nothing could have looked more welcoming.

"This is exactly what I need." She turned to Fergus. "How do I thank them for this? I've been feeling worn out and overcome, and this hits the spot."

"You won't need to thank anyone. They're just showing their gratitude for what you've done for me. But if you feel the need, a few words to Lydia would do it. Right now, I'm going to pour the champagne and bring you a glass. You can climb right in if you want and please, take your time."

The funny thing was, she could feel his alpha hunger for her like a sensual crawl over her skin. Yet he had enough restraint, despite his ever-present drive, to give her the space she needed.

When he left, she stripped out of her clothes, folding them into a neat pile. She stowed them out of sight near the hamper. Using a couple of large hair clips, also laid out for her, she drew her hair up and pinned it on top of her head.

She stepped into the steaming water then lowered herself in. The sound that came out of her throat was more a wolfish growl than the sigh she'd intended.

Her body grew light, her arms and legs floating easily, her head resting on a bath pillow. She closed her eyes and took deep breaths. The aromatic oils in the water soon had a restorative effect and her energy began to rise once more.

She heard the pop of the champagne cork, and a minute later Fergus returned carrying two glasses. Opening her eyes, she saw that he was also naked, which made her smile. Not surprising, her thoughts became much more focused on him, and the difficulties of the night faded away.

The present moment felt like a gift to her in every possible way. Fergus had survived another horrendous attack, this time through a deadly witch powder, and now he was here.

She extended both her hands. "Let me hold them, then please join me."

His smile broadened. "Was hoping you'd say that." He handed her the glasses, and she scooted forward so he could climb in behind her. The tub, thank God, was big enough that he easily stretched out his long muscled legs on either side of her. The water swirled as he slid an arm around her waist, drawing her against him.

She groaned for the pleasure of it, for the feel of his body, the water and the soundproof room. She felt some serious future howls forming in her throat. She handed him a champagne flute. When he took it, she leaned back and rested her head against his shoulder.

He brought his glass forward and tapped hers. "For everything, Mary."

He sipped, and she felt and heard him release a growling sigh. She took a drink as well. She couldn't believe she was here, lying in a tub full of bubbles, smelling a scented bath oil that reminded her of the ocean, and feeling Fergus's muscular body all around her.

"You're back where you belong, Fergus. You must be so relieved."

"I am." His rough wolf voice pleased her so much.

She continued sipping for a few minutes and when she was done, she set her champagne glass on the floor. She heard an answering clink of Fergus's flute on the opposite side of the tub which caused a shiver of anticipation to flow head to toe.

She felt his lips next as he kissed the back of her neck. Every sense she possessed became focused on each intimate pressure against her skin. The feel of his growing arousal forced her to draw air into suddenly achy lungs.

She couldn't believe she was here with Fergus, in a bathtub, naked and ready to join with him again, to be connected to him as she had been in the dreamglide for the past few weeks. The memories surged and she howled softly. Their weeks of dream-world lovemaking had primed her for an intimate relationship.

She used her hands once more to map the curves of his muscular arms, which were beautiful and perfect.

Slowly, she turned over and floated above him in the water. She kissed his chin and his nose. "You look incredibly relaxed."

"I am," he said.

He poised a hand above the clips in her hair. "Do you mind if I take these out?"

She shook her head. "Not at all."

He removed them, allowing her hair to fall to her shoulders and into the water.

He held her around the waist and drew her against his chest. He was just tall enough that his feet held him in place. His muscles might have been fairly dense as well since he didn't seem to be floating like she was.

She felt the full length of his erection against her abdomen. He kissed her, his tongue taking possession of her mouth. She felt the kiss all the way to her toes.

Before she realized she'd done it, and without meditating even a little, she'd summoned her dreamglide and pulled him inside. He laughed as he looked around since they were in the bathtub in both places. Whatever this was between herself and Fergus, her powers had been growing from the time she'd rescued him from the Graveyard. Now she could easily be with him in two places at once.

And she wasn't unconscious in real-time at all. He wasn't, either. Instead, like the last time they'd made love, she was fully in both places at once, which enhanced every move, every kiss, every touch exponentially. She drew back just a little, arched her neck and howled. His arms tightened around her waist and his hips rocked. He growled against her throat.

The possessive, erotic sound sent shivers down her chest and over her nipples. She wanted him to bite her.

Hard.

~ ~ ~

Fergus struggled to control himself. Within his wolf body was the call of his mating need and over the past few hours, since he'd bonded again with his pack, the sensations had grown almost unbearable. He wanted an alpha-mate and everything about Mary told him she was the one.

As he kissed her neck, savoring the dual sensation of the dreamglide and real-time sex, he licked her in long swipes of his tongue. Her howl sounded like a wolf and had his cock jerking with need.

He wanted to mate with her wolf-to-wolf and his new fae instincts told him somehow their unique relationship might allow him to do just that. She even sprouted a fine layer of light-colored fur at her throat, her wrists and around her nipples.

He brought the wolf part of himself to the fore and continued sniffing and licking her throat. Her soft, sensual howls, combined with sexy wolf-like grunts, kept his hips rocking into her. He was fully erect.

He began to feel an answering response within Mary, from the part of her slowly becoming wolf.

As his need for her grew, the dreamglide began to move. "Take me inside, Mary, as deep as you can get."

She moaned, then lifted her hips up just enough to reach down and guide him to her entrance. Her whole body arched as the head of his cock slipped into her well. He leaned forward and once more kissed the long slope of her neck. Arching his hips, he let her feel him deep between her legs.

She moaned. "God, that feels good."

She drew back a little more, then planted her hands on his shoulders. As she lifted her hips, she slowly came down on his cock. A mangled wolf-groan came out of his throat. The farther he went inside her, the faster his internal wolf moved.

He nodded. "This is a miracle, isn't it?" He rocked his hips slowly, letting her feel his cock.

"I still can't believe I'm here in your pack compound, sharing a dreamglide with you while still awake and conscious. Can you feel the movement of the dreamglide?"

"Like we're caught in a wind. Is that what it's like for you?"

"It carries a wolf feel as though we could run as far and as fast as we wanted, no hindrances."

"I was trying to think what it was like. But that's it, speed and distance."

His hips moved faster. "Let me do the work."

She leaned down and kissed him. "You're so damn strong."

Her words fueled him.

Within the dreamglide, suddenly the bathtub disappeared. He stood beside her. *Let's run like we did last time.*

She smiled. *I'd love to. It's incredibly erotic to have your cock thrusting in and out of me while I shift and run beside you.*

He shifted into his wolf. Mary joined him, transforming alongside him. She'd never be able to do this in real-time, but in the dreamglide, all things were possible and here she was, a blonde-furred beauty. Her light brown eyes glinted as she raced next to him once more through the pine forest of Savage.

Fergus, this is amazing. We're having sex, and I'm a wolf and we're running. I love it, more than I can say!

In real-time, he held her hips steady and thrust his cock deep into her sex. He was wolf and man, yet the drive was fae as well. At the same time, he felt more like himself than he had in a long, long time.

With his hands still holding her hips pinned in place, he drove faster in the bathtub, the water sloshing around them. In the dreamglide, he ran hard, stretching out all four paws and reaching for as much ground as he could manage. Mary tracked close.

In real-time, Mary's breathing kept changing shape. Sometimes she huffed or gasped, other times she appeared to stop breathing, her lips parted. In the dreamglide, she ran faster. Pleasure was on every feature, and that's all he wanted right now, to know she was enjoying both experiences as much as he was.

His combined awareness moved back and forth, from racing wolf to the bathtub, then back until he could feel himself doing both at the same time. His hips went faster and his wolf legs thrust forward in long strides.

Unbelievable.

Staring into her eyes, he saw a faint amber ring emerge around her light brown irises. He lifted up and kissed her. "Your eyes have a wolf glow."

She smiled faintly. "They do?"

He lowered his chin. He moved faster and faster. "I love running beside you, and I love fucking you."

She drew in a long stream of air. "Me, too. Both."

The wind of the dreamglide pushed him on. Mary held tight to his shoulders so that he pistoned wildly inside her now. He felt her sex rippling over his cock in that way of hers. Her lips parted and the sweetest yet most erotic howl left her throat.

Her internal muscles pulled on him, but he didn't come. Instead, he caught her gaze. "Bond with me, Mary."

She was breathing hard, his cock plunging in and out as he held her steady. The water splashed outside the tub. Fur sprouted on his chest, around his ankles and along the insides of his thighs.

She cried out. "Your scent, Fergus, my God! It's ten times stronger when you show fur."

"You're smelling my bonding scent. Join with me, right now. Be my alpha-mate." He didn't know how it happened, but in the dreamglide he leaped on Mary, as a wolf would, while at the same time transforming back into his human shape. She did as well, though she stayed on all fours. He bit the back of her neck hard and she arched her throat, howling.

She howled in the bathtub in the same way.

In the dreamglide, he penetrated her from behind and the dual sensation almost made him come, but he held back, gritting his teeth. He was ready to mate with her, if only she could do it.

He released another powerful wave of his bonding scent, hoping this would encourage the bond. In real-time, he watched her back arch.

"I can feel it now," she said, "deep in my abdomen, reaching into my sex. I've felt this tugging sensation before. It's a female wolf bonding response, isn't it?"

"Yes, it is. Do it, Mary. You can do it. I know you can." He felt desperate. His hips slowed, in both real-time and the dreamglide as he waited for her.

He could feel how hard she was trying, yet something still wasn't right.

And it might never be.

Then just like that, the bond failed and the moment slipped away.

Her voice entered his mind. *I'm sorry, Fergus. I can't seem to complete the process. I want to, but I don't know how. I think my faeness is getting in the way.*

He slowed the movement of his hips in both dimensions, then finally stopped though he didn't disconnect from her. In the dreamglide, he kissed the back of her neck over and over. He needed her to feel how much he was enjoying being with her even if the bond hadn't succeeded.

He knew she would feel bad about it and he could sense the shift in her. In real-time, he slid his arms around her back and brought her down to his chest, holding her close. The warm water swirled over them both.

Slowly, he pulled them both out of the dreamglide.

"I'm so sorry, Fergus," she murmured, her lips warm against skin.

"You don't need to apologize. Not at all."

He had only one goal: To take her the rest of the way.

"Hang on," he whispered against her ear. While holding her close, he levitated straight out of the tub, but remained horizontal.

With her eyes wide, she lifted her head to stare at him. "What are you doing?" She even laughed.

He smiled. "Taking you to bed. We're not done yet, Sweetheart. Not by a long shot." He zipped through the bathroom and into the bedroom. He didn't care that they were both dripping.

Slowly, he levitated them to an upright position, though he kept her cradled against him. When he reached the bed, he shifted her to hold her with one arm, then levitated low enough to grab the comforter with his free hand. He whipped it back, then let it fall to the floor. Pink rose petals flew everywhere.

He performed another aerial maneuver, stretching out horizontally once more with Mary on top of him as they'd been in the bathtub. He then dropped onto the sheets, landing on his back with a plop, which made her laugh all over again.

He loved the sound. Maybe the bonding hadn't happened, but he intended to make the most of their time together.

"I have an idea." He gently rolled her onto her back next to him. "Stay right here."

"What are you doing?" She lifted up on her elbows.

His lips quirked. "You'll see."

Hopping off the bed, he took her ankles in hand, then pulled her over to the side.

"Oh, my," she murmured, her eyes wide once more.

When he dropped to his knees on the floor and spread her legs wide, her wolf's voice uttered a howling growl. *Oh, Fergus, you do know how to please me,* slid from her mind to his.

He wasn't about to leave Mary unsatisfied.

~ ~ ~

Mary lay on her back and gasped as Fergus's tongue touched the sensitive folds of her sex. She groaned heavily. How did he know she needed this?

She'd felt like a failure, though she knew at the exact same time she didn't need to feel that way.

But Fergus asking her to bond was a huge step for him and she'd felt the answering tug in her body that had told her it was possible. And she suddenly wanted it so much.

Yet, no matter how hard she tried, she couldn't complete the connection.

She just didn't know why.

She also thought that Fergus taking their lovemaking into the bedroom was an extraordinary act of perception and kindness.

As her body began to heat up again with each lick of his tongue, as shivers chased themselves up and down the insides of her thighs, her heart warmed as well. Tears sprouted to her eyes. She felt so much in this moment. She knew she was in love with Fergus. But right now she *loved* him.

Desire began to rise again, even more intense than before He'd proven himself in a way he'd probably never understand, and she felt her heart reach for him. The deep, internal tugging sensation within her abdomen returned, and she wondered if now she could bond with him.

But her fae senses rose, and she had an insight that startled her. The bond hadn't failed because of her, but because Fergus wasn't ready.

This was about Fergus. Not her.

She glanced down at him, at the sensuality of his movements, of his tongue and his mouth, his long black hair dragging over her skin with each glide of his head. He was loving on her sex the way he'd been with her from the first, a perfect, attentive lover.

She reached down and stroked his hair, the ends wet from the bath. He looked up at her, his dark eyes laden with passion.

Are you enjoying my tongue, Mary?

"Yes," she whispered. "But I want more. Take me from behind, Fergus, right now. I want your teeth on my neck again, but in real-time."

Fergus rose and leaped at her. She was airborne before she'd finished the sentence.

As he'd been in the dreamglide, he clamped his jaws around the back of her neck, securing her before he entered her.

She howled. And with the arch of her neck, his wolf teeth moved, accommodating her, yet holding her tight at the same time. The pleasure of this act was more intense than anything she'd ever known.

She felt him take his cock in hand and position himself at her opening. He pushed inside in strong thrusts and she grunted with each one, then howled again.

When he set a strong rhythm, his wolf-jaw holding her in place, she felt the same internal bonding tug that seemed to reach toward her sex. Yet this time, she also felt the wall between them that now made sense, and it emanated from Fergus.

She wouldn't be his alpha-mate. Not tonight.

Yet right now, it didn't matter. She loved being with him, sharing his body and enjoying the wildness of sex with him. It was enough.

You're mine, Mary.

I'm yours. Love for him flowed through her, combining with a sudden wave of pure passion, driving her toward ecstasy. She loved his mind and his heart, the strength of his body, his commitment to the pack.

The feel of him holding her tight with the animal power of his jaw lit up her sex. She began to howl in long, thrilling cries.

He released her neck so he could howl as well. His hands gripped her and held her in place as he plowed into her from behind.

Ecstasy poured over her sex as he began to release into her. His howls continued to join with hers, electrifying her sex. The orgasm was like a series of tall waves that kept crashing down on her then lifting her up and taking her to the heights all over again.

She howled as she peaked repeatedly. Sweat poured from her body, and she shook all over. Fergus howled and wolf-grunted, his hips jerking as he filled her full of his seed.

When at last his hips began to slow, she found it hard to catch her breath. She felt so much in this moment, the breadth of her love for him, how much she admired him, and how thoroughly his wolfness satisfied her. She'd never known a man like Fergus before and until he'd seduced her in the dreamglide, she would never have believed she could feel this way about a wolf.

~ ~ ~

Fergus held Mary tight against him. His cock was still buried inside her, and his heart thundered in his ears. Despite the failed bonding effort, he felt satisfied beyond words. His soul was full as he held her and slowly rocked her. "Have I thanked you for you all that you've done for me?"

"It's been one of the greatest pleasures of my life to be with you and to help you stay alive." She gasped for air, still struggling to catch her breath.

Slowly he lowered her to the bed, while supporting his weight with his forearms so he didn't crush her. "I want to say the words anyway. Thank you, Mary. You've done so much for me these last few weeks, and especially over the past two days. I'm overwhelmed by how much you've changed my life."

"Same here, Fergus. And I mean that with all my heart."

He kissed her neck several times, then drew out of her. He reached for the box of tissues on the nightstand, grabbing a handful. She'd need them; he'd left a lot of himself behind.

She took them and as she rolled onto her side, she tucked them between her legs.

He turned to face her and stretched out on his side as well. She was so beautiful. Her blond hair was damp, which emphasized her strong cheekbones, her perfect straight nose, and her lips still plump from sex. Her rose-and-yarrow scent was rich in the air, swirling around her and keeping him in a partially aroused state.

His time with her had meant so much to him, but he had to address the difficulty. "We didn't bond."

She reached for him and rubbed the back of her hand down his cheek. "I wanted to."

His new fae senses told him she spoke the truth. "I know you did." In order for Mary to be accepted as an alpha-mate in his pack, she would have to release a special scent that the entire pack could recognize. It would be similar to the flowery scent he could smell right now, but it would carry his wolf musk as well. Unfortunately, she smelled the same to him, delicious and wonderful, but unbonded.

On some level, he wasn't surprised. Not even the powerful female wolves who'd tried to bond with him in the past had been able to do it. What chance was there that Mary could?

He leaned close and kissed her cheek. "I need you to understand how impossible this might be for us."

"Actually, I do understand. But there's something I feel I should tell you, about why we didn't bond just now."

He felt her hesitation and for some reason it made him uneasy. "Tell me. Whatever it is you need to say to me, I'm here to listen."

She released a rough, wolfish sigh. "First, I need you to know something else. Your wife's been here. She's been talking to me, telling me things. At first, I thought she meant only to give me a push here and there, to help me have the courage to press on. Right now, however, I'm not so sure."

"Sharon? As in her ghost? She's appeared to you and spoken with you?"

Mary nodded slowly. "Several times."

Fergus was stunned. Ghosts often made themselves known to *alter* species, but his wife addressing his current lover felt weird by any standard.

"I don't get it. What has she been saying about me?" His uneasiness returned.

"She knew I was needed in Savage to help keep you safe, for one thing. But she really hasn't talked a lot about you. Mostly, she's said things about herself, her frustrations, and her guilt."

Fergus rose from his reclining position to sit on the side of the bed, his back to Mary. He planted his hands on either side of his thighs. His heart started beating hard. He could feel a terrible truth emerging, something he didn't want to face, but which his fae senses could feel swirling around him like a swarm of wasps, ready to strike.

"I don't want to talk about my deceased wife." To say the least. "Maybe we should drop this."

He felt the mattress rock as Mary left the bed. From his peripheral, he watched her head to the bathroom. "I understand," she said quietly.

He'd never really figured Sharon out, not even before they went through the *alter* transformation. Her temperament had always been so different from his. He'd been a typical, work-focused man, ambitious, intent on building their resort and later marketing it nationwide. He'd even been considering running for state office, then the wolf *alter* serum had ended all his plans.

But he hadn't been completely blind about Sharon, either. In the back of his head, he'd known she would have hated political life. Living in Five Bridges as the wife of a border patrol officer had been equally as unfulfilling for her. The trouble was, he'd suggested dozens of alternatives through the years, before and after their exile to the province. His only conclusion had been that her chronic discontentment combined with his tunneled focus on the Gordion Pack had led her to stray. As a result, his marriage had fallen apart long before she died.

But he'd never stopped blaming himself for her death, not really. Yet, when he looked back, he didn't see how he could have made a difference in her life. Still, it was a terrible failure and he was partly to blame.

Mary called from the bathroom. "I can't resist trying on at least one of these negligees."

He hardly knew what to say to that. What did he care about lacy sleeping garments when he was so full of guilt? "They were meant for you," he said at last.

He heard the hair-blower going and vaguely wondered why Mary was drying her hair.

He sat staring through the French glass doors at the well-lit, private garden right outside the guest room. The compound had several like this. Sharon had designed them to be spots of beauty in their world. She had a gift for decor; he'd give her that. The Sedona resort had reflected her careful eye.

"This is Sharon's work, isn't it?" Mary's voice sounded from the bathroom doorway. "The patio, I mean."

He turned and the air in his lungs refused to leave his body for a long, difficult moment. She now wore the black lace gown and was so beautiful to his wolf eyes that he fell speechless. Her pale skin showed through the lace, and she'd dried and brushed out her long blond hair so that it floated around her shoulders and down her back.

She moved to stand in front of the garden. "The purple lantana is always beautiful this time of year. Even the lighting in this space is gorgeous. Sharon created this, didn't she?"

Fergus rose to stand beside her. His throat hurt. "She did. I remember how excited she was. I'd recently become alpha and one of my first projects was building a proper home for Sharon and me that would be a small adjunct to what later became the Gordion Compound."

"So you built all of this?" She waved a hand to encompass the entire complex.

"I did. We needed massive, belowground, soundproof rooms where our wolves could let loose at will. I also wanted similar communal areas, like the dining hall. But Sharon had insisted on small gardens outside our private living areas. I fought her on them."

"Why?" Mary asked. "I have gardens like this in Revel."

He literally turned his back to the space. He wasn't sure if it was guilt he was experiencing or what. "We fought constantly the first year I led the Gordion Pack." He was frowning so hard, his whole face felt like it was being punched. "But you have to understand, I was trying to keep everyone alive. I couldn't worry about plants and trees. Oh, God." He pivoted to angle himself toward Mary.

She in turn shifted toward him, though her arms were crossed over her chest. "What? Say it, Fergus. It's important."

"She said I cared more about the pack than her."

"Did you?"

"No." The idea appalled him. "Of course not."

Yet, with an astounding amount of pain he realized he felt the same way about Mary right now as he had about Sharon. "And yet … Oh, shit. It was me. I did care more about the pack." He hit his chest hard with his fist. "Fuck, it was me. I was the reason, the cause. I'd never seen it before. But the faeness now living inside me won't let me ignore the truth. My wolf … My wolf was happy to blame Sharon. How many times did I call her 'needy' when I knew she was just expressing normal wants and desires?"

He moved to the side of the bed and sat down again. He rubbed his forehead. Another truth hit him hard as he lifted his gaze to Mary once more. Earlier, she'd tried to tell him something else when she'd first mentioned Sharon, but he said he didn't want to talk about any of it. "The bond failed because of me, didn't it? That's what you wanted to tell me earlier when I shut you down? I thought it was you, but now I know the truth. You couldn't join with me, because I wouldn't let you. I couldn't. Just like I couldn't let any of my female wolves mate with me after Sharon died."

Mary nodded slowly, her expression solemn. "That's what I believe as well."

He rose once more, crossed to her, then took her arms gently in his hands. "I'm trying to understand, but you're feeling it as well, aren't you? That I'm not here with you, not as I should be for a wolf asking you to bond with him?"

She nodded. "I'm not blaming you, Fergus. You don't have to be anything to me. And I think I understand. You have the pack to think about now, and I know your wolves take precedence above everything else."

"But it's not the right way to live and my being this way won't solve anything."

She chuckled softly, her voice slightly hoarse the way a wolf's would be. "There's nothing to solve."

He stared at her. His heart ached with so many difficult realities hitting him at once. He glided his hands up her arms and caressed her shoulders. "You look beautiful in this lace."

She smiled, then drew back from him enough to see all the way down to her feet. "With my purple nail polish, especially." She even chuckled. He loved that about her, how she was lightening the moment.

"Sharon was unfaithful to me, but I never knew who the man was that killed her. Hell, maybe she'd taken up with dozens. For what I put her through, I could never blame her."

"So, were you an alpha wolf for like a hundred years or something?"

He frowned at her. "What do you mean, because that doesn't make sense? I've only been in the province fifteen years, but you know that."

"I'm saying there's nothing in your prior experience as a Sedona resort owner that could have prepared you for becoming an alpha wolf, especially during a deadly season of all-encompassing territorial war. Unless you'd lived in your role for decades, say perhaps with military experience in Afghanistan or Iraq, and had gone through the experience repeatedly, I don't see how you could have known what or what not to do. But that's just my opinion."

"Is this your subtle way of telling me I'm being too hard on myself, because right now I think I've been foolish and even cruel."

Mary glanced around the room slowly, floor-to-ceiling, side-to-side, then spoke in a strong voice. "Sharon, if you're here, I'm sorry about what I'm going to say next."

She then turned again to face Fergus. "Your wife was unfaithful to you, but that was her choice. Not every woman who's dissatisfied with her marriage, even deeply unhappy, steps outside the bounds of her commitments. Only Sharon can be held accountable for the choices she made. In the case of her last lover, it got her killed. Life isn't easy for any of us. You were learning how to serve as an alpha. It seems to me you either made a huge mistake with your wife or you're not truly fit to be an alpha leader."

"What do you mean by that?"

"Fergus, I can feel even now that you're not really with me. It's as though there's a thick steel door between us, and I'm not sure it can be breached by you or by me. You might be either an alpha or a husband, but it's possible you can't be both. It's not a crime, Fergus, but it's something you might want to think about."

"Are you saying I should have stepped down for Sharon?"

"Or divorced her. Or sought outside counseling. Our *alter* world is so new, none of us truly knows how to live this life. I mean do you realize that you are my first romance here in Five Bridges? I've been fairly happy as an *alter* fae, but I've found it extremely difficult to want to be intimately involved with another *alter* man. And look how our relationship began? You forged a dreamglide and seduced me while I was asleep. I probably would have never come to you otherwise. So, what does that make me?"

Fergus experienced that punched-face frown again as he stared at Mary. For the first time he began to ask the why of his original seduction. Why had he gone to her?

"You called to me," he said, almost to himself. He didn't look at her. Instead his gaze moved over the stone floor of the bedroom as though hunting for a place to land, where life would make sense again.

"But I didn't call to you. I swear I didn't."

He met her gaze again. "Not *you* Mary, but your *alter* self, the part of you that's no longer human. I'm not sure I'll ever understand why except that maybe it was a basic survival mechanism on my part. Look how many times you've saved my ass."

She smiled. "You're right about that."

And she was right; he had a lot to think about.

"I'll never be able to explain how I created that dreamglide in the first place."

She took a couple of steps toward him. "Or maybe your pursuit of me is something else completely."

"Like what?"

"Maybe you're not supposed to be a border patrol officer any longer or maybe not even the head of a pack. Not all alphas forge packs."

He shook his head. "Only because there isn't enough room in Savage. Trust me in this. The drive to create and head up a pack, or take another one over, is stronger than the drive to live. Look at Sydon's behavior."

"That's not a fair comparison at all. That bastard is a psychopath."

Fergus laughed. "I won't argue with you there." He considered her for a moment. "So, where do we go from here, Mary of Revel?"

She shook her head slowly. "I have no idea."

CHAPTER TEN

MARY STARED AT Fergus for a long moment. She put a hand to her chest since her heart had already started aching. Her reasoning might be rational enough, but being separated from Fergus was going to hurt like nothing she'd ever experienced in her life.

She loved him.

It was as simple as that.

But she also had clarity about who he was and to stay with him would only muddy the waters. Fergus was all for his pack. He didn't know how to be with a woman right now, in the same way he'd been an absent husband to Sharon. Fergus had issues only he could resolve and her presence wouldn't help him figure things out.

She kissed his cheek. She let her lips linger for a moment as she drew his scent deep into her nostrils: Stone, wolf musk and wild grasses.

She then straightened her shoulders and headed to the closet.

When she pulled out her flight bag, he asked, "What are you doing?"

"I think I need to head home now."

"But I don't want you to go."

Mary saw the panicked look in Fergus's eyes. She also sensed how much he wanted her to stay, which tore at her heart. "I don't want to leave, either. But it's time."

Her gaze drifted over his thick black mane, almost dry now, and the broad shoulders she enjoyed so much. Affection for him swirled through her chest. She didn't want to leave, but she couldn't stay, not when he'd built an impenetrable steel door keeping her out.

She forced herself to turn away from him and settled her suitcase on the bed. Earlier, Fergus's wolves had unpacked everything for her. She had to admit he'd built a wonderful community.

"Please don't go, Mary." His voice went straight through her as she unzipped the small bag.

She didn't look at him as she said, "You're back where you belong and well-guarded. I don't think I'm needed any longer."

"Don't you want to be here? With me? I thought we'd be together through the day, share the same bed."

She glanced at him. He was frowning again. She'd never seen a man frown harder than Fergus had over the past few minutes. "I don't think it's wise," she said quietly. "I get why Sharon was so unhappy. You're completely shut off right now but you don't see it. I'm not trying to find fault, Fergus. I just think it's an alpha-wolf thing and I'm not a wolf."

"Sharon was a wolf. She should have understood."

"Maybe, but she'd also been your wife while you were both human. She'd known you in a completely different and probably much more satisfying context. I've known you as my lover and a man who needed my help.

"Right now you've stopped being either of those things and part of you is completely closed off from me. I was so caught up in the passion of our relationship, I just didn't see it before. Now the fae in me can see little else. I would be doing a disservice to us both if I stayed."

She went to the dresser and drew out a fresh pair of jeans, a thong, one of her favorite purple bras and a light green t-shirt. When she headed into the bathroom, she shut the door to change. She needed some space.

The other negligees still hung nearby, draped over the counter. The Gordion Pack had made an effort for her. She'd never forget their kindness.

She was stunned how things had turned out, but she had to believe it was for the best. She'd gained something extraordinary from her brief time with Fergus; she was now part wolf. What her faeness had given him, she couldn't imagine or even how her new wolf would be of benefit to her in Revel.

Slowly, she took off the black lace negligee and replaced it on the hanger. She fingered the lace. Fergus had created a spirit of giving in his pack. She'd miss getting to be part of the group.

She put on her clothes and once more brushed out her hair.

Without warning, Sharon appeared, sitting on the counter with her knees crossed. *So, you're leaving?*

Mary jumped, then released a huff of air and rolled her eyes. *You're back. I wish you'd give me some warning. But yes, I'm leaving. It's time. Did you hear any of that?*

Of course I did. Sharon seemed oddly subdued. *I guess you think I need to take responsibility for my part in our failed marriage.*

No, only for the infidelity that got you killed. Your marital difficulties were a two-way street.

I suppose they were. But thanks for not telling Fergus the truth, about Sydon I mean. It may come to that, but I should be the one to tell him.

I didn't see how it would help anything. Surprising tears suddenly bloomed in Mary's eyes. She stopped brushing her hair and glanced at the bathtub. Though it was still full of water since Fergus hadn't flipped the drain, it looked strangely empty. The water would be cold by now.

Had they really just made love then broken up?

Now you know how I felt.

She shifted her gaze back to Sharon. *You're right, I do. This whole time, I've known something was wrong, but I couldn't put my finger on it.*

Fergus is all for his pack with nothing left over. Sharon directed her gaze toward the tub as well. *He stopped having sex with me completely about six months after he became alpha of the Gordion Pack.*

You're kidding? That must have been terrible.

I thought it was me. All this time, I thought he'd grown bored with me. It was one of the reasons I went outside our marriage.

Mary turned toward Sharon. *I'm still confused, though, about what you're doing here. I'm not exactly a therapist, so I can't help you gain closure if that's what you're looking for.*

It's not. She frowned and looked really perplexed. *But it's a helpful side effect. I think I'm starting to understand more and you're right, I'm getting a degree of closure I never had before.*

Maybe this is like a twelve-step recovery program for the deceased? Mary offered.

For the first time, Sharon smiled, then laughed. The ghostly sound, however, was like a raspy bark.

"You okay in there?" Fergus called out through the closed door.

Mary cleared her throat several times. "I'm fine. Just a frog."

Sharon grinned. *He's handsome though, isn't he?*

As hell.

Sharon laughed again and once more Mary pretended to clear her throat.

Mary met Sharon's ghostly gaze once more and was surprised when Sharon's expression grew serious. *I wish I could tell you more, but we have way too many restrictions. Like I said last time, you need to show some balls in the next few hours and I think you should stay here with Fergus.*

Mary let out a heavy sigh. *I know on one level you're right, but I'm completely torn. My fae instincts tell me to stick close but my wolf-side is shouting to get the hell out of a hopeless situation. Wolves are clearly much bigger on self-preservation.*

Sharon shook her head. *Men. They make life so complicated for us, don't they? And they never really understand why. But I get it Mary, and I agree. You really are stuck. If you stay, there's a chance he'll never figure things out so you'll continue living a half-life with him. But if you leave, he'll lose your ability to protect him because of your powerful fae instincts.*

You've summed it up exactly. Mary felt tears burn her eyes. *Sort of a damned if I do and damned if I don't.*

Yup. Been there, done that.

So, what should I do? Mary thought if anyone would have wisdom right now, it would be Sharon.

But Sharon barked her laughter once more, causing Mary to clear her throat yet again.

How the hell should I know? Sharon said. *I'm the woman who let Sydon break my neck with his killing wolf-bite. The only thing I know for sure is that you must beware of the witch. She's the unknown and most dangerous aspect of your current predicament.*

Mary was about to ask 'what witch', but just as quickly as Sharon had come, she disappeared.

How empty the room suddenly felt with her gone.

Mary stood very still and focused inward, hoping her fae abilities would speak to her and give her guidance. But what returned were two screaming sides of the issue: She needed to stay but she had to leave. Either option would make her vulnerable in ways she simply couldn't fully predict at this point.

In the end, she decided she had to go. Now that she could fly, Fergus was only a few minutes away. She would keep her faeness focused on him and the moment she felt he was in danger, she'd head back to Savage.

With her heart settled, Mary returned to the guest room, carrying the clothes she'd worn before her bath. She put them in the flight bag, then quickly moved about the room loading her suitcase.

When she was done, however, she turned to Fergus and saw that he'd put on a pair of black silk boxers which had her blinking hard. He looked good in black, which set off the rolling landscape of his six-pack.

Desire for him skyrocketed all over again.

He narrowed his gaze at her. "You say you're leaving, but that scent tells me you want to stay."

She cast her hands wide. "You look hot, okay? But I'm still going."

"Fine."

"Fine."

Her cheeks felt flushed the entire time she finished packing up. She left all three negligees behind, of course. They didn't belong to her and she definitely didn't want the female Gordion wolves to think she'd taken advantage of their generosity when she wasn't sticking around.

When she was ready to leave, Fergus insisted he fly her home. But Mary had other ideas. "You need to stay here where you belong. However, I will accept a couple of your guards just in case Sydon is anywhere near this part of Savage."

"If that's what you want."

"It is."

By the time he'd walked her up to the front entrance, part of her hoped he would suddenly realize how much he needed to change his thinking. But when he called for several guards, six in all, she knew it was over.

The steel door had slammed into place once more and she was heading home.

Alone.

Her throat tightened, especially when he gave her a parting hug.

But there was nothing more to be said.

With her flight bag in hand, she took to the air easily. The lead guard, Ryan, appeared startled as he caught up with her.

"Your alpha taught me how to fly," she said. Using the word 'taught' was a lot easier than trying to explain how she and Fergus had been acquiring each other's *alter* abilities.

She switched to telepathy, and asked the wolf if he wouldn't mind talking to her mind-to-mind. He had long wavy brown hair and wore two braids on the right side that interlaced to form a single braid. He had dark blue eyes and a warm smile.

When he gave permission, she said, *You're Ryan, right?*

Yes, he responded, taking up his place on her left.

Fergus has mentioned you a couple of times. He relies on you a lot.

Fergus is a good man, one of the finest I've ever known.

Wanting to hear more, Mary eased closer to him and slowed down a little. The detail matched her speed. *Have you served other alphas, besides Sydon I mean?*

I was once a member of Warren's pack early on, but asked to serve in Gordion because Fergus was new at it and needed to learn the ropes. Both Harley and I helped out a lot in the old days. I met Fergus on the Savage Border Patrol. Warren had no problem letting me transfer. He's a good man, too.

Yes, he is.

As she directed Ryan to fly northeast, Mary felt herself frowning almost as hard as Fergus had in the guest room. *Tell me what it was like when Fergus became Gordion's alpha?*

He made an almost painful snort. *There was a massive territorial war that year, worse than any that have followed. Fergus lost at least fifty of his wolves over the course of several violent battles. He took it hard. He was finally able to make a difference in the war when he got more seriously focused.*

She slowed her flying even more and as before, the entire squad slowed with her as though she'd emitted some kind of signal. Maybe it was a wolf thing. *What does that mean, 'seriously'?*

More attentive, more present. I'm not sure I can explain it.

To the exclusion of other interests, would you say? Mary definitely wanted someone else's opinion on the issue.

Yes, that's it, Ryan said. *Fergus stopped spending his time on anything else. He used to always have rock music blaring through the compound, then one day it stopped. Of course the compound was much smaller in those days, but that's what made me think of it. You could hear the music everywhere.*

And that was just one thing. I remember he had a vintage car that he'd brought over from his previous life. He loved to drive it around Savage, even on the bad roads. But he sold it. Some say he neglected his wife but I don't see it that way. She was never happy, that one. But maybe I've said too much. Shit, I think I have. Apologies.

Not necessary. She thought of Sharon and wondered if the woman knew what some of the other Gordion wolves thought of her. Even Fergus had called it her chronic discontentment.

Mary fell silent after that. Ryan had given her a lot to think about. She might have left Savage because she knew Fergus had closed off from her, but the fae part of her had started wrestling with all of it. And not just Fergus, but her own issues as well.

After thanking the men for seeing her home, she went in by way of the front door and locked it securely.

Checking her phone messages, one from her assistant let her know that all the pet patients she'd had scheduled were either given new appointments for the following week or handed off to other vets.

Mary was relieved. She went to the kitchen and the sight of the clean cat bowls meant her assistant had already taken care of her kitties. The fact that none of her felines rushed to greet her told her each had a full belly.

She poured a glass of cabernet sauvignon, then returned to the photo album and scattered pictures still sitting in front of her couch on the family room floor. The sight of them reminded her again of all that had happened in such a short time.

Her mind whirred, however, because her fae senses had locked onto Fergus's shut-down, reflex process that had first alienated his wife, Sharon. And tonight, it had given Mary a powerful excuse to leave.

Reviewing what Ryan had told her, the issue seemed to be seated within Fergus's initial rise to alpha level responsibility. That so many wolves had died on his watch must have affected his leadership, cementing his belief that while serving as an alpha, he didn't dare focus on anything else or lives would be lost.

What Mary couldn't quite figure out was where she fit into the equation. But she suspected that Fergus's narrow focus, which had created the steel door in the first place, was preventing him from gaining a critical, larger view of his pack and his territory.

Now that she had some distance herself, she could take a long, hard look at everything, especially her role and what she wanted for the future. Savage was a brutal place to live and with all that she'd just been through, including saving Fergus from a witch's spell, she had no reason to believe things would improve anytime soon.

Yet the project she'd started, of organizing her photos and creating an album featuring her family, no longer appealed as much as it had. With her sister killed accidently as a result of an out-of-control dominance fight, and her parents long dead, she was essentially alone in the world.

Her experience with both Warren's wolves and the Gordion Pack had continuously soothed her emerging wolf. Now that she was back in Revel, she felt restless and uneasy.

As she finished her wine, she began packing up the photos. She might not be certain what her life should be, but right now making an album was not going to settle her restless wolf down at all.

Maybe she'd have another glass of wine.

Or three.

~ ~ ~

Fergus busied himself the rest of the night with taking stock of every member of his pack. He was planning a memorial service for Elena, the young female wolf who had committed suicide, and the ten wolves who'd gone berserk because of her desperate act.

At the same time, he began the process of negotiating the ransoms for the return of the women Sydon had already put to work in one of the cartel clubs. He'd have them home soon.

The whole time, he kept looking over his shoulder, though he couldn't say why.

Harley finally asked, "Is there something you need to do? Do you want another guard on the door?"

"A guard? For what?" He had no idea what Harley was talking about.

"For the past quarter hour, you've looked toward the door every two minutes. Thought maybe you were worried about another attack."

"No." But he frowned. He honestly didn't know why he kept checking the doorway.

Then it dawned on him. His wolf was looking for Mary, searching for her, but she wasn't there anymore. It didn't help that her scent was still in his nostrils.

His thoughts drifted toward her as he recalled having sex with her in real-time, while running beside her in the dreamglide. She'd brought so much to his life and he'd hated letting her go.

He gave himself a shake. He couldn't afford to give in to desires that had no possible use in Savage Territory. Maybe he had built what Mary called a steel door, but he'd put it there for a reason. He'd needed to protect his pack while they'd been at war. Sharon had suffered because of it and he knew that. But he'd saved countless lives by centering his attention exclusively on the salvation of his wolves.

He forced himself to do so now. Sydon was still a serious threat he needed to address.

Summoning his top betas, he took them into his strategy room on the east side of the ground floor and settled in to discuss ways they could work to uncover the location of Sydon's headquarters. He decided Sydon must be the priority and he would do everything he could to end the bastard's destructive influence in Savage. There was no point pretending Sydon would go away all on his own, especially if he had no problem buying expensive, deadly spells to try to get rid of his enemies.

Both Fergus's wolf and his fae were in complete agreement on that front.

The night finally drew to a close and at dawn, with his compound and attached home shuttered for the day, he made his way back to the guest room.

Unfortunately, he found all three lace negligees still hanging in the bathroom.

Without warning, a wave of grief washed through him so quick and so hard he weaved on his feet. He had to grab the counter to keep from falling over. He didn't understand what had just happened. But the image that shot through his head had nothing to do with Mary but everything to do with Sharon the night before she died.

Fuck. He'd buried the memory. At the very least, he'd buried it, the way he did everything.

Sharon had dressed up in a sexy, skin tight black dress and had worn matching stilettos. She'd looked beautiful and he'd longed to take her in his arms, to hold her and to kiss her. But he couldn't let her distract him from his duties or pack members would die.

So, he'd yelled at her, saying absurd things like she needed to be more modest, to set a better example for the other female wolves, things he didn't even believe. He just didn't want to be tempted away from his job.

She'd yelled back, saying she couldn't live like this anymore. He'd given her a cold half-life that wasn't worth the trouble. She'd already found another man, in another pack, and she wanted a divorce. She was going out for the night, but when she returned, she'd be packing up all her things and moving out for good.

Then she'd left.

He'd been shocked. He'd paced the rest of the night, waiting for her to come home. He'd made a huge mistake with her and he needed to start making amends, if he could.

Yet even then, he'd doubted his ability to make things work with Sharon.

Of course, she hadn't come home and by nightfall the next day, he'd received word she'd been dumped a half mile from the Gordion Compound, near the canal. Sun exposure had damaged her corpse, but the Savage Medical Examiner said she'd been killed as a result of rough sex with a powerful male wolf who had bitten through her neck and fractured her spine while marking her.

Her death had become the final layer of the steel door he still used to keep himself focused on the safety of his pack.

As he brought his thoughts back to the present and the guest bathroom came into view again, he sank to the cold tile floor. He leaned his head against the cabinet and closed his eyes. He lifted his hand, intending to press his eyes and get rid of some of the burn, but his fingers got caught in the lace of one of the gowns, the black one that Mary had worn just before she'd left.

He'd failed Sharon.

And he'd sent Mary away without her knowing for even a second how much she really meant to him.

Suddenly, he felt inadequate in a way he couldn't explain. He'd sacrificed his life for his pack. It should have been enough, yet it wasn't.

The pack came first.

The pack always came first.

He remained on the floor for a long time. He wasn't the same man that he'd been a couple of nights ago. He'd died out in the Graveyard when Sydon had skewered his heart.

But he wasn't sure he'd truly been reborn. Instead, he'd launched straight back into his old life once his pack was secure. Yet now that everything was in order, he felt extremely restless and dissatisfied as he'd never been before.

He didn't want to keep living this way.

Even acknowledging his dissatisfaction was new for him, a sign of the fae abilities and powers that had become part of his soul since he'd been with Mary. Yet he didn't know what goal he was mentally chasing right now. Did he expect to have a sudden life-altering epiphany?

The pack came first.

But what about Mary? Where was she right now? Probably in her home and in bed for the day. Would she start seeing pet patients again? Resume her life as a veterinarian? Would she forgive him for shutting her out so completely? Would she understand? Did she want any part of him?

He finally rose to his feet, showered and headed to bed. He'd expected Mary to stay with him through the day. He'd wanted to make love to her again. But as a sensitive fae, there was no way she could have ignored the steel door he'd slammed down in front of her.

When he finally lay on his side in bed and pulled the sheet up, he relinquished his attempts to make his current situation fit into the box of the past.

Time would serve him in this situation. It would dim his memories of being with Mary and help him to recommit to the wolves of his pack. He'd find some way to chart a new path without her.

He fell asleep reasonably content with those thoughts.

Hours later and somewhere in his dreams, he smelled a female wolf scent that woke him. He smelled Mary, though he knew she wasn't with him. A longing for her so intense came over him, that even in his half-sleep, he released a howl that filled the entire soundproof room.

Then he was chasing her in his dreams through thorns that bloodied him.

~ ~ ~

Mary awoke to the sound of Fergus howling, or at least she thought that's what she heard. But the howls were full of so much pain, she could hardly breathe.

She sat up in bed.

Fergus? She tried reaching him telepathically over and over but nothing returned.

She left her bed and went into the well-shuttered living room. It was late in the afternoon, which meant she'd slept soundly for hours.

She reached out with her fae senses. The sound of Fergus's howls had created a physical ache in her body, something so deep she wondered if she would ever be free of it.

She didn't understand what she'd heard or why she was feeling this way or even what to do about it.

Except for one thing, maybe the only thing that would be of any help right now.

She lay down on the couch and stretched out. She dropped quickly into her deep meditation and created her dreamglide. She focused on Fergus and found him.

He was asleep in the guest room in his compound. She could see him, covered in sweat and thrashing. He howled in his sleep as well. But because the room was soundproof there was no one to come to him and wake him up.

She couldn't even go to him in real-time, not until the sun set.

Suddenly, Sharon was next to her. *He looks pretty upset. Wonder what he's dreaming about.*

I have no idea.

Sharon frowned. *Well, do something, would you? He's in bad shape here.*

I intend to. The problem is, it's highly illegal, but I'm doing it anyway.

Sharon's ghostly brows rose as she stared at Mary. *Good for you.*

Mary ignored her. She still wasn't sure why Sharon was hanging around, but right now she didn't care. She slowly dipped the dreamglide lower and lower onto the bed. She stretched out on the bottom of the strange dream-world vehicle until she made contact with Fergus's body. She began drifting into his mind and his dreams, without his permission. If caught doing something like this, she could be prosecuted and jailed.

She didn't see specific images so much as a boiling cloud of smoke. She began calling to him softly. *Fergus, I'm here. Come to me. Be with me in the dreamglide the way you were before Sydon tried to kill you.*

Mary?

Yes, I'm here. Relief flooded her. She hadn't known what to expect, but her greatest fear was that she wouldn't be able to reach him.

The smoke cleared and there he was, standing in front of her. She rose quickly to her feet in the dreamglide.

He looked confused as he met her gaze. *How are you here?* He asked. *Wait a minute. This is illegal.*

Yep, the same way you originally came to me. I've broken into your dreams and now I've pulled you into in my dreamglide.

As he watched her, however, she felt something change within his heart. He smiled at her and she could feel the heavy steel door open wide.

"Mary," he murmured softly. "Thank God you're here. I need you."

Before she could do or say anything, he crossed to her and took her in his powerful arms. The kiss that followed melted her all over again. When Fergus was in the dreamglide, the man she knew was all in, nothing held back, no steel doors, no the-pack-comes-before-all, just her and his profound affection for her, maybe even his love.

And she loved it. This was her profound reality as well, that when she was in the dreamglide, she didn't hold anything back either. She wasn't worried about the fact she was fae and he was an alpha wolf. All she cared about was feeling the strength of his arms around her, the feel of his muscled thighs, and the pulse of his tongue inside her mouth.

And right now, she had a glimpse of what Sharon had lost when Fergus had become alpha to the Gordion Pack.

Remembering why she'd come to him, she knew she had work to do. She drew back, though she couldn't quite bring herself to let him go completely. Since the dreamglide was still directly above his bed, she glanced through the opaque floor to where he slept. He looked calmer now, as he should since she was with him. "Why the bad dreams, Fergus? You were howling in your sleep and you called to me."

"I don't want to talk about that. I just want to be with you." He pushed her hair behind her ear. "You're so beautiful."

"And you're handsome as hell, you big wolf, but why were you howling?"

He frowned slightly. "How did you know I was? This is soundproof and you live in Revel."

"It seems odd to me as well. But your nightmare woke me up and whether you like it or not, we're connected. So, what's going on with you?"

He looked down as well this time, looking at himself through the floor of the dreamglide. But he kept a firm hold on her, his arms still wrapped around her. "Jesus, I'm covered in sweat."

"You've calmed down. When I first arrived, you were thrashing. Something's not right with you, Fergus. You've got to figure this out."

He grew very still and she felt him draw in a deep breath. "I remember now. I was chasing you through a forest of thorns. You were in danger, but every step I took cut me up a little more. I was bleeding and in pain and knew I could never reach you because you were moving too fast and you couldn't hear me call to you."

"Are you sure it was me you were chasing?"

"I know it was."

"What was I wearing?"

He met her gaze. "That's the odd part. You wore an amber trimmed tank and black leathers."

"Like your wolf pack. Was I injured or anything?"

"No." he shook his head, but she could see the wheels turning. "You represented something in the dream."

"I'd like to think I'm someone or something you care about very much. What were you thinking about when you fell asleep?

"You and the Gordion Pack. The future."

"But what else?"

She felt his hold on her diminish and though she didn't want to let him go she drew her hands from around his neck and took a step back.

He started to pace. "Do you remember the sniper incident while you and I were being shot at outside Warren's compound?"

"Of course." She repressed a shudder at the memory of Fergus almost getting killed again.

"The part of me that has new fae senses could feel something bad moving through the entire territory. You told me you felt it as well."

"You're right, I did."

"That's what I was thinking about as I drifted off, something terrible that's here, in our world. I guess it took hold."

"Fergus, I hate to say this, but in real-time you're not facing up to something critical, life-threatening even, and I don't think it's about me."

He looked like she'd slapped him across the face. "What the hell are you talking about?"

"Don't you get it? Something's going on here with you, something astounding. And I guess I think it's the same for me, I just haven't figured out what it is for either of us." She shook her head slowly, then continued, "When I got home earlier, I saw all the pictures I'd left on the floor of my family room. My sister and my parents are all gone and this is Five Bridges where I'd been called to fetch a near-dead wolf from the Graveyard because a psychopath tried to kill him." She tossed up an arm. "I don't know what I'm saying or even what I mean. But I suspect our coming together is meant to be bigger than just oh-so-fabulous sex, don't you think?"

His expression softened. "Well, I'm not sure. It's been great with you, so why can't that be enough?" He glanced around. "We could keep meeting like this, in the dreamglide, the way we used to."

He tried to take her in his arms again, but she wouldn't let him. Instead, she held tight to his shoulders to keep him at a distance, but she met his gaze straight on. "We were both living in denial back then. Now we each know more. You've walled yourself off from intimate relationships to keep your pack safe, I get that and I understand why. And I've … well I'm still not sure what's going on with me. Also, you're lying in a bed of sweat-soaked sheets. That's why we can't go back to our secret dreamglide sex." She huffed a sigh that sounded hoarse and wolfish. She pulled away from him at the same time. "And I'm sensing my life is about to pivot a full one-eighty any second now."

Fergus was scowling again, that look he'd get when he was thinking hard. "I don't want to let you go. That's what I know in this moment, in the dreamglide. I feel as though my life depends in every possible way on being with you. That any happiness I can ever have in Five Bridges is about my relationship with you.

"But once I leave this space, I know my real-time self will take over and my commitment to the Gordion wolves will become everything again. And I'll have to let you go."

Mary took a deep breath and squared her shoulders. "Fergus, you do whatever you feel you must. I'll do the same. Be well."

With that, she dissolved the dreamglide. She watched him reach out his hand to her and probably protested with a loud, 'No'. But she felt the need to disengage. They were connected, yet not well enough. And each of them had to figure this out.

As she returned fully to her couch, she realized again that she hadn't been unconscious at all. She felt the power of it as well, that she had no problem being fully aware of her surroundings in real-time while she was in the dreamglide. It was an amazing ability to have. Fergus, having been asleep when she drew him into the dream-world, had remained asleep. Otherwise, he too would have been conscious in both places.

Still lying on her back, she stared up at the dark wood beams angled at the apex of the ceiling. A French, bird-cage lighting fixture hung above her.

When she'd become an *alter* fae woman and had moved to Five Bridges, she'd created her home to be at ease as much as she could. She'd set up a veterinary practice, had kept a low profile, and assisted Officer Brannick of the Crescent Border Patrol in helping abducted women escape Revel Territory. She'd grieved the loss of her sister, but she hadn't made any real friendships and she hadn't dated seriously at all.

She'd lived a ghost's life, a very small life since she'd come here. So small, she hadn't even been willing to acknowledge to herself in real-time that she'd had an affair with Fergus for several weeks before she rescued him in the Graveyard.

She'd once been told she had enough raw fae potential that she could one day serve on the Revel Board of Sages, the central fae governing institution of her territory. But she hadn't lifted a finger to acquire a requisite mentor or anything.

Then Roche had abducted her. Fergus and Brannick had helped her escape Roche's prison and now she was here.

One of her cats leaped up on her stomach. She petted him all the way down his back and up his fluffy tail. He was yellow-striped and had been brought to her by one of her pet owners. He'd somehow found his way into Revel Territory from the human part of Phoenix but had been emaciated to the point of death. She'd brought him back from the dead.

She loved animals.

It seemed somehow fitting that now she loved a wolf.

But how odd to think that she was part wolf herself. She might have left Fergus early this morning, for rational reasons. She'd even planned to pick up her life once more.

Yet even the fae part of her had grown in strength since she'd connected with Fergus. He'd awakened something in her that stimulated every other part of her life, not just her desire to be with him. She loved her sensual connection to the new, partial wolf she'd become. She loved that she'd worked beside him in a true partnership and that she'd served essentially, more than once, as his bodyguard.

When the cat jumped off her lap, she rose to a sitting position then glanced around her family room. Plans began to move through her mind. She'd give up her practice and hand it over to her capable assistant who had already passed her exams. She might even give her house away as well because her instincts told her that she'd soon be leaving Revel, maybe even by nightfall.

She gave full scope to her faeness and directed all her attention to Savage Territory and to Fergus. She faced south and as if a switch had been flipped, she felt the pull of the territory.

She belonged to Savage now. She felt it in her bones.

She'd never once thought something like this would happen to her. But from the time Fergus had entered her life, extraordinary forces had been at work. She'd crossed some mystical threshold into unknown terrain but which felt right, though scary as hell.

She believed now that her fate, no matter which direction her relationship with Fergus took, had become entwined with Savage Territory.

As she focused all her fae energy south, toward Savage, her former sensation of dread began to hum. The territory became fixed in her mind and in her heart, the land of wolves, of packs, of too many shifters crammed into a small human space and bound by barbed wire and searchlights, and of evil men like Sydon.

She closed her eyes. She could feel all the packs of the land, writhing in their constraint.

She felt Sydon's energy as well, one that fed off so much prevalent discontent. She could feel him like a virus that had already spread thickly through the veins of the territory.

It all came back to Sydon.

And her fae senses told her that the fate of the territory rested on her ability to locate him right now.

CHAPTER ELEVEN

MARY FOCUSED HARD on Sydon. The sense that events would soon move at lightning speed had settled deeply within her. She knew in her bones she couldn't wait.

The times had come.

She brought a strong past image of Sydon into her mind. She saw him sitting on the floor of the Gordion dungeon cell where he'd been put after Fergus shot him in the leg. She could see him as he'd been in that moment, facing away from the barred cell door, very still as though in a trance.

Holding the image steady, she entered her dreamglide. At the same moment, Sydon's current location began to take shape.

She could feel him now, in the southern part of the territory, well underground and beneath one of the Savage Strip clubs, a place called the Naked Wolf. The name made her shudder. She was pretty sure this was the same club where the female Gordion wolves had ended up.

She put her dreamglide in motion. With another thought she moved within a few feet of him, off to the side of what looked like an expensive office.

As she turned the opposite direction, she could see that Sydon's space was at the head of a long series of adjoining rooms, each with a wide entrance and pocket doors kept open. The work areas looked formal, even elegant with wood paneling. The style seemed like a strange choice for a killer like Sydon.

Within the series of rooms, dozens of wolves moved around or sat at desks. They were working hard, but at what?

Several rooms down, she could see a wall of monitors.

On instinct, she piloted her craft to the much larger space where fifteen screens were mounted on the wall, each showing live-feeds of the fronts of various properties. It took her a moment to recognize both Warren's and Fergus's, which in turn meant she was looking at the front view of all the pack compounds.

A terrible feeling of dread came over her. Sydon was surveilling all the major packs of Savage Territory and probably had been for a long time.

She moved her dreamglide down through several more rooms. Each one became increasingly war-like with more monitors, finally ending in a large open space. In the center was a huge, digital relief map of Savage Territory laid out on a massive table. She felt dizzy with alarm.

Sydon had built a military operation and had kept it so secret she was sure neither Fergus nor Warren knew anything about it. But how had such a level of secrecy been able to exist in Savage, especially since she could sense his operation had been going on for months, possibly years? Wolves were gregarious by nature, even chatty at times.

Slowly, she made her way back in Sydon's direction and only stopped once because she recognized one of the wolves.

Harley.

So, her instincts had been right all along. Harley was the traitor.

He was on the phone. She drew close to listen. "Amber Flame Rising launches at nine." He hung up, punched in a few more numbers, then repeated the coded words.

Had to be an attack and the hour placed the timing well after full-dark.

Her heart beat hard in her chest. Sydon's whole operation was primed and ready, though she had no idea what 'Amber Flame Rising' would actually look like. She recalled how Fergus had been deeply troubled about the territory, fearing that Savage was on the verge of something horrific. And here it was.

She held the dreamglide in front of Harley's desk, hoping for more information. But with each phone call, he simply repeated the same message.

As she watched Harley, however, she realized something wasn't right with him. This wasn't the wolf she'd met at the Gordion Compound. His eyes were usually a clear, vivid blue. Right now they looked dull. Something was going on with him, but what?

She had to think. She had to pull all the pieces together and do it fast. Some kind of attack would occur at nine. But what was the actual scope of Amber Flame Rising?

She returned slowly to Sydon's room. She still couldn't believe all this existed and no one knew about it.

When she finally returned to her initial entry point, she found Sydon sitting at a large carved wood desk, papers scattered the entire width. His head was bent over his laptop and every few seconds he'd type rapidly. The staccato effect sounded loud in the otherwise quiet space.

His office had beautiful wood shelves, hundreds of books, and a display case housing a half-dozen antique swords. The walls bore a muted gray-patterned wallpaper, again very elegant and surprising.

Was this really Sydon's set-up?

The stone floor was covered with what appeared to be an expensive woven carpet and on the opposite wall was a large landscape painting of the White Mountains. A credenza sat below the painting. Crystal decanters, filled with amber liquid, rested on a silver tray. In front of all this was, of all things, a curved purple velvet couch.

It was the couch, however, that caught Mary's attention, not because it looked out of place, but because it belonged as surely as everything else in the room did. Yet very little about the décor seemed to match Sydon's hard, ambitious exterior. Steel and glass would have worked. Slabs of black granite, maybe.

All this wood and velvet fit someone else entirely.

But who?

The wolf in her lifted her nose and sniffed the air. The dreamglide was an amazing *alter* creation, because she could even catch odors and fragrances through the dream-world vehicle.

The scent that struck her was complex and bitter, though it carried a redolence of smoke as well. And there it was, the answer to the riddle of how Sydon had built his operation.

Another entity was present in Sydon's office, a woman who could hide herself in plain sight.

A witch.

But not any witch. This one was a dark witch from Elegance Territory.

So many elements of the past three days coalesced in Mary's mind. Even Harley's dull eyes, inexplicable defection and split-loyalties now made sense.

But there was something more. The witch carried another scent that Mary knew well, one that caused dread to spill over her in powerful waves. The woman wasn't just a witch anymore. Instead she was part wolf, in the same way Mary had new wolf instincts and abilities.

Yet Mary couldn't see the witch. The woman kept herself cloaked by means of a spell.

Extending her senses, Mary could tell that the witch was fully aligned with Sydon. They'd forged a bond and each had become more powerful because of it.

Mary knew she had to find out as much as possible about this woman in order to know exactly what Fergus and his pack would be dealing with tonight.

In real-time, she concentrated heavily on the dreamglide. She no longer needed to be asleep or even meditating, but held both realities open at the same time. The more she focused, using each mental awareness, the more her ability to see the witch from the position of the dreamglide began to improve.

At first, a vague, misty form took shape, almost ghostlike.

She concentrated harder until the mist began to coalesce and finally the witch was completely visible.

The woman levitated above the couch. She wore a long flowing garment, also in velvet though the color was a dark red, almost maroon. The bodice of the gown was cut low, exposing a long line of cleavage as well as beautiful amber flames that crawled up her throat and darkened her cheeks. Her skin was pale and she was very thin. The woman was an addict.

Her eyes were coal black and her features gaunt and sharp. She might have been beautiful at one time, now she looked grotesque.

Mary knew who she was, a powerful dark witch named Sandrine and a prime player in one of the dark covens of Elegance Territory. She had to be the source of the lethal blue powder that had come within an inch of killing Fergus.

She was famous for poisons and torture and especially liked to combine the flame drugs with her spells.

Sandrine suddenly stopped moving. She floated down to land on the floor. She was short, maybe only five-foot-two against Sydon who was well over a foot taller.

"Sydon, my love, someone is here and you'll never guess who?"

Mary held her breath. She needed to leave but she had to know whether Sandrine actually knew Mary had invaded Sydon's HQ.

"Just tell me." Sydon sounded aggravated as he looked up from the stack of papers to the right of his laptop.

"Don't get crabby with me. This is important. She's Fergus's woman, the one I warned you about repeatedly, the one I told you to get rid of. The veterinarian, Mary of Revel. Sound fucking familiar, my love?"

Sydon looked around. "What the hell are you talking about? I don't see anyone and none of the alarms went off. She can't be here."

Somehow Sandrine had sensed the dreamglide.

Fear turned to a sharp, agonizing dread. If Sandrine had enough power to detect a dreamglide, Mary knew she had to get out of there. She immediately withdrew from the dreamglide.

As she sat up on her couch, she felt horribly exposed. She trembled and for a long moment couldn't put one thought in front of the next. There was so much wrong with what she'd seen, and with what Sandrine had said, she hardly knew where to start.

First and foremost, Sandrine saw her as a threat and had for a long time.

Mary worked hard to face up to the truth. Everything she'd experienced with Fergus over the past few days told her she was in danger. But so was Savage Territory.

She glanced toward the shuttered windows and the backyard. Though it was now seven in the evening in the middle of June, it was still light out which meant Sydon's forces couldn't attack her home for at least another hour. Setting the major attack at nine would also ensure that his sun-sensitive *alter* forces would be safe once they went to war.

She put a hand to her chest and slowly worked at calming herself.

What she knew to be true was that Sydon and his counterpart were at the heart of the disaster looming over Savage. The bonded couple intended nothing less than full domination of the territory. Despite her sense of personal danger, she also knew she had to help thwart the threat that Sydon had become.

The wolves she'd seen weren't the same wolves who served as part of Sydon's rogue warrior pack. These wolves were administrators, and they'd set up a large organization, one that could rule. Harley was part of that, though he appeared to be drugged or more likely be-spelled. Mary doubted he was even aware of the role he played.

It was obvious to her now that the whole time Sydon had been in the dungeon at Fergus's compound, he'd been communicating with Sandrine and his top wolves.

What came to mind next was a frightening question: How many spells had Sandrine employed to gather so many loyal wolves around Sydon? Had she done this to Harley or had Harley gone willingly?

She felt it now, the awful truth. If she was part wolf and Fergus was developing a number of fae instincts and abilities, then why not a wolf and a witch? Worse, why wouldn't Sydon be a willing participant in the dark arts as practiced by Sandrine?

She knew the time had come to contact Fergus and she reached for him telepathically. He hadn't responded earlier, apart from the dreamglide, but at the time he'd been caught in a nightmare. If he was waking up or already up for the night, she might be able to connect with him, even at such a distance.

Fergus, can you hear me?

Nothing returned, so she tried again. *Fergus, it's Mary. I need to talk to you and we probably shouldn't use our phones.*

She kept this up for a full minute, over and over, until a sleepy wolf finally responded. *Mary, what's going on? Are you okay? Where are you?*

His immediate concern warmed her heart. She thought about mentioning the danger she was in, but right now, she wanted him to have the bigger picture.

She started, however, with what would be the most personal part for Fergus. *I believe Harley's been subverted by a witch's spell.*

She felt Fergus grow very still. *What are you saying? Mary, what the fuck is going on?*

I've been in the dreamglide and I know where Sydon is and Harley's with him.

Fergus was silent for a moment then said quietly. *I don't believe it. Not Harley. I told you that before. He's been with me for years. I trust him with my life.*

Fergus, don't take my word for it. Instead, access as much of your faeness as you can right now and see if you can locate Harley by yourself. If nothing else, check to see if he's in the compound.

All right, give me a sec.

She remained quiet, then after a moment he returned to her. *I'm here and I've opened up to my pack and the surrounding area. Harley's not in the compound and though he has a den home nearby, he's not there. And you say he's with Sydon?*

Yes, but first, before I tell you anything else, I want you to take in the full scope of Savage right now. Forget Harley and your pack. Focus all your attention on the territory.

Mary—

She felt his need to argue, so she cut him off. *Fergus, stay with me on this and let me walk you through it. Will you do that for me?*

Another long, difficult pause. Fergus wouldn't like giving up control, not even in a conversation.

All right, fine.

Good. Use your faeness and encompass Savage in your thoughts.

She could feel his fae energy rising. *I'm doing it now.*

She waited, giving him time to connect with his territory the way a powerful fae could.

After a moment, he said, *I'm sensing the same thing as before, as though every pack is on the brink of war. But I don't get it.*

She took a deep breath and launched in. *Fergus, I found Sydon in an extensive headquarter system he's built for himself. It's not as big as your compound by any means, but large enough to coordinate anything he wants. Harley's there because I've seen him, but I think he's been be-spelled or drugged, I'm not sure.*

Fergus broke in with, *Fuck.*

Mary continued, *It gets worse. Sydon isn't just a wolf anymore, he's part warlock. He's hooked up with the witch, Sandrine, and they've forged a bond. They're working together to take over Savage.*

Holy fuck! The words carried so much resonance, Mary's head rang. Fergus continued, *Sandrine is one of the most powerful dark witches in Five Bridges. Are you sure?*

I saw her. She called Sydon 'my love'. They're in this together and Fergus, they plan to launch some kind of attack tonight. They're calling it by a code name: Amber Flame Rising, and it's slated to begin at nine o'clock.

She went on to tell him about the monitors, the relief map, Sandrine's addiction to amber flame, everything she could think of. The whole time, she could feel Fergus grow increasingly quiet.

When she was done, she remained silent to let Fergus wrap his head around all that she'd told him.

Finally, he responded. *Jesus, it all makes sense now. Sandrine must have created the killing powder Sydon tried to use in the arena battle. And if what you've said about Harley is true, then he no doubt delivered the spelled substance to Sydon himself just before the last dominance match. But are you absolutely sure Sydon and Sandrine are a pair?*

I'm positive. They're like you and me right now. Sandrine is part wolf and Sydon has taken on warlock qualities. They're operating in tandem. I also think its possible Sydon, with Sandrine's dark magic, has be-spelled significant wolves from every pack in Savage.

Now that he knew all that she'd learned, he released a long string of hellish words. She couldn't blame him, not one bit.

Finally, he asked the most pertinent question. *So where is Sydon's headquarters?*

Below the Naked Wolf at the western end of Savage Strip.

You're sure?

I am. One hundred percent.

And you used your dreamglide to see all this?

Yes, until Sandrine found me out.

Even telepathically, she heard Fergus offer up a frustrated wolf grunt. *Wait a minute. Are you saying she knew you were there?*

She did, so I left.

Okay, whatever you do, don't go back. I'll come get you personally at nightfall, that is, if you want to come to me. Is that what you want?

Absolutely. There was no doubt in her mind. Whatever her life was supposed to be, it would include Fergus and Savage Territory. Whether they would become a couple remained to be seen, but she was meant to be at the Gordion Compound, at least for the immediate future.

Fergus ended the telepathic conversation shortly afterward. He would need to quickly pull all the pack alphas together in order to counteract Sydon's plans for Savage.

But as she sat on the couch, something nagged at her about Sydon's HQ. She was certain about the location. That wasn't the problem. Instead, her fae senses told her she'd missed something critical, a piece of information Fergus would need as he put together his battle plan.

She felt a profound compulsion to go back. But returning to Sydon's HQ, even in the dreamglide, would put her in harm's way. Sandrine would be on the lookout for her and might have enough power to attack her through the veil of the dream-world reality.

Mary felt dizzy. She'd never faced a situation like this before. She had a choice, a real one. And Fergus had already told her not to return.

Yet if she didn't go back, she sensed hundreds of wolves would die.

She thought about contacting him again, but she already knew he would never allow her to put herself in danger. The decision had to be hers.

But it only took her another minute of deliberation. She didn't fully understand why her life had taken such a profound turn over the past couple of nights, yet it had, and she could never simply resume her former life. That meant doing what needed to be done where the coming attack was concerned.

She would return to Sydon's headquarters and if she was clever enough, she might even survive whatever the witch threw at her.

She didn't leave right away, however. Instead, she forced herself to grow very calm since her instincts told her something else. The longer she waited to return, the greater her chances of survival.

~ ~ ~

Fergus showered and dressed for the night in fresh leathers and a black tank trimmed with amber and bearing the Gordion logo patch. As he put on his boots, a weight settled on his shoulders, something he'd never experienced before because it felt very fae.

Mary's news had confirmed his own growing concerns for Savage. He just never imagined the plot against the territory would be as involved as it was. But it definitely explained the uneasy sensation he'd had for days that Savage was on the brink of war. And if he hadn't been sharing powers with Mary, he wouldn't have had a clue that anything was wrong since it was his faeness that warned him of the looming disaster.

As soon as Mary had described the monitors, the war room containing the digital relief map, and that Harley was contacting Sydon's wolves one after the other, he understood the scope of Sydon's plans.

Savage was a hotbed of reactionary wolves. When Elena had killed herself, some of his wolves had gone berserk with rage and had attacked Sydon's forces without weaponry of any kind. They'd been slaughtered as a result. But it was this kind of erratic, impulsive, and completely irrational behavior that occurred when war broke out, only on a much larger scale.

Wolves only had to get their blood up and mayhem and death would follow. Mary's sister, Alicia, had gotten killed as a result of wild, uncontrollable wolf reactions.

A direct attack at the front of each pack compound would incite every pack to battle and violence. Blind instinct would follow and Fergus firmly believed an all-out war would ensue, which appeared to by Sydon's ultimate goal.

He'd seen it before when he'd first become alpha. A full territory war had broken out and had lasted for weeks. In the end the hellish conflict and had taken the lives of nearly a hundred Gordion wolves. The last thing he wanted was another similar, chaotic battle, each pack out for its own. Wolves from all the packs would get worked up beyond reason and indiscriminate killing would follow. The resulting death toll would be catastrophic across the board. He had no doubt hundreds of wolves would die, maybe thousands.

What happened next was on him. But he needed to act fast and at the same time he had to be thorough.

Mary's safety was his first concern so he'd keep one eye on the arrival of dusk to make sure he was at her door the moment he could leave the compound. His next priority was to contact each of the pack alphas and to coordinate counter measures with them.

Leaving his private rooms, he headed to the compound's main entrance hall. With all the exterior windows shuttered against the bright June sunlight, he called his most powerful betas together, each of them an alpha-in-training.

Fergus took a couple of minutes to engage his men individually. The alpha wolf in him demanded the contact. He either shook the beta's hand or clapped him on the shoulder. He looked into each pair of eyes and let his new fae senses roll. He needed to know right now if he had enemies in the compound. The fate of Savage depended on the loyalty of his pack.

Fortunately, what returned to him was that he could trust all the wolves in front of him. He sensed the depth of their loyalty to the Gordion pack, equal to his own.

He also knew he had to act fast and get his bridges built by the time the sun set in the west. By his estimation, he had forty-five minutes.

Ryan spoke up. "Where's Harley?"

"Glad you mentioned him. Here's what we've got." He spoke quickly and outlined everything Mary had told him.

He felt a terrible shock settle over his wolves.

"If Harley could be turned," Ryan said, his voice little more than a growl, "then any of us could fall victim to Sydon and his witch."

"How they subverted Harley is unknown, but Mary saw him and he appeared to be drugged or possibly be-spelled.

"More importantly, I believe Sydon and Sandrine have corrupted a specific wolf in each of the fifteen acknowledged Savage packs. They've siphoned off top men, probably without their knowledge, in order to learn critical details about the different pack compounds. Their plan appears to be as comprehensive as it is vile."

Ryan scowled. "But what do they want? What are they after?"

"Sandrine has found a mate in Sydon. They're bonded and her craving for power feeds off that. But she also craves chaos and murder. The dark witches are some of the most violent in all of Five Bridges. If they could get the packs stirred up, Sydon no doubt counted on our wolf volatility to dredge up old wounds and start battling each other. How many times has this happened in the past? Dozens." The team around him nodded, each expression serious.

"And Sydon?" Ryan asked. "What does he hope to gain? He can never be a recognized alpha, not after the stunt he pulled in the dominance battle."

"I have every conviction Sydon plans on gaining control of Savage through instigating a brutal war. We already know the cartels will back him so he's well motivated and extremely well positioned to attempt a takeover of the entire territory."

"Then we need to bring him down." Ryan's voice had deepened and carried a lethal edge.

Fergus nodded, a grimness filling his chest. "And we're going to do just that."

He then laid out the first part of his strategy, to contact each of the pack alphas. They would let them know what was going on and have them figure out which of their beta-leaders was missing. These would be the wolves Sydon corrupted.

Fergus said, "This will be the best way for me to confirm with the alphas that an attack is imminent. As soon as each has been alerted, we'll prepare for the nine o'clock assault. I'll want a team here to coordinate our attack on Sydon's HQ. We'll bring him to heel before he can do any more harm to our territory and with luck, we'll avoid war in in Savage."

The wolves as one howled their approval.

Immediately after, Ryan used his tablet and pulled up the central pack information, a series of files that came directly from the Savage Pack Council. "I've got the alphas and their phone numbers."

There were fifteen official packs that the council recognized and a number of rogue tribes. Fergus made the decision to limit the initial inquiry to only these fifteen. He ordered his men to divide up the list and contact each pack leader, adding he would talk to Warren himself.

Not all the wolves were as adept at telepathy as Fergus was and distance could definitely prove a difficult obstacle to overcome. So most would use their phones. He thought it possible some of the devices might be bugged, but that was a risk worth taking with less than an hour to avert disaster.

For the next few minutes, the wolves chose which pack to contact. Afterward, each man went to a different part of the room to make his call. It didn't take long for the space to hum with the sound of so many rough wolf voices on their cell-phones. For that reason, many of the wolves moved into the adjoining hallway.

Fergus focused his attention on Warren and tapped on his telepathy.

It took some time to wake him up and Warren responded exactly as Fergus expected him to. *Fergus, what the hell are you doing disturbing my beauty sleep?*

In any other circumstance, Fergus would have laughed because Warren was poking fun at his scars. But not this evening. *We've got a situation. Sydon's primed for a takeover. The bastard brought in a witch.*

~ ~ ~

Mary sat on the couch sweating. Short of sitting on her hands to keep from moving, she'd done everything she could to delay her return in the dreamglide to Sydon's HQ.

When the need to get going became an overwhelming pressure within her chest, she stretched back down on the couch and created her dreamglide.

Her heart pounded as she focused on Sydon and Sandrine. Even then, she could feel that she'd put on the brakes. The fae part of her knew she was placing herself in jeopardy and didn't want to move forward. Once more, she had a prescience that her activities were going to bring her smack up against death itself.

Still, it was a job that had to be done. She needed to find out exactly what she'd missed the first time around that would place Fergus or any of his men in danger.

Putting the dreamglide in motion, she sped in a southwesterly direction. As she drew close to Sydon's HQ once more, she stalled out. For a moment her courage flagged and her dreamglide sat just outside the suite of offices. She took several deep breaths, gave herself a strong talking-to, then pushed within.

She kept the dreamglide close to the tall ceiling as she piloted it toward the map room. She moved swiftly, hoping to avoid Sandrine's detection.

She sped all the way to the large war room, the one at the end with the digital relief map. Her instincts took her to the far wall and a door. Several bolts sealed the door shut. She glided through and found a stairwell blocked by what even she could see was a large bomb.

At the top of the stairwell, was another door.

Well, look who's back? Now you're not planning on warning anyone about this, are you? It's our little failsafe.

Mary recognized Sandrine's voice. She immediately tried to leave her dreamglide but couldn't. Sandrine already had hold of the dream-world vehicle and was pulling it toward her.

The next thing Mary knew she'd lost complete control of her dreamglide and Sandrine was taking her swiftly through the main suite of rooms. She couldn't even leave the dream-world.

She knew she had only seconds before she'd fall under Sandrine's spell. *Fergus,* she cried out desperately. *Can you hear me?*

The response was instantaneous. *Yes, but you sound like you're in a tunnel. Oh, shit, Mary what have you done?*

I'm in the dreamglide in Sydon's headquarters. Explosives. Southwest entrance, with a spell. Did you hear me? Fergus?

But nothing returned.

Fergus. Explosives. Southwest door. Fergus!

Still, nothing.

She could only hope her message got through.

Sandrine brought the dreamglide to Sydon's desk. "We have a visitor, my darling. It seems Fergus's fae lover has returned in her dreamglide."

Sydon looked up, one brow raised indifferently. "Can you bring her to earth?"

"Of course."

"Then do it because as you can see I'm a little busy."

Sandrine turned toward Mary and smiled. She floated in a slow circle around the entire circumference of the dreamglide. As she moved, Mary's thoughts grew loose and distant.

When Sandrine closed the circle, the dreamglide fell hard to the stone floor at Sandrine's feet as though wrecked.

Mary lay prone in the dreamglide as well and she grew dizzier with each passing second, though she could hear Sandrine on her phone.

"I want you over at Mary Somers's house, the one on the street that backs up to the Graveyard. Yes, the veterinarian. You'll find her on her couch. I want her transported immediately to Sydon's HQ. If you value your lives, you'll be quick about it. Oh, and shoot her up with amber." There was a pause, then a snap to the witch's voice. "Yes, you heard me right. Flood the bitch with amber flame."

Mary processed these words and finally realized that Sandrine had called for a physical pick-up at Mary's home. Since it was still light out, she could only suppose that Sandrine and Sydon had humans in their employ.

Her last thought, before she passed out, was an awareness she'd be shot up again with drugs. Last time it had been dark flame. But this time, it would be with the horrendous amber flame, a substance used to tame female wolves who worked in the Savage Strip sex clubs.

~ ~ ~

Fergus stood very still at the head of the table in his strategy room. He was surrounded by his team, but had never felt more isolated or alone than from the moment he'd lost contact with Mary.

She'd provided extremely valuable information with her warning about explosives at the southwest entrance and had probably just saved dozens if not hundreds of lives because of it.

But had she lost her own in the process?

He tried repeatedly to reestablish contact with her, but couldn't. Was she being silent in order to protect herself or had something else happened?

As the minutes passed, he grew increasingly uneasy that he couldn't reach her. By the time dusk was falling, he was on a group communication with the alphas from the remaining fourteen packs. Each would protect his pack and keep his wolves from going war-mad, while Fergus would take a team to Sydon's HQ as soon as full-dark arrived.

When at last the automatic steel shades came up, he glanced out at the dark night sky. He tried reaching Mary again, both telepathically and through her dreamglide, but got no response.

Because of his fae senses, he knew she was no longer in her home and that she'd been unable to escape Sydon's HQ. He sent his squad over to her house anyway, just in case he was misreading the signals.

Ryan reported back two minutes later. "When we arrived, the front door was off its hinges and Mary was nowhere to be seen. But there's more. We found a syringe reeking of amber flame on the floor next to the couch. We've searched the house. Mary's gone."

CHAPTER TWELVE

FERGUS GREW VERY still. He tried to reach Mary a couple more times, but nothing returned. His fae senses confirmed what he already knew, that Sydon had sent humans to shoot Mary up with amber flame and drag her out of her home.

The war room disappeared from his vision and every one of his wolves fell silent.

He heard only the sound of his rough breathing, which came out in short gusts, like intermittent gunfire.

Mary was gone, taken by a monster.

He could hardly think, and he sure as hell didn't know what to do. Only one thing became clear to him. He had to get Mary back. But how?

He felt his neck arch and knew he was close to letting loose with an agonized howl. But he couldn't do that right now, not in front of his pack.

He contacted Warren telepathically and let him know what had happened. Warren already knew that Mary had gone back a second time in her dreamglide to gather the information about the bomb.

What do you need me to do? Warren asked.

You'd better get over here and bring a squad with you. At the very least, I'll need you to liaison with the rest of the packs.

I'm with you, brother.

Fergus's throat tightened. *Thanks.*

Whatever happened with Sydon's assault, Fergus had to find some way of getting Mary safely out of the bunker. The counter-attack wouldn't begin for at least a half hour, so he had time to figure things out and put a plan together.

Needing a minute alone, he turned the pack over to Ryan, then left the room. He couldn't feel his feet as he moved. Maybe he was levitating; he wasn't sure. His heart pounded in his chest.

Sydon and his witch had taken Mary well before sundown.

Jesus. They must have used humans.

His limbs shook with a profound drive to go after her. But a hasty move could jeopardize not only her life, but the counter-attack as well.

He headed back to the guest room and shut the soundproof door. He paced at the foot the bed. 'Fuck' became his mantra. The word burned the air repeatedly.

He clenched his fists. The wolf in him wanted to run, something that would help the raw state of his nerves, but he didn't have time for that. He had no way of getting to Mary.

Frustration caused the dam to break. He dropped on all fours, shifting at the same time, then lifted his neck and howled over and over.

Fully wolf, he called for his alpha-mate, for Mary, for the woman he loved.

There was his greatest truth, fully acknowledged: He loved Mary and he needed her. He had from the moment he'd held her in his arms during her rescue from Roche's sex club. His wolf had recognized her for exactly who she was in his life, his woman, his mate.

He'd known it all along, of course, but he'd refused to allow himself to see it. He howled some more, then guilt struck because if he'd permitted himself to bond with her when he'd had the chance, she would never have gone back to her house. She'd be with him right now. She'd be safe.

After a minute, his howls ceased and his mind began to grow calm.

Reason returned.

He'd kept himself separated from Mary in the same way he'd built a heavy steel door between himself and Sharon.

But the same door that had been useful to keep his pack safe in his early alpha days now seemed obsolete. Maybe it had been for a long time.

With powerful intent, he mentally bulldozed the damn thing down. And as he did, a fresh breeze blew through his soul.

A familiar woman's voice entered mind. *Fergus, I'm here. Let me help.*

Fergus turned and saw a misty form taking shape. He recognized Sharon immediately and flowed back into his human form to speak with her.

She floated above the dresser but appeared to be sitting with her knees crossed. She had a quirky smile on her lips as she looked him up and down. *Damn, you look good. Were you always that tall?*

He slipped into telepathy as well. *And you look the way I remember you, Sharon. But I'm so fucking sorry for the way I treated you.*

She nodded. *I know and its okay, all of it. So many of our wolves died the year you took over and I know their deaths caused you to shut down. I also understand that I could have helped you through the transition, but I didn't. I was too self-absorbed. Fergus, I never took to Savage like you did and I never liked being a wolf, though you seemed okay with all of it.*

He nodded. *I don't know how it happened, but I accepted my transformation pretty quickly and I always liked serving on the border patrol. But what are you doing here and why have you been hanging around Mary?*

To make sure you didn't do anything stupid, of course. But there is something you need to know. She hesitated for a moment before continuing. When she did, she looked guilty as hell. *Our friend, Sydon, was the wolf who killed me.*

He stared at Sharon uncertain he'd heard her right. *You had sex with Sydon?*

He'd been after me for a long time and finally persuaded me to meet him. Her misty nostrils flared. *The sex wasn't exactly consensual.*

He raped you.

She nodded slowly. *But right now, that's not the important part. It was Sydon's plan all along to get rid of me. He and Sandrine had been planning this whole thing for years, starting with the takeover of the Gordion pack and ending here with a full-on Savage territory assault. In an attempt to weaken you, he got rid of me.*

Until this moment Fergus hadn't quite realized how nefarious Sydon's plan had been. *Sharon, I knew little about Sydon back then. If I'd understood what we were up against, maybe I could have prevented what happened to you.*

I'm not sure about that, she said. *Sydon is a devious monster and he's had Sandrine's help all along the way.* Her lips slowly curved, *But you know what? Neither of these assholes counted on Mary.*

At that, his spirit grew deeply settled, purposeful. He sat down on the end of the bed and watched Sharon, knowing she'd deliberately come from the other side to help him. *You like her, don't you?*

Sharon floated to the floor and moved to hover in front of him. *Oh, hell, yeah, but she's way too good for you.* Her ghostly lips quirked again.

You won't get any arguments from me. He felt as though he'd already lived an entire lifetime with Mary.

He shifted his gaze away from Sharon, then continued, *She'd taken her dreamglide into Sydon's den the second time, but Sandrine was right there, probably waiting for her in case she returned. I lost contact with her but not before she relayed a critical piece of information, about a bomb on the southwest entrance, then nothing. I'm pretty sure Sandrine did something to her in the dreamglide.* Reverting his gaze to her, he asked, *Do you know what happened to her?*

Sharon nodded, which moved the ghostly mist around. *Sandrine brought Mary's dreamglide straight to the floor. And in case you're wondering, she sent a team of humans to kidnap Mary from Revel.*

That's what I thought. He had to figure all of this out. *But based on what Mary had told me earlier, I've been able to mobilize all the pack alphas in anticipation of the assault. And I have a team ready to attack in their bunker beneath the Naked Wolf. I take it she's there?*

She is. But, hold on a minute. You mean you've even gotten cooperation from packs you've gone to war with?

Sure. What choice did any of them have? Sydon has been cultivating traitors in each of our packs. They're with him now, in his bunker.

Fergus, you've built a lot of respect in Savage over the years. I was there to watch some of it develop and seeing what's happening here, you've accomplished a lot.

He stood up and met Sharon's gaze. *That's one of the nicest things you've ever said to me.*

Her quirky smile returned. *Just giving you a hint about the future.*

Is that why you're here?

In part. Mostly, I'm supposed to tell you to do everything you can to save Mary.

She's the key for you and for Savage. Also, she knew she might not make it out of there the second time she went back in her dreamglide. She's basically sacrificed her life for you and for all the packs. The least you could do is get her the hell out of Sydon's bunker.

He watched her for a long moment. *I'm sorry I didn't stop you from going out that last night, the night you died. I waited up for you. I'd intended to make more of an effort. I know I failed you.*

She drew close to him, her form little more than mist. She lifted her arms and the next moment he felt a drift of fingers down his face. *And I apologize for cheating on you, especially with a bastard like Sydon. If I'd been a better mate to you, I could have helped. Instead, I don't think I ever got over losing my human life and that beautiful resort we built together. But I am sorry. I know I caused you a lot of grief.*

All is forgiven then? he asked.

Of course. Now, I'm going to tell you one more thing, then my job here is done. When you draw close to the Naked Wolf, make contact with Mary and have her tell our heinous pair that if they kill her, the moment she dies, you'll know of her death and you won't hesitate to bomb the hell out of their bunker. Have her inform them that you're part fae now and that you'll know exactly if and when she dies. That will keep her alive long enough for you to get in there and take care of business. Got it?

I do. And thanks.

At that, she smiled. *And one last thing. Sandrine will soon think about using a killing spell on Mary. Apparently, Sydon is about to show a little too much interest in taking Mary to bed.*

These last words created the right imagery to spur Fergus forward. He headed toward the door.

Sharon called after him. *I won't be back, Fergus. Be sure to let Mary know I think the world of her and that I wish you both well.*

Reaching for the door, he glanced at her over his shoulder. *Will do. And thanks, Sharon.*

With another quirky smile, she saluted him then disappeared.

~ ~ ~

Mary's eyes rolled back in her head and she couldn't focus. Her vision was blurred. She ached in strange places, which made her howl softly.

The humans, four strong men, had come to her front door and broken it down. She'd tried to fight them off, but they were heavily muscled and knew what they were doing. They'd pinned her to the couch, roped off her arm, and shot her up with amber flame.

She'd passed out.

Now she lay on the purple velvet couch in Sydon's office. She could smell Sandrine's dark, smoky scent nearby, and she could feel the witch's powerful drive to kill her.

But there was another smell now, very wolf that kept teasing the insides of her legs all the way to her sex.

She ground her hips into the cushion. She needed sex and she needed it now.

Oh, dear God, she'd forgotten this aspect of amber flame, how it affected female wolves, making them ready to work the sex clubs. All she wanted right now was a man between her legs, any man, and the scent that kept her in an aroused state was very male.

Her first impulse was to sit up and maybe attack the next male wolf she saw. Instead, the fae part of her kept her very still. As much as she was able, she needed to think.

Her gaze became fixed on Sydon. A very distant part of her brain despised him for the killer he was. But the part doused with amber flame thought he'd never looked better in his snug gray t-shirt and leathers. Right afterward, however, the fae part of her made a disgusted snort inside her head. That helped.

She looked away from him.

What she didn't understand was why she was still alive. What was Sydon's game? Or Sandrine's, for that matter?

"Looks like our guest is waking up."

"Would you just kill her, Sandrine, and get it over with? I have a territory … to take … over." Sydon must have caught Mary's scent, because he stopped what he was doing and turned to stare at her.

He moved suddenly in Mary's direction.

"Sydon, my love, what's going on?"

"Can't you smell her? The woman is part wolf now."

"What?" Sandrine almost shouted the word.

"Yes, she's wolf the way you are and she's ripe. Her scent is pouring off of her now because of the drug. A good fuck is just what I need before we launch. Besides, if you didn't want me to take her, why did you shoot her up with amber flame?"

"I didn't know that it would affect her like this. She can't be part wolf. She's a Revel fae."

"You're part wolf," Sydon state reasonably.

"Shit. You're right."

She then moved to float in front of Sydon, levitating to compensate for their height difference and took his face in her hands.

Mary still had enough of a survival instinct not to get caught between Sandrine and her man, but it was hard as hell to stay put. Amber flame was doing a number on her libido.

"Look at me." Sandrine's voice carried a dedicated resonance. She followed with a soft speech Mary could hardly make out, though she kept repeating something about staying focused on 'Amber Flame Rising'.

But in the exact same moment, Fergus broke through the witch's control over her and entered her mind. *Mary, are you there?*

Fergus? How did you reach me? I couldn't make contact because of Sandrine. She spelled me or something.

I'm not sure, but Sharon was just with me. She said you need to remind Sandrine and Sydon that if they kill you, or even try to, the fae part of me will know exactly when that happens. And if they take your life, I'll happily bomb their bunker to hell and back.

Got it.

And Mary?

Yes?

I'm coming for you. His wolf's voice, even inside her mind, was low, hoarse, and sexy as hell.

At the same time, her heart melted. *I love you, Fergus. No matter what happens, I need you to know that.*

Without a beat, he responded, *I love you, too, and when this is all over I'm going to show you just how much.*

Because he was a wolf and because amber flame had hijacked her brain, she did a full body undulation on the couch. *Can't wait.*

I'm going now. But I'll have you out of there in a few minutes. I promise.

Mary felt him disconnect. Her body was on fire for him even in the middle of a nightmare. At the same time, her heart slammed around in her chest. She was grateful Sandrine was working to keep Sydon's attention on her, otherwise she might have detected the telepathic interference.

She watched the couple carefully as she forced herself to calm down. Sandrine was still talking her mate down, diminishing the possibility she'd discover that Mary had alerted Fergus to their plans.

"It doesn't matter what any of the packs know about Amber Flame Rising at this point. They'll be too late. Once our rogues start attacking and get all the Savage wolves stirred up, chaos will do the rest." Sandrine still caressed Sydon's face.

Sydon glanced at Mary. "And I say we don't take any chances. Just kill the bitch."

Those words were Mary's cue. "If you do," she called out, though her voice was slurred since she was still horribly weak, "Fergus will know I'm dead because he's part fae now, in the same way you're part warlock." She drew a deep breath and pressed on. "If he thinks for a second I'm gone, he'll blow this place up, my corpse with it. Face it, I'm your best insurance to keep your enemies from dropping a bomb on the Naked Wolf and destroying this bunker."

Sandrine nodded. "The woman is right. We have to keep her alive until the very last second. Then I'll gut her myself."

Sydon's nostrils flared. "Fine, but in the meantime, can you get rid of the wolf smell?"

"Of course I can, my love. You only had to ask." Sandrine reached into the black leather pouch at her waist, withdrew her hand and flicked something in Mary's direction. A teal powder flew through the air straight for her.

Mary held her breath, but the airborne substance clung to her nose and mouth. It wasn't long before her body forced her to open up her lungs. As soon as she drew the spell into her throat, a new kind of dizziness assailed her. At least she didn't black out. But whatever it was, she became too weak to move.

The new spell, though easing the reaction of the flame drug in her body, also created a profound layer of fatigue. She could barely keep her eyes open.

Fergus came to mind once more. She knew there was a strong possibility he wouldn't be able to get her out of the bunker in time, but she didn't regret returning to Sydon's HQ. Alerting Fergus to the presence of a failsafe bomb had been worth the risk. If only there was a way out for her.

She tried to create another dreamglide, but found it impossible. Whatever Sandrine had done to the first one, she felt broken in that respect, at least while the witch had control of her.

She felt the energy in Sydon's office intensify, and she knew the hour was closing in on nine. Dread seized her once more at what he was about to unleash on Savage.

She held her eyes open the barest crack to watch events unfold. Sydon rose to his feet, his dark eyes glinting. He rounded the desk and held his hand out to Sandrine. "Are you ready, my love?"

Sandrine smiled. "I am."

He inclined his head toward the couch. "Will she give us any more trouble?"

"No. She won't be able to move for at least another hour. By then, she won't even belong to this earth."

"Excellent. Then let's move this party to the war room."

Mary lay very still. She heard their footsteps as they left. Now that Sandrine wasn't in the immediate vicinity, Mary didn't feel nearly as tired, but she still couldn't move. She couldn't rebuild her dreamglide, either.

Then another idea came to her and since Sydon and Sandrine were gone, she decided to try to reach Fergus again. She opened her telepathic channel. *Fergus? Are you there?*

~ ~ ~

Fergus had made his way to his gun cabinet off his study, when Mary's voice once more entered his mind, this time loud and clear.

Checking his Glock, then sliding it into his holster, he asked, *Is everything all right? Has anything changed?*

Yes. Right now Sandrine, Sydon and his entire administrative staff have moved to the strategy room ready to launch Amber Flame Rising. But I have an idea that might help you and your troops as you bust into Sydon's HQ.

Fergus drew a steel, half-sword from the several he owned and slowly slid it into its sheath on his left side. He couldn't get over Mary's extraordinary presence of mind. She was in a terrible situation, but she had enough inner calm to be thinking about the upcoming assault. *Have you uncovered more information?*

Not exactly. Do you think you can still build a dreamglide?

Yes, of course. Why?

I'm thinking that if you could pilot your dreamglide into the bunker, you could gather the intelligence you'd need to attack Sydon's HQ with very little loss of life. What do you think?

Fergus made quick calculations in his head, his nostrils flaring and elongating with the exciting possibilities inherent in her proposal. It hadn't occurred to him to make use of his dreamglide ability in the course of a battle. He'd been thinking more like a wolf and a warrior. But Mary's idea might be the turning point.

However, there was one thing he had to know. *Didn't Sandrine bring you down in your dreamglide?*

That's right, but she wasn't as preoccupied as she will be now. I think you can get in without being noticed. Besides, the last thing she'll expect is a wolf in a dreamglide.

Then I'll give it a shot because this could change everything. I'll get back to you when I'm in position. It won't be but a couple minutes now.

He heard the amusement in her voice as she responded, *Well, you know where I'll be.*

God, I love you.

Back atcha, wolf. Now get going.

Fergus returned to his strategy room and saw that Warren had arrived. "I'm going after Mary right now."

Warren's green eyes glittered. "And you're sure she's in Sydon's bunker?"

"I am."

"So, she's not far from the bomb you told me about."

"That's right."

"Why is that bomb even there?" Warren asked.

"Best guess? Sydon could detonate it anytime he wanted, especially if the place was overrun. He could escape his bunker at the last minute, and still take out a lot of lives in the process."

Warren's expression grew solemn. "From the size of it, I think he could take out half the block. So, what's the plan?"

Fergus tried not to think about Mary's proximity to Sydon's contingency explosives. "I'm about to find out Mary's exact position within Sydon's HQ."

"How are you going to do that?"

Fergus smiled slowly. "I'm going to use my dreamglide."

Warren held his gaze. "So, you're like the other border patrol men who've bonded with their women and now you have fae powers."

"That's the way of it."

"Then you'd better go get her."

The wolves all around him began to draw close, the wolf pack at its best. He felt their energy as if it was his own.

He glanced around. "I need all of you to know that Mary is my alpha-mate, even though she's not a wolf. When I've secured her safety and her freedom, I intend to bring her back here to be with me, permanently. If the pack needs a different leader, then I will step aside. But she's the woman for me. Besides having served unwittingly as my bodyguard since she first came here two nights ago, she may have just given us the key to ending Sydon's assault with minimal loss of life."

Before he said anything more about sharing powers with Mary, he took a moment and with every fae ounce of his body, he formed his dreamglide. He didn't have to meditate or shut down his conscious mind in any way. He could now be in both places at once with barely any effort at all. Somehow he wasn't surprised. Having vaporized the steel door of his soul and confessed his love for Mary, new power flowed through him in heavy waves.

To the warriors gathered around him, he explained his faeness briefly, then added that Mary had several wolf powers of her own. He told them about his dreamglide and that he was headed into Sydon's HQ bunker to have a good look around even as he stood in the Gordion Compound.

Ryan smiled. "You're going to spy on the bastard."

"I am. Then I'll let all of you know exactly how we're going to take him down."

The wolves as one lifted their fists, then gave a shout. Each wore a battle uniform with black tanks bearing amber logo patches, black leathers, sword and Glock. The bulk of his army and a portion of Warren's waited outside for the go-ahead.

He was essentially in two different realities at the same time.

As he put the dreamglide in motion in what was the dream-world, he spoke aloud to his men in real-time. "I'm piloting over the forest. I've reached the edge, and I'm passing above the central housing tracts." He put on some speed and got the dreamglide to his destination. "All right, I'm at the Naked Wolf at the west end of Savage Strip. Warren, you know about the bomb. Get the border patrol over there to clear everyone out of the surrounding clubs and buildings. The streets need to be empty as well, but tell them to do it fast. I have a feeling Sydon's bomb will be going off at some point in the next ten minutes. Let's keep our Savage wolves safe."

"You got it," Warren responded.

Still focused on the dreamglide, Fergus sensed Warren was on his phone.

While Warren made contact with the Savage Border Patrol, Fergus continued to relay information to his top betas. "I'm easing inside the HQ at the north end which is where Sydon's office is located. I can see Mary. She's on the couch. She's safe there for now. I'm heading toward the strategy room which is through a series of offices at the south end of the bunker. All the offices in between are empty, but I can see Sydon and his team clustered in the last large war room. This is it. Sydon is laying out his attack as we speak. I'll have details about Amber Flame Rising in a matter of seconds."

His wolves remained silent, but their joint intensity fired him up. He remained focused on the dreamglide, hovering as high against the ceiling as he could to avoid detection by the witch. Fortunately, Sandrine had her head bent over the digital relief map right next to Sydon, so he knew he had a shot.

Fergus reported to his men. "I'm looking at the entire battle plan. Warren, get ready to transmit information to all the alphas."

"They're on standby with their coms. Everyone's in position. Just waiting for you."

Within the dreamglide, he took a long hard look at the map, then began, "The plan is simple but insidious. Its clear Sydon gained critical information about each compound. If there is a vulnerable or secret entrance into a compound, Sydon intends to use it. His wolves will attack at two points: they'll create a lot of noise at the entrance, but a larger force will attempt entry through the most vulnerable points in each home or compound. He has pictures, for instance, of my hidden entrance behind the bookcase."

He glanced at Ryan in real-time and said, "Put some of our men inside the hidden passageway right now, the one on the third level. Hopefully, Sydon's forces won't even get that close, but I want a team there just to be sure. In a minute, we'll set up a perimeter to catch the rogue wolves assigned to our compound. When you've got the men set up inside, come back here. I'll want you with me when we head to the bunker."

Ryan nodded. "I'm on it." He took off on a run and a few seconds later shouted orders to several of the warriors waiting in the entrance hall.

Fergus turned his attention to Warren. "You need to get back to your compound."

Warren's brow furrowed. "Some of my troops can remain here. Hell, I can stay here, if you need me to help with Mary, I'm with you. She's risked everything for Savage."

Fergus stared at him for a long moment. He clapped him on the shoulder and let his hand rest there for several seconds. "Thank you for that Warren. I'll never forget it. But the Gordion Wolves have got this."

As Fergus drew his hand away, Warren offered a crooked smile and inclined his head. "We'll catch up with drinks afterward."

"Damn straight we will." Fergus checked his internal clock. "Thirty seconds until nine."

Warren nodded twice in response, then turned on his heel. He called out for his pack and offered a long, loud howl.

Fergus waved his team forward. He moved to the open doors of the compound entrance and tracked his friend as he headed into the skies. It was an impressive sight to watch a powerful man like Warren whipping through the night air, his blond hair flowing behind him like a mane. What couldn't Savage accomplish with men like Warren in charge?

Fergus returned to his team quickly and once more focused on the dreamglide. The energy in Sydon's war room had ramped up. "On my mark," Sydon called out in a strong voice, "Engage Amber Flame Rising."

Fergus contacted Warren telepathically to let him know that Sydon had just given the order. Warren would let the rest of the alphas know.

For his own compound, he delivered a brisk series of commands and watched as one group of wolves either transformed into their wolf shapes and ran into the forest or levitated to take up hidden places high in the trees in order to intercept Sydon's forces. He sent a second group to the east of the pack's property specifically to wait for the rogue wolves who would try to enter the compound through a side window in order to gain access to the secret passageway.

He had a third of the wolves positioned to guard the entrance, while the remainder filled the large front foyer to engage the enemy as needed.

All that remained was for Fergus to get his team of ten to Sydon's bunker. He took to the skies, and Ryan and the rest levitated with him, rising at least a quarter mile up to avoid being seen by any of Sydon's rogue wolves. Their job was treacherous and the last thing Fergus wanted was for Sydon to know ahead of time what he'd be facing.

Fergus focused on his dreamglide, which still hovered above the relief map. Sydon and his wolves remained clustered in the larger war room, listening to squad reports as they came in.

In real-time, Fergus heard several shots as he passed over the heart of Savage, yet still a mile away from Sydon's bunker. More shots followed.

When he looked down and could see some of the different pack wolves battling Sydon's forces, it was hard to pass by. His wolf battle instincts wanted to engage then and there. But he had to get Mary out of the compound, and it was time to run Sydon to earth for good. His fae senses warned him that once Sydon got the first reports back from his army, he'd realize his plan had been compromised and Mary would be in serious trouble again.

He told his wolves to hold steady as they passed over yet another compound and heard more shots being fired. When a couple of minor explosions went off, one to the east and the other in the north, he flew faster. The whole territory was now in full engagement as Sydon's plan unfolded.

By the time he'd reached the Naked Wolf, however, the border patrol had cleared the streets as well as the clubs in the surrounding area. A line of cars intent on leaving the territory was grid-locked all the way to Defiance Bridge. The Savage Border Patrol had done a quick and excellent job securing the street since the immediate area around the Naked Wolf was now free of its normal traffic.

He held his team hovered over the strip club, reminding each member of his team to avoid the bomb on the stairs of the southwest public entrance.

He continued with group telepathy. *I'll use the dreamglide to find the best point of entrance for us. Be ready to battle. This is it.*

He felt a profound warring spirit bind his wolves together. They were a unified force in the best sense.

Within the dreamglide he saw Sydon listen intently to reports coming in from all over the territory. He was frowning hard and finally said, "Why aren't the wolves going berserk and tearing at each other, pack-to-pack?"

When Sydon glanced at Sandrine, Fergus took it as his cue to get his dreamglide the hell out of there. He swung the dream-world vehicle north and flew swiftly in the direction of Sydon's office. Once there, he checked on Mary, then contacted her. *We're right outside, Mary. Can you move at all?*

The sound of her voice reassured him even though she lay inert on the purple velvet. *Sandrine be-spelled me. Can't move a muscle yet, but I'm doing better. Ready when you are.*

Won't be long now. I'm taking my dreamglide out of here.

Facing south, he saw a second door that opened onto the east side of Sydon's bunker. Passing through, he found a long conference room and a large door with an 'exit' sign above it.

Moving in a quick burst of energy, he passed through the door, which led to a wide flight of exterior cement stairs. When Fergus flew his dreamglide up, he realized the stairs led to street level and he could see himself and his team hovering high in the air. Mary had been right. Sydon had built his HQ directly below the Naked Wolf.

He addressed his team in real-time, letting them know the layout and that he'd guide them in using the dreamglide.

Ready? he asked, meeting each man's gaze.

The question was rhetorical, though a lot of dipped chins and snarls followed. Each wolf drew his Glock as well.

With his wolves in position, he piloted the dreamglide back into the still empty conference room. In real-time, he directed his troops to follow behind him.

He landed on the sidewalk, then levitated quietly down the cement stairs. He opened the door, and the man behind him came forward and held it open for the rest.

Fergus moved inside, still holding his dreamglide tight. He moved it into the suite of offices and took a look, but Sydon's staff was still in the war room.

He reminded his wolves of the biggest danger. *Remember, the southwest door leading out of the strategy room is armed with a bomb that will level this building and several others around it if detonated. Avoid that door.*

His wolves offered huffing grunts in response, a unique sound mind-to-mind.

Fergus moved into the offices with the wolves. Each now had his Glock in one hand, short sword in the other.

Fergus carried only his Glock in case he needed to grab Mary. He went through the north door first and found her still safe on the sofa. He put his hand on her shoulder. "Mary, can you hear me? Can you wake up?"

She mumbled in her twilight state, then switched to telepathy. *It's a combo of the drug and a spell. Sorry.*

No worries. But I've got to help my team secure the bunker.

Go for it, wolf.

He heard shouting and gunfire as his troops engaged with Sydon and his team in what had to be the war room.

Ryan contacted Fergus telepathically. *Half the wolves present seem to be coming out of their stupor. Harley's here. He's shaking his head and rubbing his eyes.*

Is the room contained?

No. Oh, shit. I was looking at Sydon, and suddenly he vanished. I think he might be headed your way.

CHAPTER THIRTEEN

FERGUS COULD SENSE the wolf, but he couldn't see him. As he waited for Sydon to appear, he could feel his rage, but for whatever reason, the wolf-warlock wasn't moving fast.

Ryan's voice hit Fergus's mind again. *How the hell did he make himself disappear?*

Sydon is part warlock now. He probably used a spell, but I've got this.

Shit. Okay, we'll secure the war room.

Fergus extended his fae senses. He could feel that Sydon was headed toward him though he'd barely moved beyond the doorway of the war room. What was he waiting for?

He tapped Ryan's telepathy again. *Where's Sandrine? Do you see her?*

No. She's gone as well.

Fergus accessed his dreamglide and sped quickly to Ryan's location. Sandrine wasn't there, but he sensed her and followed his instincts.

When he found her, a new wave of adrenaline hit his system. *Holy shit, Ryan. I'm looking at the witch now. She's near the bomb and she's just activated the timer. Fuck, we've only got five minutes. Get our men out of the bunker now. And any of the wolves affected by Sandrine's spell! Make sure the area near the Naked Wolf is clear as well.*

I'm on it! Ryan started shouting orders.

Fergus returned his focus to his real-time self. Sydon had suddenly shifted to high gear and was closing in on him fast. Because he sensed Sydon was armed only with his half-sword, he holstered his Glock, then unsheathed his sword.

He contacted Ryan once more. *Sydon's coming for me now.*

Take him down, Fergus. And don't worry. I'm getting everyone out as we speak.

With only his sword in hand, Fergus moved away from Mary's couch. Sydon's choice to use his blade instead of his gun was a good thing. Mary could easily get hurt or even killed in an exchange of gunfire.

Without warning, Sydon let go of the invisibility spell. He was only twenty feet away, lips snarling, half-sword held in a tight fist.

"You did this?" Sydon shouted. "You and your woman? You figured out our attack plan?" His face turned a reddish hue. "How? I had every contingency covered."

Well beyond Sydon's shoulder, Fergus watched Ryan swiftly usher the Gordion team and what was left of Sydon's staff, through the door that led into the large conference room.

Fergus shifted his full attention back to the wolf and shared a small portion of the truth. "A ghost sent Mary to Savage. But does it really matter? It's just you and me now, Sydon." He lowered his shoulders, bent his knees, then growled heavily. "As it should have been from the beginning."

Sydon's nose elongated wolf-style and he pulled his lips back. Fergus could feel his intention and wasn't surprised when Sydon disappeared again, no doubt assuming it would give him the advantage.

But Fergus wasn't just a wolf anymore and used his dreamglide like a visual tracking device. He could see Sydon easily and met the downward slice of his unseen sword as though he was watching it in real-time.

"What the fuck?" Sydon shouted as their swords clanged together. But the wolf still didn't show himself.

"You're not the only half-breed in the room," Fergus said. "I'm looking at you through the dreamglide."

"You can build a fucking dreamglide?" Sydon shuffled backward several feet, eyes wide.

"Surprise. But did you know your witch activated the bomb?"

Sydon smiled. "So she did. By my estimation, I've got four minutes to put you in the ground."

Fergus countered his taunt. "I thought maybe the two of you were planning to die here together. I think it's a very romantic idea. In fact, I intend to help you both toward that end. Right now."

"Like hell." Sydon growled and came at Fergus again, whipping his sword through the air at waist-level. Fergus pivoted and with his own sword caught Sydon's blade hard so that Sydon leaped backward several feet.

Sydon then struck out again, creating a series of thrusts and swipes that had Fergus's feet hopping. He moved in tandem with what he could see easily through his dreamglide.

Sydon was a better swordsman than he was a fighter, however, and each attack came faster.

The whole time he battled with the wolf, Fergus felt the click of the bomb's timer like a heartbeat pounding inside his head.

Three minutes and counting.

Fergus's sword arm vibrated with each strike of steel against steel. Finally, he saw his opportunity, whirled and sliced swiftly across Sydon's abdomen. He could feel his blade catch flesh, thank God. He had to get Mary out of the bunker.

Sydon levitated backward several feet and looked down at his bleeding abdomen. "You bastard."

Sandrine suddenly called out, "Sydon, my love, I can smell your blood. Did the wolf hurt you?"

Through the dreamglide, Fergus watched the also-invisible witch fly quickly through the several adjoining rooms toward Sydon. She was still wearing a long red velvet gown.

As Sandrine caught up with Sydon, she pulled something from her pouch, dabbing it on the wound.

How fucking tender.

Fergus was breathing hard as he checked his internal clock. Two-and-a-half minutes til detonation.

Fear gripped him. If Sandrine got involved, he wasn't sure what he could do. Mary was still incapacitated on the couch because of the spell, as well as the amber flame drug. But he'd never be able to get Mary out in time if they kept stalling.

He called out, "Couldn't fight this battle on your own, is that it Sydon? Didn't have the balls, the power or anything else, did you?"

He shifted his sword from hand to hand, moving it back and forth, getting ready. "And you, Sandrine, you're about as worthless as they come, using your power to take the lives of others. But here's what I know about you. You're an insect, nothing more, something I could crush easily beneath my boot."

Sydon gripped Sandrine's arm. "Don't let him get to you."

"That's right, Sandrine. Don't let me get to you. But I know why you hooked up with a wolf. You couldn't make it on your own in Elegance, could you?" He could feel the bomb ticking away. Two minutes to go.

The witch's face twisted up, taking a demon's shape. Her coal-black eyes flashed fire. She jerked her arm away from Sydon, reached into her pouch, then flew like lightning at Fergus.

"Sandrine, don't!" Sydon shouted.

He knew she carried a spell in her hand. But the witch had made one fatal mistake since she clearly didn't know Fergus could see her through the dreamglide.

When she was four feet away, he flipped in the air and with years of practice, brought his sword down on the back of Sandrine's neck. He felt the connection with blood and bone, then felt nothing but empty space. He'd severed her head.

At the exact same moment, his fae senses warned him of the sudden, overwhelming rage now flowing from Sydon.

He turned to face him, sword upright. Through the dreamglide, he watched Sydon come down fast through the air, sword high.

Fergus barely had time to counter the swift strike, but he pivoted just enough to catch Sydon's blade with the edge of his sword. The vibration rang up his arm.

The battle was on. He met each strike with a counter strike, the sounds of metal-on-metal filling the air.

Sydon flew at Fergus, pivoting at the last second, blade coming in from Fergus's left. But unlike Sydon, Fergus had battled for years. He leaped in a levitating move straight up, then flipped in the air to come down in front of him. His blade struck Sydon deep in his abdomen. Sydon fell backward onto the floor, screaming.

The spell lost its power and Sydon was now visible. He held his hand to his gut, blood pouring through his fingers. The cut was deep. Though Sydon might yet survive, Fergus had to get Mary out of the bunker.

He flew like a bullet in her direction.

Her voice penetrated his mind. *Fergus, Sydon is up.*

Using the dreamglide, he saw Sydon's move as he threw his blade toward Fergus in one last attempt to take him down.

While still in the air, Fergus whipped off to the side just in time. Sydon's blade flew past Fergus and struck Sydon's desk. At the same moment, Fergus flew as high as he could toward the ceiling, then came down above Sydon. With his blade point first, he struck Sydon at the base of the neck. Blood shot through the air in a broad, pulsing pattern. Nothing could save Sydon now.

Fergus had only seconds, however, to get out of Sydon's HQ, twenty at the most.

He lifted Mary swiftly into his arms and levitated at light speed through the conference room, then toward the north exit point. Thank God Ryan had propped the door open for him. Fergus flew up the outside cement stairs as fast as he could straight into the air.

He headed at an angle into the night sky away from the Naked Wolf. With a quick glance, he saw the flash of distant border patrol vehicles and that the streets had been cleared of wolves and humans.

A civic alarm sounded in heavy booms through the air.

As expected, the blast sounded behind Fergus. He continued to race north as fast as he could, but even then heat and debris caught up with him. Small bits of shrapnel hit him, but nothing major and he really didn't care. He'd self-heal quickly and he'd gotten Mary to safety. Nothing else mattered. He held her close to his chest as he continued to fly north.

Warren's voice entered his mind. *Fergus, did you make it out?*

I did. I've got Mary with me.

Thank, God. I'm contacting the rest of the alphas now. I'll report back in a few minutes.

Finally at a safe distance, Fergus slowed, then drew to a stop to hover in the air. Holding Mary close, he turned to look at the bomb's wreckage. The Naked Wolf was no more, just a flattened, burning building, with smoke billowing in a thick upward stream.

Mary lifted a hand and squeezed his shoulder. She was already coming out of the spell's effect. *Are we safe, Fergus?*

We are.

Good.

From his current position, he could see Ryan fifty yards to the east, levitating in the air with at least twenty rescued wolves as well as Fergus's security force. Fergus let him be for now. He'd need to debrief the bespelled wolves and see that each one was returned to his pack. But that was a job for another night.

Mary's voice touched his mind again. *Did Ryan get everyone else out?*

He did. They're all safe. He's taking care of them now.

That's wonderful. And our favorite pair? Please tell me they're gone.

Fergus realized she might not have been able to see his battle with Sydon given her drugged out state.

The witch died by my sword and Sydon was mortally wounded when I took you out of there. The blast no doubt obliterated their bodies.

Warren hit his telepathy. *I've just heard from the remaining alphas.*

Mary's with me. I'm bringing her in on this conversation.

Good deal.

Mary's soft telepathic voice entered the conversation. *Hey, Warren. We made it.*

We sure did. First, I need to know if you're okay.

I'm fine, she said. *Not a scratch.*

Good. Good. So, Fergus, have we seen the last of Sydon and his witch?

Fergus relayed the details, then said, *Tell us what you learned from the rest of the pack leaders.*

Fergus could feel Warren's pleasure as he offered up the details, *We only lost a few wolves. Sydon's rogue pack was hit hard at every compound they attacked. Each of our alphas has already checked in and is celebrating a victory. As far as I can tell, we didn't have one incident of a wolf losing control.*

Fergus was relieved beyond words. *No reports of inter-pack battles?*

Nothing. And I've had contact with all the alphas. This is a real victory, Fergus. You and Mary have prevented an all-pack war.

Fergus released a heavy rush of air. At the same time, he experienced a lightening of spirit he hadn't known for the past several days. The greater risk had always been that Savage would fall into a state of war.

Ryan's approaching, Fergus said. *I'll make sure he updates you as the evening progresses. For now, I'll be signing off.*

Fergus, you do whatever you need to do. Mary's your priority right now and I've got my pack to tend to as well. I'll catch up with you tomorrow night at the White Flame.

Sounds good.

When Ryan drew near, he signaled for five members of Fergus's security force to create a protective array around them.

Fergus still held Mary close, her head cradled against his neck.

"Is she all right?" Ryan asked. He moved next to Fergus, levitating easily in the air beside him.

"She will be. But I'd like you to get the guest room set up with drug-flushing equipment and I want a nurse to be with Mary the entire time. She has amber flame in her system."

"You got it." As he flew a few yards away from Fergus, he whipped his cell from his pocket and started issuing orders.

The remainder of the Gordion detail levitated within a few feet of Fergus, their backs to him as they constantly surveyed the skies.

Knowing his wolves were protecting him, Fergus finally eased down and directed the team north toward the Gordion Compound. He kept the pace slow to have a good look at the land below and to gain a sense of Savage. Overall, he could feel that Sydon's attempted takeover of the territory had failed.

It was time to go home.

Adrenaline had driven him for the past hour and his head pounded as a result. Not that he cared much. Mary was his primary concern now. He'd make sure she had good medical attention, then he'd ask her the really hard questions about their future.

He heard her moan softly, a wolfish sound he loved. She shifted in his arms so that he had to slow down and readjust his hold on her. She ended up with her face pressed against his neck this time.

Did she just sniff his skin?

Fergus, I'm feeling better already. The witch's spell is completely gone.

Something about the sound of her voice in his head went straight to his groin. Was it the timbre? The Savage hoarseness? Then he felt guilty for having a purely sexual reaction to an injured female. *You okay?*

You smell so good. Her whole body writhed against his.

He remembered the effects amber flame could have on female wolves and wondered if her current reaction was as a result.

He was about to ask her if she'd experienced anything unusual because of the drug when she lifted her chin, then clamped her teeth around his throat. *You're mine, Fergus, and I'm not letting you get away from me. Not tonight, at least.*

A full body shiver went through him.

Two images got stuck side-by-side. One was of the medical equipment in his guest room where he needed to take her. The other was his private den home with a soundproof room which happened to be closer to his current in-air position than the Gordion Compound.

The former, however, called strongly to his sense of duty.

But the latter...

He flew even slower as he wrestled with his conscience. He should get Mary clean of the amber flame drug, but his body rolled with his need and longing for her.

Her voice penetrated his head abruptly. *Take me to your den home. Now.*

His conscience won. *Mary, this isn't right. We need to get you free of the drug, first.*

Actually, I don't have it in my system anymore. The spell that rendered me so weak has just finished bleeding the effects of the flame drug out of my body.

Fergus was confused. *Then what's with your teeth on my neck? Are you saying this isn't about amber flame?*

Not even a little. This is all about what I'm feeling for you, Sweetheart. She released his neck and leaned back to meet his gaze. She even smiled. "Check it out, if you don't believe me. But you won't find a single flame mark on my body. And don't worry, you can let go of me now. I'm good to levitate."

Fergus drew to a complete stop midair and his squad around him pulled up once more in a tight, protective formation.

He released Mary so that she floated next to him. She had amber rings in her eyes, which had nothing to do with the flame drug either.

He pushed her hair away from her throat and sure enough he couldn't find the smallest flame sign on her skin. If she'd had the drug in her system, she'd have corresponding flames all up her neck and on her cheeks. But her complexion was as pure and as beautiful as it had always been.

Which meant she'd spoken truthfully about her current state: Her reactions were all about him.

She smiled again. "See what I mean?"

While levitating beneath a swathe of stars and surrounded by his security detail, he took her arms gently in hand. "Mary. I ..." He had so much to say to her, but not in front of his pack. The words he needed to speak were for her alone.

She switched to telepathy. *I know. How about we finish this in your den home?*

He drew in a deep breath, then nodded. *Good idea.*

Realizing that Ryan had caught up with them and flew close, he said, "The drug has left Mary's system because of something the witch did, which is a good thing. But this also means we won't be needing the hospital equipment so you can cancel the order. Also, she and I are going to my den home."

Other than watching Ryan draw his phone to his ear to revoke his earlier order for medical equipment, Fergus didn't wait to see any of the other responses. His wolves would do whatever he said, no question, and the time would come very soon when the pack would have to decide about his leadership and about Mary.

But not tonight.

He pulled Mary back into his arms and sped in the direction of his forest home.

She wrapped her arms around his neck and entered his mind once more. *I need to be with you, stripped down naked.*

He growled heavily.

I love that sound, she said. *Makes me want to be on all fours.*

He got so distracted he almost clipped the top of a pine tree and had to jerk sideways to avoid it. He needed to concentrate, but Mary was making it hard. Real hard.

As soon as he descended to the front of the den home, he posted four guards to walk the perimeter until dawn. He had no doubt that there was a remnant of Sydon's rogue wolves still active in every part of the territory. If any of them happened to come near his home, he wanted to be ready.

With his guards in place, he sent Ryan and the last wolf back to the compound.

He levitated close to the walkway leading to the front door, but didn't let Mary go. Instead, he continued to fly, since he could move faster without using his feet.

He pushed the door open and barely got it shut before he was speeding her down the narrow stairwell. He held her tight against him, including her arms, to protect her.

Once in the den, he all but threw her on the bed, then started stripping out of his clothes.

Mary's light brown eyes glowed amber now. She was fully with him as she let her wolf rise to the fore. He kept growling, which in turn had Mary rolling her hips and touching her breasts as she watched him. With the steel door no longer blocking his heart, he could feel her mating need as strong and as straight as his cock.

Tonight, he'd make Mary his once and for all.

She hadn't taken her clothes off, but lay with her hand pressed between her thighs as she looked at him. Her eyes widened as her gaze fell to his fully erect cock.

When he was undressed, he drew close to the bed and made short work of her shoes and jeans. Her thong disappeared about the same time.

She tried to leap on him, but he pushed her back. "Hold still. I want you completely naked."

She released a growl of her own and her legs scissored trying to reach him, but he wasn't kidding. He didn't want one scrap of fabric separating her body from his.

He had work to do and a job to get done.

Once her clothes lay in a heap on the floor next to his, he returned to the door and slammed it shut. This was going to get loud.

He headed back to the bed. "I'm going to fuck you, Mary, and we're going to bond. You okay with that, because this is your last chance?"

"Do it now, wolf." She spread her legs, then arched her neck, offering up her throat. He leaped on her and felt his maw lengthen wolf-style. He took her neck in his mouth and clamped down hard. Her body grew very still and submissive, exactly the way he needed it.

With his cock centered on her sex, he began to push inside, firm thrusts that glided because the fae-wolf was wet for him.

Fergus, this is everything.

I know.

I don't want to leave you again. I belong in Savage now.

He loved her voice in his head. *You're staying with me for good. If the pack can't accept you, then I'll walk away and we'll figure out the next step together.*

Soft chuffs came out of her throat. *I love you, Fergus. I have from the moment I woke up from Roche's attack a month ago. Your scent was all over my skin, like stone, grasses and wolf. I fell hard for you before I ever saw you.*

He released her throat and rose up enough to look down at her. He savored her rose and yarrow scent, now blended with a true wolf musk. He kept his hips pumping into her slowly, knowing his cock would give her pleasure. "I love you, Mary. You were the beginning for me, of a new life here in Savage. I just couldn't see it. I feared the change it would bring, but being here with you, having my cock buried deep, this is what I want." He rolled his hips to let her feel him.

She arched her back and moaned, the sound low and wolfish. Her hands gripped his shoulders. "I'm here, Fergus, and I'm yours."

"Will you bond with me?"

She smiled softly. "My fae to your wolf?"

"Yup. And mine to yours, in whatever combination our strange powers will allow us."

"Then let's do it. I'm ready."

Her words spurred him on. He thrust faster, his gaze fixed to hers. He felt his mate-bonding drive take over his body, but this time he held nothing back.

Her back arched, she closed her eyes and her head rolled. "Your scent. Fergus, my God!"

Her answering bonding scent grabbed his balls. He wouldn't last long, not like this. "Mary, look at me."

She shifted her wobbly gaze to meet his. He let more of his scent and his mating drive flow over her. He watched her lips part as she drew in a long rush of air. He felt his power spread over her body as she undulated again.

He leaned down and kissed her. She parted her lips for him and he drove his tongue inside. He felt the bond grow, then tighten. His wolf wanted to howl, but instead he kept his lips pinned to hers, his tongue in her mouth.

~ ~ ~

Mary felt lost in time and space. Fergus was moving over her, making love to her, kissing her. His alpha wolf power was spreading through every part of her body and at the same time, something was leaving her and moving into him, the part of her that was fae. *Can you feel that Fergus, what I'm giving you?*

I can. I hadn't expected a return offering, but it's beautiful, like you. And full of amber light all the way to my soul.

He moved faster now, his cock driving in and out, quick like a wolf and erotic as hell. His lips worked hers, plucking at her and at times, his tongue thrust into her mouth duplicating what he was doing down low.

She loved him and she was bonding with him. The tugging sensation in her abdomen reached toward her sex, made contact and tightened.

A rush of light headed toward her as well, full of amber fireworks and shot through with the depth and magic of Fergus's masculine soul.

He was heavy on her now and it felt spectacular. The light filled her and surrounded her.

Ecstasy rolled through her body, taking the dark that was Fergus, and the light of her faeness, blending them together. She had no idea what a normal alpha-mate bonding would feel like, but this was like being transported into the heavens and sustained there by forces beyond her understanding.

She loved him and she wanted to be with him more than anything else she'd known her entire life.

He drew back and she met his gaze. His eyes glowed amber as well. *I love you, Mary.*

She wasn't sure she could even speak, so she stuck with telepathy. *I love you, too.*

Are you ready?

I am.

The bonding came at the same moment as her release as well as Fergus's. A sound came out of her throat, a wolf's cry but shaded with everything she was as a fae woman so that it sounded like a beautiful melody. Pleasure gripped her between her legs and a new rush of ecstasy poured through her.

She was caught up in the blending of her fae to his wolf, and the bond that suddenly settled in place, created a tremendous anchor to the earth and to Fergus. Though it was new it felt as old as time and as solid as the earth.

She felt different, yet the same. Just … *more.*

~ ~ ~

As Fergus felt the last of his seed leave his body, he slowed his hips down. He didn't want the moment to end because what he'd experienced had belonged to another world and ecstasy held his body in a tight beautiful grip. A bond existed now that hadn't been there before, something that could never be broken.

Looking down at Mary, he felt a tremendous connection to her and he knew his pack would never come first again. Mary would be his priority, yet not just her, but what they were meant to accomplish together.

He recalled her saying that essentially he should think outside the box, possibly leave the pack. He would have never considered it before, yet everything had changed.

And it wasn't just because of the bond. He saw his pack differently and Savage as well.

"What are you thinking about?" Mary's hand rested on his cheek and he turned just enough to kiss the palm of her hand.

"Nothing much. Just you and me and the future."

She smiled. "Nothing serious at all."

He chuckled, then slowly pulled out of her. He reached for a handful of tissues, tucked them between her legs, then stretched out beside her.

When she turned to face him, he drew her close. She angled one of her legs over his thighs.

He was content as he'd never been before. She continued to caress his cheek, his neck, then moved to his shoulders.

"It's as though I was blind," he said.

"But now you're not?"

"No. I'm seeing clearly for the first time in years."

He drew a deep breath. Even the air in his lungs felt different, cleaner. His fae senses felt fired up and the future appeared to him in full, but nothing like he'd expected. "I think you and I will be leaving Five Bridges."

At that she rose up on her elbow slightly. "What do you mean? If we leave the province, we'll be caught, possibly killed."

He chuckled. "I didn't mean illegally. And by-the-way, this is my fae speaking. I'm still caught up in what just happened between us, but I'm looking into the future. It appears we're headed to Washington D.C. for a series of brief visits."

A sharp intake of breath followed. "To lobby for wolf-rights."

"Yes," he said. "We've got to have more space. Savage will always be on the verge of war if we don't get a few hundred square miles of open land."

"Will anyone listen to you? To us?"

"With the *alter* wolf population growing as fast as it is in the U.S., they'll soon have to start listening. Wolves won't stay bound by barbed wire very much longer. It's just a matter of time. We were close to a full-on war tonight and not only because of Sydon."

She nodded. "I feel how edgy all the wolves are. They can't howl and shift as they need to, or run."

He held her gaze. "Are you willing to do this with me? I don't want to make the same mistake as before. We need to be a team, but I won't step one foot outside this room if we're not in agreement."

"Are you giving me veto power?"

"I am."

She leaned close and kissed him on the lips. "Good, because I promise you there will be times when I'll say no to you."

He felt how serious she was, even adamant.

He kissed her back. "And I'll need you to say no whenever your fae senses tell you to. I might fight you now and then because I'm damn stubborn."

"And I'll fight back, so beware."

He couldn't help himself. He smiled and caught her chin in his hand and kissed her again. "I'm duly warned."

"As for these jaunts to D.C.," she said, "my faeness is with you one-hundred percent. I know Savage is in deep trouble, that your wolves, *our* wolves, need land and lots of it. We can go see the council right now, if you want. I'm ready."

He smiled again. "I think we can wait a few hours."

"Fergus?"

"Yes?"

His gaze followed her hand as she planted it between her breasts. "This bond is amazing. I can feel your heart beating here, inside me. I swear I can."

He realized he could hear her heart as well, like a second beat within his own skin. "Me, too."

He'd spoken truthfully when he'd told Mary not long ago that she'd changed everything for him. He'd been a solitary wolf, though he headed up the Gordion Pack. Now he was connected to Mary, to his wolves, and to all of Savage in ways he'd never dreamed possible before.

~ ~ ~

A week later, Mary sat beside Fergus on a dark red couch in the sitting room of his newly remodeled master suite. When he'd begun work on the space, he'd brought in a trusted witch to cleanse the entire area of the horror Sydon had committed in his bedroom. The original furnishings had been burned on a sacred pyre, a potion added to the fresh paint, and new, consecrated furniture brought in.

She curled her knees up beside Fergus and worked on the intricate braid design that Sharon had created, but she struggled to get it right.

"Why don't you make up a pattern of your own?" He offered. He caressed her thigh as he spoke, a gesture that sent delightful shivers up and down both legs. She made love with him frequently and howled her head off in the soundproof chamber. He did the same.

She released a lock of his hair, separated the recent untidy bit, then tried again. "I've thought about it, but I really like your former wife and without her, I wouldn't be here in Savage. No, we'll keep her design and I'll learn to make it, even if it takes me the next decade trying." She just didn't have Sharon's nimble fingers.

She worked at it again for a few minutes, huffed an exasperated sight, then pulled the braids apart once more. She changed the subject. "Warren has grown really comfortable around me since the bond. Have you noticed?"

Fergus growled softly, a sound she loved. "He touches you more than he should. He's taking advantage of the bond. I need to have a talk with him."

Mary grinned. "You'll do no such thing. Warren's lonely, that's all. The way you were before you took me illegally in the dreamglide."

"I don't care if he's lonely. I want his paws off you. I mean, when we met at the White Flame the night after we defeated Sydon, he must have hugged you three times. How is that right on any level? You're an alpha's mate?"

She let the braids go, caught his scowling face in her hands, then kissed him. "Tell you what. Every time you feel he's being inappropriate with me, I'll make it up to you." She then slid one hand slowly to caress him between his legs. He was in a half-aroused state, something very usual for him when they were this close. "I'll use my tongue and my lips and take you all the way if you want. Deal?"

He groaned heavily. "You strike a hard bargain. But with that kind of offer, I might start encouraging Warren to come over more often."

She laughed and though he tried to pull her on top of him, she gave him a shove and brushed out his long black hair once more. "Not yet, Sweetheart. I need to get this right."

"Fine."

He settled down as she worked his hair once more. But she sensed the shift in his thoughts as though they were her own. "Are you thinking about the memorial service?"

He nodded slowly. She let her fingers drift with his movements. "It went well."

"I don't think it could have been more beautiful," she said. "And I loved how your wolves howled so softly throughout, like a choir."

"The pack at its best."

"I was so moved and caught up at the same time. I felt the deceased nearby as well."

"Did you see them, I mean like you did Sharon?"

"No, not at all. I just felt their presence and afterward each passed on. It was sad yet beautiful at the same time."

"Mary?"

She kept her fingers pressed to what was becoming her best braid yet, then shifted enough to meet his gaze. "What?" She could feel his need to say something.

"I'm glad the pack accepted you as it did."

She drew a long, slow breath. "When we first emerged from our bonding, I was so afraid."

"I know. I could feel you shaking."

"But it was amazing, wasn't it?" Tears rushed to her eyes. "They kept coming up to me, one at a time. I could feel their acceptance and how much I already belonged. I'm still overwhelmed when I think about it. I'd lost my entire family to the *alter* serum. But I gained six hundred brothers and sisters."

"You did. Though I was ready to step down and wouldn't have thought twice about it, if they'd found our union unacceptable. The way they embraced you, however, confirmed that everything you and I had been through was meant not just for us, but for Five Bridges as well. The new fae part of me recognizes that we'll become a force for meaningful change in the entire territory."

Mary could feel it was well, that she and Fergus had forged their bond for something much greater than just their private relationship. "And together," she said, "We'll help build a better future for all the segregated provinces in the U.S."

His answering smile was full of affection and his bonding scent suddenly whirled around her. Without giving it a thought, she released the braids. As she slid her arms around his neck, she quickly found herself airborne as he carried her back to bed.

~ ~ ~

After Fergus made love to Mary again, he held her close, loving that she fell asleep in his arms. She was right, he could sense her heartrate within his chest and how the beats slowed as she fell deeper into her dreams.

His own heart was full and changed. He still wished he'd been a better husband to Sharon, but her forgiveness had meant everything to him.

Sydon and Sandrine were gone and couldn't hurt anyone in Savage ever again. The spells the witch had used to cast over each critical pack member dispelled the moment she died. He couldn't fathom the level of power she'd possessed that she'd been able to corrupt so many wolves all by herself. He hoped a force would arise at some point to end the influence the dark witch covens had in Five Bridges.

Harley had been devastated to learn of his role in Sydon's attempted hijacking of Savage. So much so, that Fergus had brought in the good witch, Emma, to help him overcome his guilt.

Emma was now working with a large number of the previously bespelled wolves, healing their minds from the distortion Sandrine's spells had caused.

Fergus knew that one day Harley would be restored to his usual confidence and pack rank. For now, he let the powerful beta work through his issues and heal.

Ryan had stepped up to fill Harley's place. Fergus smiled. He knew Ryan was almost ready to challenge Fergus in a dominance battle, something he would welcome. All alphas enjoyed a solid, legitimate battle. His fae senses also told him this fight would be the first of many and that one day, years from now, possibly even decades, Ryan would break off and form his own pack, something he'd be able to do because of the work Fergus and Mary were just beginning in D.C.

Fergus would hold the reins of the Gordion Pack for a long time to come, especially since he now had a powerful alpha-mate. Mary would help secure his pack bonds and would bring an even greater communal sense to his family of several hundred wolves.

A woman's voice suddenly entered his mind. *Okay, I lied, Fergus. Though it wasn't exactly a lie. I didn't think I'd be coming back, but I begged to have one last word with you, and I was allowed.*

Fergus shifted his head on his pillow and couldn't help but chuckle. Sharon floated nearby as though sitting on a chair, her legs crossed at the knees. She wore her favorite black boots, laced up the front and tied with small neat bows.

Still holding a sleeping Mary tight against his side, Fergus smiled. *I'm glad you did. But Mary's asleep. Should I wake her?*

Sharon's quirky smile appeared. *Nah.*

How did you get permission to come back?

She pretended to fluff her non-existent cropped hair, which only caused her ghostly mist to move and swirl. *My supervisor said I did really well, on all fronts, so he said yes.*

Mary suddenly stirred and leaned up on her elbow. Her voice entered their telepathy. *Sharon? Is that you?*

I didn't mean to wake you.

I heard you in my dreams. Oh, I'm so glad you're here. Did you see it all? The battle against Sydon, I mean.

Sharon's expression grew affectionate as she looked at Mary. *I did. You were brilliant. Both of you.*

We couldn't have done a damn thing without you, Fergus said. *You know that.*

Sharon smiled and looked really pleased. *I admit I had a hand in things.* She screwed up her face. *Confronting my flaws was hard as hell, but it was worth it to see that pair get blown to pieces.*

Thank you so much, Mary said, *for making the effort to come to me that first time in my house. I know I wouldn't have made a single move toward Savage without your encouragement.*

Sharon glanced from one to the other. *I'm really happy for you both. Just wanted you to know.* She appeared for a moment to be listening to someone else. She made an odd disgusted sound with her voice, and addressed her ghostly mentor. *Hold on. I'm getting to it. Don't be so impatient, Gabriel. Jesus.* She gave herself a shake and shifted her gaze back to Fergus.

I have one last message. You might want to keep an eye on your friend, Warren. Seems like some dark witch in Elegance has it in for him, though I don't know why.

Fergus felt a ripple of dread pass straight through the fae part of his soul. *Sharon, what witch? Do you have a name?*

She shook her head. *I have no idea and now I'm being called away for good. You two kids behave, or not!* She blew a misty kiss with her hand and was gone

Fergus could feel her absence in the room like some of the air had just been sucked out of the space.

"That was weird," Mary said. "But typical. She's funny, your deceased wife."

"You know what else is weird? That we've both been talking to my 'deceased wife'. Sometimes the reality of the *alter* state blows me away."

Mary relaxed against his shoulder, laid her arm over his chest and hugged him. "But what are we supposed to do about Warren?"

There was a time when Fergus would have been all-wolf and launched into attack mode. He would have contacted Warren right away, offered his help, made up a list of some of the worst dark witches in Elegance

Territory, then suggested his wolves track each of their movements. Yup, a whole host of let's-take-care-of-this-now.

Instead, he took a deep breath and accessed his faeness. Peace descended in the same moment and what came to him was simple. "Warren will let us know when he needs our help. And when he does, we'll be ready."

Mary chuckled softly. "You know, I confess I was thinking like a wolf. I was ready to leap from bed, fly straight to his compound and repeat everything Sharon just told us."

"Couldn't let you do that," he said, rubbing her arm.

"Why not? I mean maybe we should."

"Well, here's the problem, you're naked. There's no way you're going over to the Caldion Compound without anything on."

"Oh, you're so funny. I'm laughing so hard."

Fergus sighed deeply and smiled up at the ceiling. He was thinking about adding beams like the ones Mary had in her family room. "I have a surprise for you," he said.

"What's that?"

"I hired an architect to draw up new plans for us. I want to add on a wing to our private residence."

Mary lifted up just enough to meet his gaze. "What for? I mean your home is plenty big as it is right now."

He'd never felt so much love in his entire life as in this moment, staring into her light brown eyes. "For your cats of course and your birds. And if you want, I was thinking we could add a surgery, some exam rooms, an office, hire some staff for you. What do you think?"

"Fergus, really?"

"But only if that's what you want."

"It is. It is. I've been thinking something similar. I know you wolves heal up fast, but sometimes those dominance fights end with brutal gashes and crushed bones that could use some intermediary work."

He laughed. "I was thinking of small, domestic pets."

"You need to think bigger."

He took her hand and held it against his half-erect cock. "I am."

She made a very wolf-like snorting sound. "You're ridiculous."

"But you love me."

Her expression softened. "I do, with all my heart."

A swell of emotion washed through him so profound, that he rolled her suddenly onto her back. His lips found hers once more and with her answering response, he was soon making love to her again.

He had no doubt his life with Mary and with his pack would be full of challenges, impossible conflicts to resolve, and perhaps even the occasional visit from an unexpected ghost.

But for now, all he wanted was to hear Mary's soft melodious howls and join her with a set of his own.

The End

I hope you enjoyed reading AMBER FLAME! And remember, you can claim a free e-book of mine right now by signing up for my mailing list on my home page: http://www.carisroane.com/

If you enjoyed AMBER FLAME, I'd love it if you took a minute to leave a short review at your favorite online retailer! And you don't have to be a blogger to do this, just a reader who loves books!

Especially for you! I run giveaways all the time on my website. Be sure to check out my contest page today! Enter here: http://www.carisroane.com/contests/

Do you love cocktails!?! I've been working with the awesome paranormal romance writing duo, Trim and Julka, who have developed a series of Flame Drinks that correspond to each of the flame books. You can find these specialty cocktails and their recipes at: http://www.trimandjulka.com/flame-drinks/ Please remember: Don't drink and drive and don't light these drinks on fire! Enjoy!

COMING UP NEXT:

Are you ready for the 9th and final installment of the Blood Rose Series? EMBRACE THE POWER will be my next release after AMBER FLAME and I'm writing it as we speak! Here's some info: http://www.carisroane.com/9-embrace-the-power/

In the meantime, be sure to read the 8th book of the series, EMBRACE THE HUNT!

A powerful vampire warrior. A beautiful fae of great ability. A war that threatens to destroy their love for the second time…

Find out more about EMBRACE THE HUNT: http://www.carisroane.com/8-embrace-the-hunt/

LIST OF BOOKS

To read more about each one, check out my books page: http://www.carisroane.com/books/

The Flame Series…

BLOOD FLAME
AMETHYST FLAME
DARK FLAME
CHRISTMAS FLAME NOVELLA, A Holiday Novella for any time of the year

The Blood Rose Series...

BLOOD ROSE SERIES BOX SET, featuring Book #1 EMBRACE THE DARK, Book #2 EMBRACE THE MAGIC, and Book #3 EMBRACE THE MYSTERY
EMBRACE THE DARK #1
EMBRACE THE MAGIC #2
EMBRACE THE MYSTERY #3
EMBRACE THE PASSION #4
EMBRACE THE NIGHT #5
EMBRACE THE WILD #6
EMBRACE THE WIND #7
EMBRACE THE HUNT #8
LOVE IN THE FORTRESS #8.1 (A companion book to

EMBRACE THE HUNT)
BLOOD ROSE TALES BOX SET

Guardians of Ascension Series...

VAMPIRE COLLECTION (Includes BRINK OF ETERNITY)
THE DARKENING
RAPTURE'S EDGE – 1 – AWAKENING
RAPTURE'S EDGE – 2 – VEILED

Amulet Series...

WICKED NIGHT/DARK NIGHT

You can find me at:

Website (http://www.carisroane.com/)
Blog (http://www.carisroane.com/journal/)
Facebook (https://www.facebook.com/pages/Caris-Roane/160868114986060)
Twitter (https://twitter.com/carisroane)
Newsletter (http://www.carisroane.com/contact-2/)

Author of:

Guardians of Ascension Series (http://www.carisroane.com/the-guardians-of-ascension-series/) **– Warriors of the Blood crave the breh-hedden**

Dawn of Ascension Series (http://www.carisroane.com/dawn-of-ascension-series/) **– Militia Warriors battle to save Second Earth**

Rapture's Edge Series (http://www.carisroane.com/raptures-edge/) **(Part of Guardians of Ascension) – Second earth warriors travel to Third to save three dimensions from a tyrant's heinous ambitions**

Blood Rose Series (http://www.carisroane.com/the-blood-rose-series/) **– Only a blood rose can fulfill a mastyr vampire's deepest needs**

Blood Rose Tales (http://www.carisroane.com/blood-rose-tales-series/) **– Short tales of mastyr vampires who hunger to be satisfied**

Men in Chains Series (http://www.carisroane.com/men-in-chains-series/) **– Vampires struggling to get free of their chains and save the world**

The Flame Series (http://www.carisroane.com/flame-series/) **– Hunky 'Alter' warriors battle for control of their world**

ABOUT THE AUTHOR

Caris Roane is the New York Times bestselling author of thirty-four paranormal romance books. Writing as Valerie King, she has published fifty novels and novellas in Regency Romance. Caris lives in Phoenix, Arizona, loves gardening, enjoys the birds and lizards in her yard, but really doesn't like scorpions!

Find out more about Caris on her website!

http://www.carisroane.com/

CPSIA information can be obtained
at www.ICGtesting.com
Printed in the USA
FSOW02n1258101116
27232FS